F
GILMORE   Gilmore, Susan
               Gregg.

               Looking for salvation
               at the Dairy Queen.

                                    218826
$23.00
               DATE

3 08

BAKER & TAYLOR

Looking
for Salvation
at the
Dairy Queen

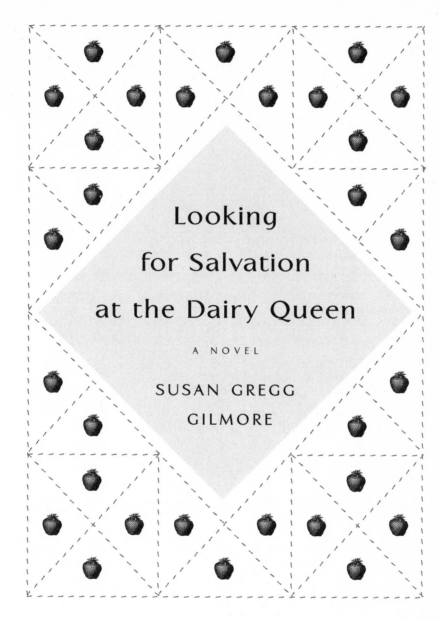

Looking
for Salvation
at the Dairy Queen

A NOVEL

SUSAN GREGG
GILMORE

SHAYE AREHEART BOOKS
NEW YORK

Copyright © 2008 by Susan Gregg Gilmore

Published in the United States by Shaye Areheart Books,
an imprint of the Crown Publishing Group,
a division of Random House, Inc., New York.
www.crownpublishing.com

Shaye Areheart Books with colophon is a registered
trademark of Random House, Inc.

Library of Congress Cataloging-in-Publication Data
Gilmore, Susan Gregg.
    Looking for salvation at the Dairy Queen : a novel /
Susan Gregg Gilmore.—1st ed.
    1. Young women—Fiction.   2. City and town life—
Fiction.   3. Self-actualization (Psychology)—Fiction.
4. Ringgold (Ga.)—Fiction.   I. Title.
PS3607.I4527L66   2008
813'.6—dc22   2007032673

ISBN 978-0-307-39501-6

Printed in the United States of America

Design by Barbara Sturman

10 9 8 7 6 5 4 3 2 1

First Edition

For my family

husband, daughters, mother, father, sisters, brother

without you, there would be no story to tell

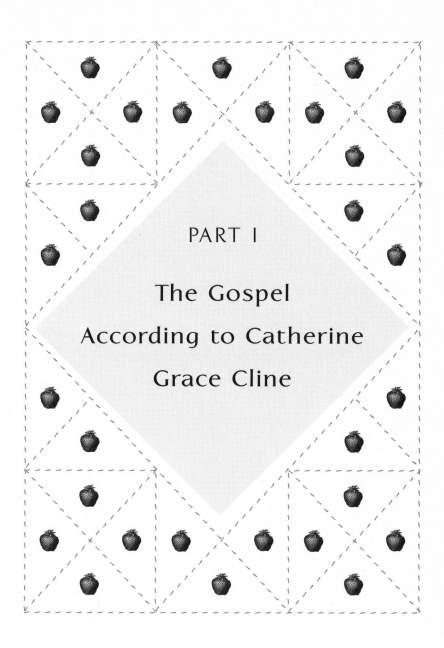

PART I

The Gospel
According to Catherine
Grace Cline

CHAPTER ONE

In the Beginning

My daddy always said that if the good Lord can take the time to care for something as small as a baby sparrow nesting in a tree, then surely He could take the time to listen to a little girl in Ringgold, Georgia. So every night before I went to bed I got down on my knees and begged the Lord to find me a way out of this town. And every morning, I woke up in the same old place.

It was a place that I, Catherine Grace Cline, never wanted to call home, even though I was born and raised here. It was a place where everybody knew everything about you, down to the color of underwear your mama bought you at the Dollar General Store. It was a place that just never felt right to me, like a sweater that fits too tight under your arms. It was a place where girls like me traded their dreams for a boy with a couple of acres of land and a wood-framed house with a new electric stove. It was a place I always planned on leaving.

When I was no more than nine years old, a tornado tore right close to my house. I remember yelling at my little sister to run and hide in the basement. "Martha Ann," I warned her, "if that twister hits this town, nobody's even going to notice it's gone."

She started crying for fear she was going to be swept up in the clouds and carried away, and nobody, not even our daddy, would be able to find her. Turned out the only thing of any importance swept up in the sky that day was Mr. Naylor's old hound dog. People said that Buster Black flew some fifteen miles, those long lonesome ears of his flapping like wings, before landing in the middle of some cornfield over in the next county.

Mr. Naylor walked for miles looking for that dad-gum dog till finally my daddy and the sheriff had to go pick him up. And just when that poor man finished planting a wooden cross by Buster's little house, darn it, if that four-legged fool didn't come limping back home, wagging his tail and acting like he'd found the Promised Land. Mr. Naylor was crying, praising the Lord, holding Buster Black in his arms. The local newspaper ran a color picture of them both right on the front page, like that dog was some kind of prodigal son.

"You know, Martha Ann," I told her after reading about Buster's triumphant return, "a tornado like that just might be our ticket out of here, but unlike that stupid old hound dog, we are not going to limp back home."

My daddy said I was a little girl with a big imagination. Maybe. Or maybe I was a patient girl with a big dream, or a despairing girl waiting for her divine deliverance. But either way, I was going to hitch a ride out of Ringgold, whether it was on a fiery twister ripping a path through the Georgia sky or on a Greyhound bus rolling its way down Interstate 75.

Truth be told, I never even liked the name Ringgold. I mean, there's nothing in these green rolling hills that even faintly resembles a ring of gold, a ring of anything for that matter. And believe me, me and Martha Ann looked, somehow figuring that if we could find a ring of trees or ancient rocks, then just maybe our living here would have some kind of meaning. But after years of searching, the best I could figure was that it was just these darn hills that I had stared at every morning from my bedroom window that formed the ring, the ring that had kept me hostage for the first eighteen years of my life.

Nobody much ever bothers to visit this town except the truckers who stop to fill their fuel tanks because they can get some of the cheapest gas in the state here and Mrs. Gloria Jean Graves's second cousin, who has come up from Birmingham every year for the Thanksgiving holiday since before I was born. She always said it was refreshing to get away from the big city for a few days.

One time the governor came by for about twenty-five

minutes to cut a ribbon at the new elementary-school library. Everybody in town came out to see him. Daddy made me wear a dress and tie my hair back in a ribbon, just like I was going to church. Six days a week my daddy didn't care too much how I looked, but on Sunday mornings there was no negotiating the dress code. My sister and I wore our very best dresses with a fresh pair of cotton panties underneath, out of respect for the Lord, Daddy said.

I really didn't think Jesus cared what I wore to Cedar Grove Baptist Church, or to see the governor for that matter, considering the fact that in every picture I ever saw of the King of Kings, He was wearing sandals and bundled up in nothing more than a big, baggy robe. But I figured this governor must be the most important person I was ever going to meet if Daddy was making me wear my navy blue Sunday dress with the white lacy collar and my patent-leather Mary Janes.

Martha Ann pitched such a fit about wearing her Sunday clothes that Daddy ended up leaving her at home with a neighbor. My little sister is a couple of years younger than I am, but she has always been a couple of inches taller, my guess from the time she came into this world. She has thick, dark brown hair and deep brown eyes like our mama. I have blue eyes like my daddy and straight brown hair that looks more like the color of a field mouse.

Martha Ann was a pretty baby and a pretty girl. Everything on her face just fits together so perfectly. When we were little, people said we looked just like twins for no better reason than we might have been wearing the same color shirt. You had to wonder if they were truly looking at us. But one thing was for certain, Martha Ann hated putting on her Sunday clothes even more than I did. She'd have much rather been in the library picking out a new book to read than waiting to look at some strange man cut a ribbon.

I told her that if she didn't stop all that stomping and snorting, she was going to get left behind. And sure enough, she did. She had to spend the entire afternoon with Ida Belle Fletcher shucking eighty-four ears of corn for Wednesday-night supper over at the church.

Ida Belle said she cooked for the Lord, but all I knew was that she smelled like an unsavory combination of left-over bacon grease and Palmolive soap. She kept her big, round tummy covered with a tattered, old apron permanently stained with the meals of another day. The only time I saw her without that apron was when she was sitting in church, and then she kept it folded in her pocketbook.

My patent-leather shoe rubbed a blister on my big toe, but it was worth it. The governor turned out to be, if nothing else, the most handsome-looking man I'd ever seen. He wore a dark navy suit and a crisp white shirt that must have been starched so stiff, it could've stood up on its own. A red-and-blue-striped tie was pulled around his neck, and the tip of a white handkerchief was peeking out of his suit pocket. I had never seen a man dressed so fancy. He was in Ringgold for only a few minutes, and then he jumped in the back of a long, black car and sped off down

Highway 151. I wanted to go with him so bad that for weeks after that, when I went to bed at night, I got down on my knees and begged the Lord to make me the governor's daughter.

But He didn't bother to answer that prayer either, not that I really thought that He would. God put me here for a reason, Daddy kept telling me; I just hadn't figured it out yet.

Now I know my father was a certified man of God, but at a fairly young age, I decided that when it came to my destiny, he did not know what he was talking about. He certainly did not understand that there was nothing for me here in Ringgold, Georgia. Sometimes I wondered if he had noticed that this town had only one red light, one part-time sheriff, and one post office, which was nothing more than a gray metal trailer perched on a bunch of cinder blocks in the back of the Shop Rite parking lot.

There was one losing high-school football team and one diner, which has been serving pork chops on Thursdays since 1962. There was one fire station, but it burned down five or six years ago when the entire fire department, which amounted to the sum total of Edward and Lankford Bostleman, were spending the night at their aunt's house over in LaFayette.

And there was, thankfully, one Dairy Queen, where Martha Ann and I spent the better part of our childhood licking Dilly Bars and planning our escape. We spent every Saturday afternoon sitting on the DQ's only picnic table, sticky from the drippings of a thousand ice cream cones, thinking about a world the kids in the 4-H club couldn't even begin to imagine.

I'm talking about a world with department stores and movie theaters and fancy restaurants that require a reservation and keep candles burning on the tables. A world with enough lights turned on at night that it makes it hard to see the stars. A world that for so many years seemed well beyond our reach. A world where girls like me and Martha Ann could dream of being more than country girls content to raise a family and grow a crop of tomatoes in the backyard.

Martha Ann and I had visited this world a couple of times already. Daddy had taken us to Atlanta twice, once to see Santa Claus at the Lenox Square mall. Santa sat on his ruby red velvet throne at Davison's department store where hundreds of Barbie dolls and all her clothes were on display for every little girl to admire. I remember Martha Ann sitting on the floor of that toy department, for what seemed like an hour, just staring at the fancy gowns and plastic shoes in Barbie's endless wardrobe. Most of our doll clothes were homemade from pieces of dresses Martha Ann and I had outgrown. Our poor Barbies looked pretty pitiful compared to these big-city dolls waiting for a winter snow in their pink coats and slick white boots.

The other time we went to Atlanta was to see Daddy's beloved Georgia Bulldogs play in the Peach Bowl. Daddy said we were watching history being made when the Dawgs squeaked by with a one-point victory over the University of Maryland. But as soon as the final second ticked off the clock, Daddy was herding us back to the car. We begged him to take us to the Varsity so we could get a chili dog and a chocolate milk shake. We could see it from the highway, but Daddy said we needed to hurry on home.

We weren't in Atlanta long either time, but it was sure long enough for Martha Ann and me to figure out that the world we kept dreaming about was no more than a hundred miles from our front door.

Daddy, on the other hand, couldn't see the good in leaving Ringgold. He was born and raised there, and he couldn't imagine being happy any place else. Ringgold, he always told me, had everything a man needed, and what it didn't have, a man didn't need.

Truth be told, I think Daddy was a little bit scared of the world beyond the Catoosa County line. And I guess I can't blame him. Every night he would get comfortable in his reclining chair, turn on the television, and then let Walter Cronkite convince him that the world was much too dangerous for anyone he loved. Boys were getting themselves blown up every day in some country I knew nothing about. Grown women were pulling off their bras and burning them in broad daylight for everyone to see. And a man named Martin Luther King was telling the black people they deserved a better life, and everybody around town seemed afraid that they might actually get it.

Daddy said the devil was sneaky, that he's been known

to take the shape of ordinary-looking people. That's why, Daddy said, you always had to look someone in the eyes, because that's where you could see the greed and the hate and all the impure thoughts. But from where I was sitting on the brown braided rug on our living room floor, all I could see in my daddy's eyes was fear. I think he thought that here in Ringgold he could keep his babies safe, just like his daddy had done and his daddy's daddy.

You see, three generations of Cline men had been known for three things—their love of the Lord, their devotion to their family, and their commitment to growing the perfect tomato. And even though this was not my life's ambition, unfortunately it was in my blood. I am convinced to this day that even my own mama considered the tomato a symbol of a person's God-fearing commitment to biblical and civic values. It may be hard to believe all that's wrapped up in one little, red tomato, but that's the gospel truth.

Martha Ann and I weren't falling for it, though. We didn't care what Mrs. Gladys Gulbenk, our eighty-year-old home economics teacher, tried to tell us. There were not enough ways to prepare a tomato to keep us entertained for a lifetime.

"Remember, guls," preached Mrs. Gulbenk, always holding the most perfect red tomato in her hand for all of us to admire, "you can fry 'em, bake 'em, stew 'em, and congeal 'em. A good wife and mutha will always have a tomata on hand."

I can still hear those words rumbling around my head

some nights when I'm lying in bed and can't sleep. And the worst part, the really tragic part of it all, is that now, all grown up, I always have a couple of tomatoes sitting on the kitchen counter. That's just how strong a hold the tomato can have over a Southern girl. But when I was little, perched on that picnic table at the Dairy Queen, with Martha Ann sitting right by my side, I never once dreamed of tomatoes, not for a single, solitary minute. No way. I spent my time thinking about being a Hollywood movie star or some famous doctor who cured hard-to-pronounce diseases.

But one thing was for darn sure, after licking a thousand Dilly Bars, we had successfully traced the roots of our discontent to one man, our great-granddaddy William Floyd Cline. William Floyd is still considered a very important man in Ringgold, although he's been dead for a long, long time now. To this day, people talk about him as if they know him, kind of the same way they talk about somebody famous like Hank Aaron or Dolly Parton or Abraham Lincoln. The talk about him was always so big that sometimes Martha Ann and I wondered if he was still living, hidden somewhere up on Taylor's Ridge.

William Floyd was one of the most prolific bootleggers the state of Georgia has ever known. He brewed and ran illegal moonshine throughout northern Georgia and Alabama and southeastern Tennessee. His whiskey was corn-based, bitter, and wickedly potent. Everybody knew his was the best, and his customers paid top dollar for one of his little brown jugs. Mr. Tucker, down at the Dollar General

Store, said he heard that a man over in Bledsoe County, somewhere up in Tennessee, slept for three whole weeks after drinking some of our great-granddaddy's moonshine.

Standing no more than five feet three inches tall, William Floyd weighed about a hundred and seventy pounds, but Daddy said it was all muscle. He said he had a barrel-shaped chest and arms as big and round as watermelons in July. He didn't have one single strand of hair on his head, and legend has it, his steely blue eyes could pierce through a man and see inside his soul. The shining business was a dangerous trade and William Floyd found himself hunted, chased, and shot at, but, fortunately, never caught.

Then one sticky, Georgia afternoon in the middle of August, William Floyd made a spur-of-the-moment decision that changed his life and my family's fate forever. Smelling of corn mash and cigar smoke, he stumbled into a white tent propped up in the midst of some lonesome field next to some unmarked country road. And under that tent, with its canvas sides flapping in the gentle summer breeze, William Floyd found the Lord somewhere in the congregation's third singing of the fourth verse of "Just As I Am."

The preacher, who had found the Lord himself only the week before, took my great-granddaddy by the hand and led him down to the banks of the Tallapoosa River. And in the middle of that river on that hot August day with the cool water moving against their backs, the preacher lowered my great-granddaddy under the water a sinner and raised him up a man of God. Without much more than an "Amen," newly found Brother William Floyd quit drinking, fighting, and cursing and dedicated his life to his Savior Jesus Christ.

My great-granddaddy didn't remember much of the days following his salvation. Story has it he walked miles and miles in some sort of divine daze so high on the Lord that he glowed like the Angel Gabriel. When he finally stumbled into Ringgold, the townspeople took one look at him and figured he had been specially delivered by the Lord himself. They called him Preacher, and within days he was sermonizing from his own makeshift pulpit next to a grove of cedar trees. And during the course of the next forty years, he built a church and nurtured a flock, all the while delivering another type of libation just as intoxicating as his moonshine.

When William Floyd passed on, Daddy said the towns-folk mourned for weeks. They had lost their spiritual leader, their confidant, and their friend. Their only comfort was knowing that his son, Floyd Marshall, would take over the pulpit at Cedar Grove Baptist Church. Floyd Marshall followed in his daddy's footsteps, all right, but I'm not sure it was as much a divine calling as it was a fear of breaking the Fifth Commandment, more loosely translated to mean *Thou shalt do what your daddy tells you to do.*

People don't talk as much about Floyd Marshall. Even I know it would be kind of hard to follow in the footsteps of someone who's been divinely delivered. And I think my poor granddaddy struggled with his destiny long before Martha Ann and I ever sat down on that picnic table at the

Dairy Queen. We never did get to meet him. He died shortly before I was born. But from the stories my daddy has told me about him, I always felt like he would have understood me. I always felt like he would have enjoyed a Dilly Bar of his own.

Daddy said Floyd Marshall was a quiet man who loved to read books and work in his garden, the one he sowed directly behind the church. He planted squash, strawberries, okra, green beans, watermelons, and four different kinds of tomatoes. He grew some of the biggest, reddest tomatoes this town has ever seen, and he grew these little, yellow, pear-shaped tomatoes that Daddy said he could pop in his mouth and suck like a piece of hard candy. But best of all, he grew these deep purple ones that Daddy said came from the Cherokee Indians over in Tennessee. That's right, a real live Indian gave my granddaddy his first vine.

Granddaddy watered, fertilized, pruned, and talked scripture to those vegetables every day. I imagine they heard every sermon he ever preached. Daddy said his daddy would come in from the garden with dirt on his hands and sweat dripping off his brow and say with a smile on his face, "Now son, those there are some true Baptist vegetables."

Daddy said he marched into his Sunday-school class one day with his chest all puffed up, holding a yellow squash so big that he had to carry it in both hands. He informed his teacher that his daddy was such a powerful man of God that even his vegetables had found the Lord. His Sunday-school teacher told him that may very well be, but she hoped his son and his vegetables remembered that the meek and the mild were the ones who were going to inherit the Kingdom of God. Then she took that squash home and fried it up for supper.

Of course, I imagine those poor plants also heard a thing or two about the choir director driving down to Florida during the dead of night so he could bet on the greyhounds. Or about Brother Hawkin's baby daughter who was shipped off to Texas to live with an aunt because she had gone and gotten herself in the family way in the back of her boyfriend's pickup truck before taking the time to say, "I do."

Granddaddy must have grown tired of listening to people complain about the color of the cushions in the pews or the cost of the new hymnals or how much meat loaf the young deacon, Brother Fulmer, whose faith in the Lord was as big as his appetite, ate at Wednesday-night suppers. Every preacher must need a place where he can hide from his flock, and that garden must have been my granddaddy's secret hiding spot. He probably felt closer to God hidden among those stalks of corn than anywhere else on this earth, probably the way I felt sitting on that picnic table at the Dairy Queen.

When my daddy was only eighteen years old, Floyd Marshall asked him to come and join him behind the pulpit. He said he was getting tired and needed his son's strong back and patient ear to help keep his flock from falling from grace.

I think my daddy had been ready to step behind that pulpit since he was old enough to talk. He loved all people, and they loved him right back. He was named Marshall William, after both his daddy and granddaddy, and he had a good portion of each in his blood. He was tall like his daddy but solid and thick like his granddaddy, and he looked like he could save you from a burning building just as easily as from the fires of hell.

He spoke with such confidence and persuasion that it wasn't long before everybody in town started comparing him to the great William Floyd, and people from as far away as Dalton started coming to Cedar Grove Baptist Church just to hear him preach. Daddy kept photographs of William Floyd and Floyd Marshall on his desk at the church. He said their faces reminded him every day of his reason for being.

Not more than a year after assuming his new position, he married my mama, Lena Mae Pierce. My mama's family was from Willacoochee, a town even smaller than Ringgold situated down in the southern part of the state. She had come north one summer with a girlfriend who was visiting relatives, and she and Daddy met at the Fourth of July fireworks celebration on the field behind the high school.

Daddy said it was love at first sight. Mama was beautiful, and he said he took one look at her with those big brown eyes shining like moonbeams and knew there was no other woman for him. By Labor Day, they were engaged, and they married the following month on Mama's birthday, the twenty-fifth of October. She was only sixteen when they married, but Daddy said she was mature for her years. Sometimes I couldn't help but wonder if Mama had just been looking for a way out of Willacoochee, and sometimes I wondered if she wished she had stayed. I've never met any of my mama's family. Daddy said Mama leaving Willacoochee was the best thing that ever happened to Lena Mae.

Granddaddy died shortly after their wedding, and Daddy said the day he left this world was one of the saddest days of his life. But he also said the day I was born, nine and a half months after they returned from their honeymoon in Gatlinburg, was one of the happiest. He said that for every angel that leaves this world there's another waiting to take his place. And I guess I was the one waiting in line to take my granddaddy's place.

Mama stayed home and took care of me. She tended to the house, the one Daddy said he bought just for her. It was a white-framed house with a big porch that stretched clear across its front. All day long Mama cooked and washed and cleaned. She even tended to the tomatoes she planted right outside the kitchen door. But when the day was nearly done, Mama would rock on that porch and watch the sun fall behind Taylor's Ridge. Sometimes Daddy would sit along next to her with a big smile on his face. He had everything he ever wanted.

Daddy worked at the church almost every day. When his granddaddy started preaching, Cedar Grove was nothing more than a lean-to in a little clearing of cedar trees not far from where our house stands now. But today there's a real brick building and a fellowship hall and eight class-rooms for Sunday school. Daddy hoped that in the next few years he could build a swimming pool right behind the pul-pit so he could baptize people inside the church building.

One thing was for darn sure, my daddy never needed to grow a secret hiding place. He could listen to people chatter on and on about the silliest things in the world and always seem interested. He just saw the best in everything and everybody, and I think people really felt like they were in the presence of God when they were with my daddy. They must have been because he even found it in his heart to love Emma Sue Huckstep.

Every Saturday before Easter, Emma Sue's grand-mamma planned a big egg hunt at Cedar Grove Baptist Church. Hidden in the bushes and the tall green grass were all sorts of candy eggs—brightly colored, speckled eggs with malted milk inside and creamy marshmallow eggs with dark chocolate shells. There were even plastic eggs filled with jellybeans and pieces of bubblegum. But the egg to be had was the golden egg. It was the biggest, most beautiful egg of all, made of solid milk chocolate and wrapped in shiny gold foil. The sunlight reflecting off that egg was almost blind-ing. When I was real small, I was convinced Jesus Himself had sent this egg to Cedar Grove. He had sent this egg hop-ing it would be found by little Catherine Grace Cline.

But every year, Mrs. Roberta Huckstep took her grand-daughter by the hand and led her right to the holy egg.

Mrs. Huckstep owned a small gift shop in town and for some reason seemed to think that because she knew something about leaded crystal and fine bone china that she was better than the rest of us and that her precious Emma Sue was the only one among us who could appreciate such a heavenly piece of chocolate.

With her blond, curly hair tied back in a big pink bow, that bratty Emma Sue would sit on the front steps of the church, and with a big stupid smirk stretched across her face, would hold that golden egg in her hands as if she'd won some first-place trophy. She was rubbing my face in it, and I just wanted to rub her face and that big pink bow in the mud.

"Looks like Jesus was smiling down on you again this year, Emma Sue," Mrs. Huckstep would say, like she actually believed her precious little granddaughter, in her precious little white smocked dress, had found that egg on her own, her uncanny sense of direction coming straight from the Lord above.

I know I was taught that Jesus loves all the children in the world, but sometimes I wished He had made one exception with that Emma Sue. Martha Ann and I would stomp our feet and beg Daddy to make Emma Sue give back that egg. "It isn't fair," we'd cry in unison, sounding almost as though we'd been practicing our refrain.

And we weren't the only ones complaining. Three or four deacons were regularly standing right behind us, waiting their turn to talk to the preacher. But as usual, Daddy knew just what to say to calm the crowd, something about the real gift of Easter not being hidden in the bushes or something Christian like that. Then one year, when Brother Buford Bowden, the town's only doctor and the same Brother Bowden who had donated all the money for the Bowden Fellowship Hall, finally threatened to join the Presbyterian Church in Fort Oglethorpe, Daddy came up with the idea of hiding two golden eggs, the second secretly placed well out of sight of Mrs. Huckstep's roving eyes.

It seemed to make the hunt a little more equitable, at first. But funny thing, Brother Bowden's niece, Mary Cummings Bowden, was always the lucky girl who found the second egg.

Walking home with Daddy after the hunt one year, Martha Ann and I were kicking up the dirt on the road, griping about Emma Sue and Mary Cummings. Daddy calmly looked at us and said, "Girls, life's not fair. You know that by now. But I promise you there is a golden egg waiting for you, somewhere, someday."

Maybe, but one thing I had already figured out was that *my* golden egg was not hidden anywhere in Ringgold, Georgia.

CHAPTER TWO

Dreaming of the Promised Land

My mama died when I was six years old. I don't remember much of anything about her dying. I imagine I pushed those memories about as far out of my head
as possible. All I really do remember was Ida Belle Fletcher
and the blue-haired ladies from the Euzelian Sunday-school
class who came and cared for Martha Ann and me in the
days right after Mama's accident.

I called them the Zillions, partly because I couldn't pro-
nounce their name and partly, I think, because there seemed
like a million of them huddled in my house. I know they
meant well, but I just wanted them to go home and leave
us alone. They didn't make peanut-butter-and-jelly sandwiches like my mama. They didn't brush my hair like my
mama, and they certainly didn't smell like my mama. And

they kept saying the same thing over and over again like a choir singing some plaintive hymn, "Oh, you poor little children, your mama has passed and left you and your daddy alone. Oh, sweet Jesus. Oh, sweet Jesus."

Funny thing is, "passing" didn't sound like dying to a little girl. At first I thought Mama must have passed on over to the next county like Buster Black or some bird flying across the sky. But surely if she had passed over, she would pass on back soon. Even Buster came home. She wouldn't leave me and Martha Ann like that. Years later, Daddy told me that after Mama died, I watered her tomatoes every single day, all summer long, just waiting for her to come home and tell me what a good job I'd done.

I begged and begged Jesus to bring my mama back to me, but He didn't answer that prayer, either. Finally, I decided that heaven must be something really special, like the picture in my Bible where the streets are paved with gold and the blue sky goes on forever. It had to be more beautiful than even I could imagine if my mama couldn't bring herself to walk out those pearly gates and find her way back to Ringgold, Georgia. Then again, I figured Ringgold probably wasn't much of a temptation for an angel living in a golden paradise.

After the funeral, nobody really talked about my mama much, not even my daddy. I guess everybody thought it would be too painful for me and Martha Ann. I think it was just too painful for them, because I could never hear enough about her. I was always thirsty for more.

Mama drowned in Chickamauga Creek, which is known on occasion to run pretty fast, especially after a thunderstorm. Daddy said she had gone down to the creek to pick some blackberries late one afternoon in the middle of July. She loved the taste of those wild berries, and she always picked enough so she could make a batch of blackberry jam. That way, Mama said, she could eat her berries all year long.

Daddy said she walked along the creek a mile or so south of town to a small clearing just beyond the old gristmill where the blackberries grew particularly thick. She must have gotten hot and waded out into the water to cool herself off and wash the chiggers off her legs. I can still picture my mama standing in the middle of the creek in her white cotton slip, with her long, brown hair hanging down her back, dripping with water.

Mama was a good swimmer. She had already taught me to keep my head above water. But the sheriff told Daddy that she slipped, hit her head on a rock, and fell, unconscious, into the current. The water wouldn't let go and took her away from me and Martha Ann.

The blue-haired ladies kept whispering in each other's ears. I knew they were talking about the poor preacher's wife, but all I really knew for sure was that when the sun set on that hot, sticky summer day, my mama was gone forever.

I've kept the same picture of her on my dresser for as long as I can remember, and then I've kept another one locked in my head, which I can see better than any old piece of paper. And even now when I'm lying in bed at night with my eyes closed tight, I can see her pretty face with her deep brown eyes and full, pink lips. I can touch her soft skin and smell the Jergen's lotion that she rubbed on her arms and legs before going to bed. In this picture, she talks to me. She tells me that she loves me. She tells me that she's sorry she had to leave me. She even sings "Hush Little Baby," her perfectly pitched voice lulling me back to sleep.

Then I wake up, and she's gone.

I have lots of little pieces of memories of my mama and then I have one very vivid one, and I've guarded every detail of it as if it's some secret golden treasure. I was playing in the backyard with my baby doll, pushing her around in a little carriage Mama got me at the S & H Green Stamp store down in Dalton. The carriage was white with a delicate navy pattern scrolled around the sides, and it had a matching navy hood I could pull up to protect my baby's eyes from the bright sunlight. Mama had collected those green stamps for months at the Shop Rite before she could get me that stroller. It took five whole books of stamps, most of which I licked myself. Mama placed them all real neatly on each page until the books were full.

"Catherine Grace, I do think your tongue is going to turn green licking all those stamps," I remember her saying. "Sweetie, that's why I put the kitchen sponge there, so you don't have to do so much licking and tire your tongue out so."

Daddy said I pushed that buggy around the backyard

for hours while Mama did her chores. She'd prune and water her tomatoes and then let me pick the really red ones, the ones she was going to serve with dinner. She'd hang the day's laundry on the clothesline that stretched from the house to a pole stuck out in the middle of the yard, making our house look like a ship about to set sail. All the windows were wide open and Loretta Lynn, Mama's favorite singer, was playing on the radio in the living room. Loretta's voice just floated across the backyard serenading us both. Mama sang along, like she was standing there with her onstage at the Grand Ole Opry.

It's funny how you can take just one memory of someone and create a lifetime of feelings and attachments. Sometimes I think I'm really lucky. Martha Ann was only four when Mama died. She doesn't have any memories of her at all, only the same black-and-white photograph I have sitting on my dresser. I think she carries another one around in her head, too, but I think to Martha Ann, Mama sounds more like Miss Nancy on *Romper Room*.

The Lord would heal our hearts, Daddy kept telling us. But mine never did quit aching, and eventually I decided that the Lord had forgotten about Catherine Grace and Martha Ann Cline. He had forgotten about the preacher's daughters in Ringgold, Georgia, who needed their mama.

But Daddy never lost his faith, not for one minute. He said God didn't take Mama away. It was an accident, and God doesn't cause accidents. He just helps us cope with them. Then he'd call to mind some part of a hymn, trying to comfort me with a bunch of rhyming words.

"The Lord will strengthen and help thee, and cause thee to stand upheld by His righteous, omnipotent hand." Daddy always spoke the words 'cause he knew, unlike Mama, he couldn't carry a tune.

One day, I asked Daddy what *omnipotent* meant, and he said it was a big fancy way of saying "more powerful than anybody or anything in the whole wide world." "In other words, hon, it means there's nothing the Lord can't do."

Yeah right, I thought to myself. If God was really, truly omnipotent, He could have kept one needed mama from slipping on a stupid rock. But I still went to Sunday school every week wearing my best dress and my patent-leather shoes, looking like I had absolutely no complaints with the all-powerful One. I had everybody at Cedar Grove Baptist Church, even my own daddy, thinking I was the most Jesus-loving girl in town. Sometimes I wondered if I even had the Omnipotent One fooled, too.

Truth be told, even though I had grown a bit tired of waiting on the Lord to get around to answering some of my most pressing questions, I found an unusual amount of pleasure in reading His good book. Well, at least the stories. I figured if Noah could survive a flood that covered the entire earth while rocking around in a homemade boat filled with a zooful of animals, and David could beat up a giant with nothing more than an old slingshot he fashioned together with a sturdy stick and a piece of leather, then maybe little old Catherine Grace was going to find her way out of Ringgold after all.

But Moses was my favorite. His life was exciting from the minute his mama birthed him. This mean, old Egyptian king commanded that all the Hebrew baby boys be killed, including Moses. So his mama put him in a basket and floated him out into the river so the king's daughter would find him and protect him. Then his mama, who must have loved him something awful, pretended to be some kind of maid or something and offered to help the princess take care of her newly found baby boy.

When he was all grown up, Moses got a message from God telling him he was going to lead all the Hebrew people out of Egypt. Moses was sure God had gone and gotten the wrong man for the job, apparently forgetting momentarily that He was the Omnipotent One. But God reminded him, even parting the Red Sea square down the middle so Moses could walk the Israelites right out of slavery once and for all.

Miss Margaret Raines, our Sunday-school teacher, illustrated these stories using the green-felt board hanging on the front wall of our classroom. She moved from Tuscaloosa when I was about eight and taught the one and only first-grade class at the Ringgold Elementary School. She said she had come to teach for only a couple of years before moving on to something better. Well, she didn't say it quite like that, but I knew what she meant. Anyway, that was so many years ago now, I've lost count, and Miss Raines is still teaching the only first-grade class at Ringgold Elementary School.

I always figured she would be kind of tired of looking at kids by the weekend, but she was in Sunday school every week, although she looked different when she was at church. At school, she wore her long, blond hair tied back in a ponytail or a bun. But on Sundays she wore it hanging down in pretty soft curls.

She's the only adult I know who's won the perfect-attendance pin three years in a row, although I was never quite sure if she was coming to church with such regularity to praise the good Lord or to admire the handsome preacher. Miss Raines and my daddy were more than friends. I knew that, and I knew why. She was smart and nice and loved the Lord and definitely was the only Bible teacher at Cedar Grove who didn't have blue hair.

I could never admit this to my daddy, but I probably learned more about the Bible from her than from anybody else. She could move those paper figures on that felt board so smooth that sometimes I thought I was standing right there in Palestine witnessing it all with my very own eyes. The first time I saw her separate the Red Sea, I just sat there, speechless, amazed and angry all at the same time. God Almighty could part an ocean for this crowd but couldn't even bother to clear one narrow path in Chicka-mauga Creek for Lena Mae Cline. I sat in my chair getting madder and madder. He could have saved my mama if He had wanted to. I knew it, and I had known it all along, but now I had proof.

"Boys and girls," Miss Raines continued, not even noticing my personal indignation, "this was the handiwork of the Lord Himself. This was a miraculous event. This was an exodus of biblical proportions."

Maybe. But I still wasn't happy about it. And Martha Ann, well, she was more impressed with Miss Raines's choice of words than with what she had actually said. My sister admired all sorts of pretty things, like the daffodils that bloom as soon as the winter days start to turn warm and the full moon that hangs over Taylor's Ridge. But more than anything else, Martha Ann admired words, especially those that just rolled off her tongue in some sort of melodic rhythm like butter rolling off a hot biscuit.

Martha Ann loved to read, and she always had a book in her hand. She swore reading was even better than eating a Dilly Bar. By and by, she developed a real appreciation for the English language, and when she heard words put together like "of biblical proportions," she would try to squeeze them into every possible conversation for the rest of the day.

"Daddy, that pot roast is so good it is of biblical proportions," Martha Ann announced at the dinner table later that night.

Sometimes she didn't make any sense at all, but it didn't change the fact that Moses had led God's people into freedom. And after giving it more thought, I finally decided that even if the Lord didn't save my mama, and even if Moses did end up wandering around the desert for forty years, it was still an exodus worthy of admiration, if not an inspiration for my own eventual great departure.

My wanting to leave town had nothing to do with my daddy, although sometimes I wondered if that's what he thought. He really did do a good job of mothering us. He cooked our dinners, washed our hair in the kitchen sink so the soap wouldn't get in our eyes, and even dried our tears when our knees were bleeding or our hearts were aching. But I'm not sure if he really ever did understand my wanting to know something different.

Daddy was just more concerned with raising us right than dreaming of places he'd never seen. He always said the good Lord had one Golden Rule, but I think Daddy had two: *Go to church on Sundays and set a good example every day.* And that was what we did. Our pigtails may not have looked as even and tidy as the other girls' and our dresses may not have been as perfectly pressed as theirs, either. And maybe we never learned how to embroider or needlepoint, but there were two things we knew better than any other girl in town: the Bible and Georgia football.

Come September we understood that the weather was about to change and so was our way of living. It was time to put away the baby dolls and start tossing the football. We could throw a tight spiral fifty yards by the time we were nine and talk the game as much as the boys, something most of the other girls thought was very unladylike.

"Catherine Grace, I swear it does sound like you are speaking gibberish when you start that football talk. Screen passes and draw plays, you know the boys aren't gonna find that attractive," announced Ruthie Morgan at the lunch table one Monday when I was in the midst of recounting the winning drive that led the Bulldogs to a come-from-behind, six-point victory over the Tennessee Volunteers.

Ruthie Morgan lived next door and was about as girly a girl as you could ever hope to find. She always wore a pink dress and had a pink barrette clipped in her hair. I bet it took her mama at least three tries to get that barrette hanging so straight. From time to time, Ruthie Morgan and I would jump rope together or play badminton, not because we particularly liked each other but because there was nothing else to do. Of course, it should be no big surprise that Ruthie Morgan and Emma Sue were good friends, even though Ruthie Morgan was a full two years older. I always called Ruthie Morgan by her first and last names, placing just enough emphasis on the first syllable of her last name to convey my abiding irritation with her.

During football season, Ruthie Morgan would not step foot in our house, not that I really cared. Too bad for her, I always said, 'cause on game days we drank red Kool-Aid, ate red Jell-O, and dressed our Barbies in little red dresses all in honor of the fightin' Dawgs. We screamed and yelled at that television set while Ruthie Morgan was probably stuck inside ironing her mother's linen napkins for Sunday lunch.

Even though I would have never admitted this to her, or my daddy, I would have loved to iron some napkins for Mama. She would have set the temperature gauge on low so I wouldn't get burned, and I'd press on that iron till I smoothed every single crease and wrinkle out of that linen. I envied all the ironing Ruthie Morgan got to do, all the pretty white napkins and her daddy's big, square handkerchiefs.

My daddy didn't much believe in ironing. He said if you couldn't wash and wear it, it wasn't worth buying. Even at the Sunday dinner table we wiped our hands on paper napkins Daddy bought by the hundreds at the Shop Rite.

Once I tried ironing one of Martha Ann's dresses, the one she was planning on wearing to Emma Sue's tenth birthday party. Mrs. Roberta Huckstep always felt obligated to invite at least one of the preacher's daughters, and thankfully for me, Martha Ann was her favorite. She told Emma Sue that Martha Ann was a lovely young girl, but she had to wonder if my mama's tragic accident, as she always called it, had left me scarred. She said that it was fortunate for Martha Ann that she was barely four at the time and would have been too young to have been damaged by the tragic-ness of it.

Scarred or not, if Martha Ann was going to a Huckstep party, I was determined she was going to look just as pretty as the birthday girl and all her prissy little friends. Unfortunately, by the time I was done ironing, the dress had a big brown burn mark on the back. I told her nobody would notice, even though I knew I was lying. I tried tying the sash so it covered most of the burn, but it's hard to shape a bow as big as that one needed to be. Martha Ann wore that dress anyway, never letting on that she was upset with me.

At least the Lord left us one female in our lives who was willing to teach us some of the more womanly things we needed to know. Gloria Jean Graves was the most feminine woman I knew, and she lived right next door. When Daddy worked late, Gloria Jean took care of us, but, more important, she was the one we went to when we needed help making cookies for a Valentine's party or our hair fixed smooth and neat for our annual school picture.

She was the one who taught us how to shave our legs without drawing blood and to put on a pair of nylons without causing a run. And she was the one who told me what to do when my period started, the mechanics of which I would never have been able to discuss with my daddy.

Gloria Jean insisted we call her by her first name. She said Mrs. Graves made her sound too old, like one of those blue-haired grandmamas with one foot in the grave. Gloria Jean was definitely not our grandmama. She was real handsome but in a different way than any of the other women I knew. She looked more like she belonged in the television set with all the other beautiful people. Nothing about Gloria Jean was simple or plain.

God Almighty only knows the true color of Gloria Jean's hair. She went to the beauty parlor every other week, without fail, and had it colored a bright, beautiful shade of auburn. Your hair, she said, was your crowning glory, and it should be given the proper attention. Every day she'd tease and pile her hair on the top of her head and then spray it in place. Not even the wind blowing before a thunderstorm could knock a hair on her head loose. She kept a small bottle of Aqua Net in her purse because a girl, she said, had to be prepared for any emergency. She would even spray it on her skirt if it started clinging to her nylons.

One Fourth of July, she stuck real-live lightning bugs inside her hair and then covered it all with netting. Her head glowed like some kind of fancy firecracker till all the lightning bugs choked on her hairspray and died. She paid Martha Ann and me fifty cents apiece to pick all those poor little bugs from her hair. Nope, nothing about Gloria Jean was ever simple or plain.

Her face was made up with all sorts of pretty colors, all the time. Martha Ann and I spent the night with her once and when she tucked us into bed her eyelids were blue, and when she called us to breakfast the next morning, her eyelids were green. Looking at her face was kind of like looking at a rainbow.

She painted everything, including her fingernails and toenails. And they were always the most beautiful shade of pink or red, depending on what color outfit she was wearing that day. She had a collection of nail polish that even Ruthie Morgan found enviable. There must have been thirty or forty bottles of polish, from Chrysanthemum Pink to Paris Evening Red, neatly stacked on the bottom shelf of her bathroom closet. And when it was raining and we couldn't go outside and play, Gloria Jean would give me and Martha Ann a manicure, just like in a real beauty parlor.

Sitting out on her television set was a photograph of herself. She was standing in front of the fountain at city hall with her legs positioned just like a model in one of those *Vogue* magazines she kept laying around the house. She looked so fancy in her full, pleated skirt and her high, pointed heels. Her hair was swept up on her head and her lips were painted a deep ruby red. Gloria Jean had been a sure-enough beauty in her day. Even Martha Ann and I could figure that out.

Apparently a lot of men had figured that out, too. She had been married five times, something I considered an amazing accomplishment but something you could tell didn't impress my daddy much. Gloria Jean said herself that she hadn't given up on love, just the official marital ritual. In fact, she had a steady boyfriend who lived down in Calhoun. His name was Meeler Dickson, and he worked in a carpet mill, and that was all I knew about him. She visited him the third weekend of every month without fail, but she never once let him come to her house.

She said she wouldn't feel right about a man in her house with the preacher living next door. But I think she was more concerned about Ida Belle Fletcher, who lived two doors down, spooning out the details of her private life just as freely as she did the creamed corn at church suppers.

Martha Ann and I loved it when Gloria Jean talked

about her husbands and her weddings. She'd begin with some simple piece of advice like, "Oh girls, don't you ever marry a man that comes to the church late for his own wedding." Then we knew it was time to pay close attention because Gloria Jean was about to share a story even juicier than those soap operas she loved to watch on the television.

"My first husband, remember girls, Cel Beauchamp, from Louisiana. He was late to the church, and I just knew that was a sign from God that I should hightail it out the back door. If a man can't show up for his own wedding on time, girls, then he'll never be able to keep a woman happy," Gloria Jean said with the conviction that comes only from experience. "But the church was already filled with people, the candles were lit, my veil was on, and my mother said, 'Unless that leg of yours is in a cast, you are walking down that aisle.'

"Girls, hear me out, there is always time to turn back. You know why he was late? 'Cause he was getting drunk at some bar up in Soddy Daisy. I left him after three months of wedded bliss. He come home one too many nights smelling of Jack Daniel's and homemade cigars. But I did all right. I walked away with one fine diamond ring, a brand-new double-wide, and a set of Corning Ware that's still sitting in my kitchen cupboard, never even taken it out of the box."

"Oh Daddy, Gloria Jean is just so neat," I told him when he got home from visiting the sick late one night. "You know she wore white at all five weddings. She says that is a bride's prerogative. She even said that when I get married, I can wear one of her dresses."

"Catherine Grace," Daddy replied in an unusually firm tone, "there's a reason a bride wears white on her wedding day, and we will discuss that when you're a little older. But remember this, husbands and wedding dresses are not meant to be collected. You only need one of each."

Daddy never seemed particularly fond of Gloria Jean. I guess he considered divorce to be one of those get-down-on-your-knees-and-beg-for-forgiveness kind of sins. And the colorful way she lived her life probably didn't seem like that of a repentant woman. I wasn't troubled by the number of times she'd been married. It could have been twenty for all I cared. She was one of the most loving and exciting people I knew.

But I think, more than anything, I liked being around her because she would talk about my mama. She was the only person in town who ever talked about my mama. Any old thing might remind her of her friend Lena Mae, like when the clouds in the sky come together to look like a bunny rabbit. Then Gloria Jean would say something like, "Oh honey, your mama loved to sprawl out in the grass and look for animals floating across the sky. She was nothing more than a little girl herself when she married your daddy."

Gloria Jean said she and my mama had been friends ever since Lena Mae came to town. Turned out our mama's aunt in Willacoochee was Gloria Jean's fifth husband's first cousin. "It's a small world, girls," she'd laugh, "especially when you've married half of it."

You could tell Gloria Jean really loved Lena Mae Cline. She was just extra special, she'd say. And you could tell she saw something in my mama that nobody else saw. "Catherine Grace, I knew it from the minute I laid eyes on her. She was such a pretty thing. She didn't need all these creams and powders I wear to be pretty. She just was. And she was so eager to be a good wife and mother. Yep, she was a real beauty, hon, inside and out," she'd say, making me feel so proud to be her daughter.

"And, boy howdy, could she sing like a bird. She had the best voice in the Cedar Grove church choir. I told her that voice of hers surely made the Lord smile. I even begged her to take what the Lord had given her and head on over to Nashville and give it a go. There ain't no sin in singing for money. The Lord loves Loretta, Dolly, and Tammy just as much as He does Lena Mae Cline."

Gloria Jean really believed my mama could have been a country music star. Sometimes I tried to imagine what life would have been like if she had been, me and Martha Ann and Mama and Daddy driving around in Mama's big fancy tour bus, stopping in a place like Ringgold only to buy some gas and sign a few autographs. But that dream, just like all the others crowding my head, always ended with me waking up the preacher's daughter in my bed in Ringgold, Georgia.

"Yes, sirree, girls, your mama had what it took to be on

the stage of the Grand Ole Opry. But the minute she'd start dreaming, well, she was real quick to remind me that her place was here with you girls and your daddy. I guess that don't really matter now. Either one of you know what time it is?" she'd say, always looking for a way to change the subject whenever my daddy's name drifted into the conversation.

Gloria Jean never said a mean thing about my daddy; that wasn't her way. But I knew that since Mama died, she quit going to church. She said it was just too painful to look up in the choir and not see her friend standing there singing her praises to Jesus. But sometimes I wondered if Gloria Jean thought my daddy hadn't treated my mama quite right, that maybe he hadn't appreciated all of Lena Mae's God-given gifts and talents. I don't know, but somehow I knew that was her business, not mine.

"Come on, girls. Let's get out the marshmallow whip and Ritz crackers and make us a little snack before the *Guiding Light* comes on," Gloria Jean would say, and then we'd sit and watch the heartache and drama in somebody else's life for an hour.

CHAPTER THREE

Wandering Through the Desert
with a Jar of Strawberry Jam

When the lightning bugs came out to decorate the night sky, my daddy started working overtime, redeeming Ringgold's unsaved souls from an eternity of hellfire and damnation. He figured he had only three, maybe four, months at best when the water at Nottely Lake was warm enough to baptize those willing to dedicate their lives to their Savior Jesus Christ. Even Daddy knew that God's beloved children wouldn't go looking for salvation in freezing cold water.

So by the middle of June, Daddy's sermons were running a good fifteen minutes longer than normal, and the choir's singing of the final hymn seemed never ending. Daddy wouldn't give the poor choir a rest until he was convinced he had collected as many recruits for the Almighty as possible, which can be a tedious task in a town where 99 percent of the population has already committed itself to the Lord at least twice. He would stand in front of the pulpit, rocking back and forth as the choir sang softly behind him, and remind his flock that the time had come for them to reexamine their lives because tomorrow could be too late.

These were particularly trying times for Brother Fulmer and his aching stomach. He knew the meatiest pork chops and the freshest fried tomatoes at Morrison's Cafeteria over in LaFayette were going to be gone by the time he got there. I always considered him to be one of the most faithful men in town because not once did he sneak out the back during the closing hymn just so he could get to the cafeteria ahead of the Presbyterians, something the Bostleman brothers did with great regularity, claiming they needed to get their aunt some food before her blood sugar level dropped again.

Sometime after my ninth birthday, Daddy started asking me if I was ready to accept Jesus into my life as my Lord and Savior. I think I would have preferred he'd taken me shopping for my first bra than talked about something as personal as my salvation. "Not yet, Daddy," I'd say, avoiding his eyes for fear that I was disappointing him.

"Are you sure, Catherine Grace?" he'd say. "I mean, you'll know when it's time. You'll feel it in your heart. Are you sure you haven't felt anything in your heart? A stirring of any kind?"

I think being the preacher and all, he was eager for me

to make my walk with the Lord a public one. Truth be told, I wasn't sure I was ever going to be ready for that journey. Everybody else who walked down the red-carpeted aisle at Cedar Grove Baptist Church and into my daddy's open arms was crying and shaking, acting like they were possessed or something. I didn't feel anything like that, and I wasn't so sure I wanted to. I mean, I hadn't really known Jesus to go out of his way to do anything special for Catherine Grace Cline.

But for a preacher's daughter, I guess this transformation was as inevitable as all the other changes a young girl must endure, except this one happened without any advance warning—no pimples, no tender breast buds, nothing. Martha Ann and I were minding our own business, sitting on the back pew of the church so Daddy couldn't see Martha Ann reading the hymnal and me drawing on the backs of the offering envelopes. My friend Lolly Dempsey slipped in next to us halfway through the sermon, and we started playing a three-way game of hangman.

Lolly's mama and daddy were the only two people I knew who never came to church, not even on Christmas Eve or Easter Sunday. Lolly's daddy would drop her off right in front of the church, barely stopping his Chevy truck long enough for Lolly to jump out the door. I imagine he thought if he hesitated for more than a second, Daddy might try to save his soul, too. He was probably right.

None of us were paying much attention to what Daddy was saying except when he pounded on the top of the pulpit for added emphasis. Then we'd look up as if to say, "Amen to that."

Mrs. Roberta Huckstep was perched on the piano bench, preening like a beauty contestant as she waited for Daddy's cue to start playing. Betty Gilbert, the regular church pianist, had gone to Macon for three weeks to visit her sister, and Mrs. Huckstep was reveling in her new, albeit temporary, position. She missed as many notes as she hit but since she's completely deaf in her left ear, she kept smiling, thinking she sounded like some kind of famous concert pianist.

When Brother Fulmer started holding his stomach, Daddy knew it was time to bring the service to a close. He looked over at Mrs. Huckstep, and speaking in a kind of hymn-talk, said something like, "Remember, we all need to cling to that old rugged cross, so then one day, one glorious day, we, too, can exchange it for our heavenly crown." This was her cue to start playing softly in the background as Daddy made one final pitch for salvation.

Any other darn day, I would have kept on playing hangman. But for some reason, which I'll never understand, I put down my pencil and listened to the words of that hymn I had sung so many times before:

> In the old rugged cross, stained with blood so divine,
> A wondrous beauty I see;
> For 'twas on that old cross Jesus suffered and died
> To pardon and sanctify me.

Pardon *me?* Sanctify *me?* Catherine Grace Cline? I mean, I hadn't really been all that nice to Jesus since my mama died. And I certainly hadn't given much thought as to how Jesus was feeling about me. But I guessed if He could love Catherine Grace even after all the mean, hateful things I'd been thinking, well, maybe He was more omnipotent than I had given Him credit for.

All of a sudden, tears started welling up in my eyes and rolling down my cheeks. I didn't feel particularly sad, yet I couldn't stop crying. It was more like an urging, an urging in my heart, just like Daddy said it would be. Next thing I knew I was walking down the aisle toward my daddy, dragging Martha Ann along with me.

Lolly followed right behind us both, I guess not wanting to be left in the pew by herself. She said she wasn't sure if her mama and daddy were going to approve of her committing herself to the Lord, especially if that was going to mean taking time away from her household chores.

"You precious girls are the beloved children of the Lord," Daddy said as he pulled us, even Lolly, into his arms.

Daddy announced to the congregation that we would be baptized in two weeks, the first baptisms of the salvation season. An "Amen" chorus swept through the room, and then he encouraged all the remaining sinners to come and join us in our walk with the Lord. I felt like he was holding us up in front of everybody like some kind of fish bait, luring the others into the net. Then he said this was truly one of the happiest days in his life. Poor Martha Ann and Lolly,

I thought to myself, they have gone and given themselves to the Lord without even knowing it.

Baptism Sundays were all-day events that were as social as they were ceremonial. Immediately following the church service, everybody piled into cars laden with blankets and casseroles and drove the thirty-something miles over to Nottely Lake. The blue-haired ladies all rode together, safely following at least one mile behind the rest of the caravan, our very own Caravan for Christ, as Daddy liked to call it. Brother Fulmer always volunteered to leave church a little early so he could claim a green, grassy spot by the water and most likely a hot corn dog and French fries at the Dairy Queen along the way. It was kind of amazing that for as many corn dogs as Brother Fulmer must have sneaked behind his wife's back, his stomach was always flat as a board.

After Brother Fulmer, Ida Belle was always the next to arrive, and she would jump out of the front seat of her station wagon already dressed in her dingy, old apron that she must have tied onto her body on the ride over, one hand working the apron strings while the other was holding onto the steering wheel. She would start barking orders at the men, telling them to set up the folding tables and portable grills. "We got to get those burgers and hot dogs going for the chil'ren," she'd say, all the time directing the women to cover the picnic tables with red-checked cloths and citronella candles.

She even brought a box of empty mason jars and told

the kids to pick some wildflowers so she could place an arrangement on each table. Mrs. Gulbenk had taught her years ago that picnicking was no excuse not to set a nice table. When everything looked just right, Ida Belle would reach into the back of her old, red Rambler and start unpacking mounds of country ham, coleslaw, potato salad, sliced tomatoes, deviled eggs, green bean casseroles, freshly cut watermelon, and, her crowning glory, hundreds of homemade brownies, covered with her very own milk chocolate icing. And when all was said and done, there on the bank of Nottely Lake, it looked like the Fourth of July had run right into Thanksgiving Day.

No one was allowed to eat one bite until all the baptisms had been performed and Daddy had blessed the food to the nourishment of our bodies. Martha Ann could be heard repeating Daddy's words, "That's right, to the nourishment of our bodies."

Brother Fulmer said the sight of that country ham waiting to be carved was enough to make even a saved man feel weak in the knees. And I believe he must have been right, because just when you thought your stomach couldn't wait any longer, Daddy, dressed in a long, white robe, would appear from inside a small green nylon tent. The crowd would fall silent, and everyone would part in front of him as if they were seeing Jesus for the very first time.

Mama made that robe for Daddy right after they got married. She even sewed weights into the hem so it wouldn't float above his waist when he walked into the water. And on the left cuff, she had embroidered in gold thread the words, "Oh Lamb of God, I come!" taken from Daddy's favorite hymn, "Just As I Am." Being that it was the same hymn that had serenaded his own granddaddy's salvation, Daddy insisted that it be sung before every baptism at Cedar Grove Baptist Church. Miss Raines brought a battery-operated cassette player from our classroom, and as soon as Daddy walked out of the tent, she pushed a button and the music started filtering through the hot summer air.

Daddy walked to the lake's edge and stepped into the water and smiled reassuringly as though he had just put his foot into a warm, soapy bath. He waded farther and farther into the lake until the water was around his waist, and then he turned, with his arms outstretched toward his congregation. All the candidates for baptism were lined up on the water's edge dressed in their bathing suits and wrapped in towels. I still wasn't sure what I was doing there, and I still didn't understand why I had started crying in church in the first place. Maybe I was just missing Mama. I used to get to feeling that way at the beginning of summer when I had more time on my hands to think about things other than long division and dangling prepositions. But no matter what the reason, I was minutes away from getting right with the Lord and there was no turning back now.

Martha Ann and I were first in line with Emma Sue standing right behind us and Lolly standing right behind Emma Sue. Mrs. Huckstep was not about to see us redeemed before her precious granddaughter, so Emma Sue had found herself on the banks of Nottely Lake, looking as confused as we did. Martha Ann didn't like the water. She never had. I think she was afraid she'd be swept away like Mama. And she particularly didn't care for water getting in her nose or her ears, so she stood there with little pink plastic plugs stuffed in every hole above her chin except her mouth, which she kept locked tight.

Daddy looked toward Martha Ann and with his eyes motioned for her to join him in the water, but she didn't budge. He paused for a moment, and then waved his left arm, signaling again for her to step into the water. Before we left the house that morning, Daddy had spent a long time talking to Martha Ann about the baptism and how she'd be safe in his arms. But all that talking didn't seem to matter much now. She just stood there, frozen, like she didn't even see him standing right there in front of her. Miss Raines stepped toward her and put her arm around Martha Ann's shoulder, trying to coax her into the lake. But as the cassette player crackled in the background, everybody began to whisper. I could hear words like *scared* and *naughty* swirling about the water's edge.

Then Emma Sue poked me in the back with her scrawny little finger and whispered, "Looks like your sister's a heathen after all, Catherine Grace."

I heard Lolly warning Emma Sue that she better shut her trap real quick, but it was too late. Stealing the golden egg had been bad enough, but calling my sister a heathen was not something I could leave to the Lord to punish. My body started moving before my head could catch up with it, and before I knew what I was doing, I had taken that curly-headed, prissy brat by the shoulders and shoved her right into the lake. All I could see was a big white bow floating on the surface of the water.

Miss Raines pulled me back from the bank. Mrs. Huckstep took turns screaming at me and then at my daddy.

"Look what your little de—, Yes, that's right, devil has done to my Emma Sue. Emma Sue, stand up on your feet. Quit splashing. Reverend Cline, do something!"

Daddy took two steps toward Emma Sue, scooped her into his arms, and then in a warm but commanding tone said, "Emma Sue, looks like you've gone and gotten yourself saved without me."

Everybody laughed, except Mrs. Huckstep, me, and Martha Ann, who still seemed lost in some sort of hypnotic trance. Daddy gave me a look that was very unfamiliar and something told me that my pending salvation was not going to be enough to save me from my daddy's wrath.

Still holding Emma Sue, Daddy told her that the Lord loved her and forgave her, that she had been born a sinner, but she would be raised a child of God, then he dunked her one more time for good measure. If I'd been him, I'd have dunked her three or four more times just to be certain I had washed all the meanness out of her.

Then Daddy motioned for me to join him in the water. I took my sister by the hand and pulled her along with me, thinking Daddy might not be quite so mad if I could get

Martha Ann baptized without any further commotion. Daddy said the exact same thing to us as he had to Emma Sue, and then dunked us both at the same time, one in each arm. Martha Ann came up spitting water but other than that she was okay. I took her hand and walked her to the shore, and there I sat on the bank of Nottely Lake feeling like the most doomed child of God there ever was.

Daddy didn't say much to me the rest of the day. After lunch he asked Miss Raines if she would take Martha Ann and me on home ahead of him. I was actually relieved to be making the drive without him. I wasn't ready to come face-to-face with my earthly maker in the confines of a 1968 Oldsmobile.

Miss Raines offered to come in and wait with us. I guess she figured even the condemned might need a little comfort. But I told her it wasn't necessary. She was only being nice and all, but I didn't want her in my house trying to mother me, not today.

I turned on the bathwater for Martha Ann and helped her wash the lake out of her hair, careful not to get any soap or water in her eyes. Then I took an extra-long bath myself, trying to wash the memory of the day down the drain. We were already in our pajamas and ready for bed when Daddy got home a little before dinnertime. We were working a jigsaw puzzle that Gloria Jean had brought us from Ruby Falls. I had probably worked that puzzle a hundred times. I knew where all the pieces went, but going through the motions seemed to quiet my nerves.

Without even taking the time to hang up his robe in the hall closet, he told Martha Ann to go on to her room. He said that he needed to talk to me in private. All afternoon I had felt like I was going to throw up. Now I was certain of it, and I started scanning the room, looking for the trash can.

"Catherine Grace, you are a lucky girl that I have had some time to think and reflect on your behavior today. Needless to say, I was very disappointed. I know Emma Sue gets under your skin. But you, Catherine Grace Cline, must love your enemies, all of your enemies, especially the ones that test you the most—even the ones wearing big bows in their hair."

"But she called Martha—"

"Catherine Grace, I don't care what she called your sister."

"But Martha Ann was scared—"

"Catherine Grace, that doesn't change what you did. I expect you to be better than that. I expect you to set an example for the others to follow. You are the preacher's daughter and with that comes a certain amount of responsibility, like it or not. Now I'm sorry, but you have to be punished." He hesitated a moment before delivering my sentence, as if he didn't want to hear it himself. "I've given this a lot of thought, Catherine Grace, and you cannot go to the Dairy Queen for the rest of the summer. It is off-limits till the first of September."

My daddy had never done anything like this before.

The worst he'd ever done was smack me on the bottom once when I grabbed Martha Ann's Raggedy Ann doll while we were standing in the checkout line at the Dollar General Store. She had been cranky all afternoon, and Daddy's nerves were already frayed. But I started crying so hard, more from the embarrassment than from the sting his hand left on my backside, that we had to leave our basket on the counter and go home without the toilet paper and toothpaste we had come to buy. He apologized later that night for spanking me. He said he knew the good book advised pulling out the rod once in a while, but it just didn't feel right striking one of his little girls. He said he'd never do that again.

But Daddy knew that taking the Dairy Queen away from me was worse than any spanking. I couldn't remember a time when going to the Dairy Queen wasn't part of my weekly routine. Mama had taken me every Saturday, after all her chores were done. We would sit there on that picnic table and eat our ice cream. We always left Martha Ann at home with Daddy or Gloria Jean because that was our special time. Then when I was old enough to walk there on my own, I started taking Martha Ann myself. Daddy knew it was where I went to reflect on the week gone by and get ready for the week to come. He had no right to take that away from me.

"Daddy, that's not fair," I screamed. "I hate being the preacher's daughter. I hate being your daughter. I don't care what anybody in this stinking, rotten town thinks.

I don't want to be an example. Everybody in this town is stupid anyway. They're all stupid for staying here." And then I screamed even louder, "I hate Emma Sue Huckstep. I wish she had drowned in that damn lake."

I couldn't believe I had said all of that out loud, not even stopping to take a breath.

"Catherine Grace, you better get to your room before I get my belt."

Daddy had never used his belt for anything but holding up his pants. And even though I really didn't think he would do it, I knew I had pushed him too far. I ran into my room and slammed the door, my last desperate act of defiance. I threw myself across my bed and cried and cried until a big wet spot had formed on my pillow. I hated my daddy for being so unfair. I hated Emma Sue and her stupid-looking bow. I hated Martha Ann for being afraid of the water. I hated my mama for drowning and making Martha Ann such a scaredy cat. And I hated John the Baptist for starting this whole baptism thing in the first place. Only eight hours earlier I was freed and forgiven from a lifetime of sin, and now I hated everybody, even the people I loved the most.

I woke up the next morning to find Martha Ann nestled against my back. She couldn't stand it when I was upset, and she probably figured sneaking in when I was asleep was the safest time to make amends.

"I'm not mad at you, I never really was," I said, without even rolling over to look her in the face.

"I'm sorry Daddy got so mad at you. It's all my fault. If I wasn't such a . . . well, maybe he'll change his mind in a day or two," Martha Ann said with a strange mix of regret and hope in her voice. "But I promise I won't go to the Dairy Queen without you. It just wouldn't be right."

"I hate this place, Martha Ann," I said softly, feeling the tears welling up in my eyes again. "It's never gonna feel right, and finding the Lord in some lake hasn't changed that one little bit."

Maybe my exodus needed to be now, not when I'm eighteen, I thought to myself, knowing good and well Martha Ann would start crying too if she heard me talking like this. I could go to Willacoochee and find my mama's family. None of them had ever been to Ringgold, not even when Mama died. But I had gotten a card from Mama's sister on my birthday for as long as I can remember; so had Martha Ann. I could live with her. I bet she'd be happy to have me. But Martha Ann would want to come along and traveling with a child might slow me down.

I spent the next two days holed up in my room figuring out what to do with the rest of my life, or at least the rest of the summer. I was still mad at my daddy, and I had decided that part of my plan was not talking to him. No good-night kisses, no warm morning exchanges, nope, nothing.

On the third day, I decided I was doing a better job of punishing myself than my daddy and decided to come out of my room long enough to visit Gloria Jean. I hadn't had a chance to tell her about the baptism yet. Gloria Jean had never cared too much for Roberta Huckstep, especially after she told Ida Belle that Gloria Jean was nothing more than a modern-day Jezebel. I figured she'd enjoy hearing that precious, darling Emma Sue had had an ill-timed swim in the lake.

Besides, Gloria Jean would agree with me that life was treating Catherine Grace Cline just plain rotten. She'd understand. She always did. She never called my dreaming foolishness, not once. She believed me when I said I was leaving town, and she always said she would help me figure out how to do it when the time came. She said she understood what it felt like to land in a place where you didn't belong. I always figured she was talking about Ringgold and yet she had lived here since before I was born, since she married her fifth husband, Darrell Hixson. Sometimes I wondered if Daddy really knew how supportive Gloria Jean had been if he'd have let me spend so much time with her.

Gloria Jean listened patiently to my sad story. She tried not to laugh thinking of Emma Sue's bow floating on the surface of Nottely Lake, and then she turned to me and looked me straight in the eyes. "Honey, if you want to get out of here as bad as you say you do, then you're going to need some money, a little *do re me,* if you know what I mean," Gloria Jean said very matter-of-factly. "So why don't you put your energy into making some change instead of sitting around moping all summer long. Dreams don't just happen, baby, you got to go after 'em."

Then Gloria Jean started talking about my grand-daddy's vegetables. I wasn't really sure where she was going with this, but I knew it would be someplace good. She explained that she had been over to Floyd Marshall's garden just the other day to help Ida Belle pick some corn. Even all these years after my granddaddy had passed on, Ida Belle still insisted on planting the corn and green beans for Wednesday-night suppers on the church grounds. She said it pleased the Lord that she fed His flock with vege-tables grown on such blessed land.

"Anyway, I hadn't been back there in a year or more, and I was surprised to see that the strawberry plants have taken over half the plot. I thought about picking those berries myself and making me some homemade strawberry jam, but you girls could do that. You know your mama used to make some of the best blackberry jam I've ever tasted, and I bet you two could do something just as special with those strawberries."

I was practically jumping off her sofa with excitement. I was going to make my dream come true and all the while working in the kitchen just like my mama used to do. Gloria Jean called it divine intervention. She said maybe my granddaddy left those strawberries there for me so I could turn them into something more valuable than I could have ever imagined. She figured I could sell the jars for a dollar a piece and that Mr. Tucker, the manager at the Dol-lar General Store, might even let me display them on one of his shelves, if we asked him real sweet.

"Gloria Jean," I said, suddenly sounding deflated. Mama died before she taught me how to do much of anything in the kitchen. "I don't know how to make jam or jelly or anything like that. I helped Ida Belle pickle some cucumbers once, but I just did what she told me to do."

"Lord child, I know you don't know how and that's why I'm going to show you. Who do you think taught your mama? That's right," she said, acknowledging my surprise. "But you need to pick those strawberries first and there are hundreds of 'em. You know how to do that, don't you?" she asked, already knowing the answer.

"All righty then, you start picking, and in a couple of days, I'll take you to town to buy the jars and pectin and sugar and everything else you're going to need to go into business. I'll even loan you some money, as a good-faith gesture, and you can pay me back when you sell all your jam."

I ran home and grabbed my blue jeans and old sneakers, explaining the whole plan to Martha Ann as I changed my clothes. I told her I'd give her fifteen cents from every jar I sold if she'd help me pick the strawberries.

Martha Ann didn't like to get dirt on her hands any more than she liked water in her nose. She always put up a fuss when it was her turn to water the tomatoes because Daddy also made her pull any weeds that had popped up around the vines. But the idea of making money was too tempting even for Martha Ann, so she agreed to help as long as she got to wear Mama's old gardening gloves that Daddy kept in the garage hanging next to the watering can.

We ran the whole way to the church, carrying baskets in both hands and kicking up the dirt behind us. As I put one foot in front of the other, I kept thinking that maybe, finally, the Lord was listening to me.

When I got to the garden's edge, something inside told me to stop. Something said I was about to step on holy ground and I ought to say a little prayer or something respectful before taking my next step.

I knew my granddaddy was watching over me. And I suspected he had left me this garden as a present that had taken me some time to appreciate, kind of like the porcelain dish Gloria Jean had given me for my tenth birthday. It had a picture of a little fairy painted on it, and she said the fairy's sweet smile reminded her of me. When I opened the box and she saw my disappointment that it wasn't that pink leather wallet I'd been admiring in the window at Mrs. Huckstep's gift shop, she promised me that someday, when I was a little older, I was going to love that dish more than any old worn-out wallet. It was a keepsake, she said, and you grow to love them more as each year passes.

I knelt down on my knees and squished my fingers in the warm, dark brown dirt as if to introduce myself to the same piece of earth my granddaddy had tended so lovingly for so many years. I reached for a red, plump berry, and as I pulled it off the runner, I said a few words of thanksgiving. Then I dropped it into my basket. Every strawberry I picked that day felt like another little keepsake he'd left behind for me to find. Martha Ann and I picked strawberries until the sun started to fall behind the roof of the church, casting a shadow over our heads. Our baskets were overflowing and the tips of our fingers ached, but neither one of us wanted to stop.

We sat by the garden before heading home and sucked on the berries we'd picked but couldn't fit into our baskets. We looked at each other and started to laugh. Our lips had turned as red as Gloria Jean's favorite shade of Revlon lipstick. We blew each other kisses like we were famous movie stars stopping to greet our fans.

We walked home that night without saying a word. My body was tired but peaceful. I wasn't mad at my daddy anymore. I wasn't mad at anybody anymore.

For the next two days, Martha Ann and I worked on our knees, picking and eating dozens of strawberries. We brought peanut butter sandwiches with us and cut up some berries and placed them between the two slices of bread. When we got tired, we would sit on the grass by the garden and eat our peanut butter and strawberry sandwiches and drink a cold bottle of Coca-Cola we had carried from home in a small plastic cooler. When we had finally filled all the baskets, Gloria Jean said we had what we needed to start making jam.

The next morning, I was standing on Gloria Jean's front porch a few minutes before seven. "Lord, child, I haven't had my coffee or even begun to put on my face. Come on in and you can eat some breakfast with me."

Gloria Jean couldn't have moved any slower that morning if she had tried, and it took almost as much energy to hide my frustration as it had to pick all those strawberries. Couldn't she just once in her life throw on some clothes like Martha Ann and me and forget about putting colors on her face? I wanted to be at the Dollar General Store the very minute Mr. Tucker unlocked the doors. I even cleaned the breakfast dishes, hoping to hurry things along.

But Gloria Jean never threw on anything, especially her makeup. And finally, at about a quarter to nine, she walked out of her bedroom, wearing high heels and a linen dress, looking more like she was headed to a party than to town to run some errands.

"Now, honey, I am ready to go," Gloria Jean announced, pointing to her pocketbook sitting on the table by the door. I grabbed her purse, ran ahead of her, and jumped into the front seat of her silver Buick LeSabre. By the time she got behind the wheel and started the engine, Martha Ann was running across the yard waving at us to wait for her. She climbed into the backseat with her flip-flops still in her hand.

Gloria Jean wanted to stop at the Shop Rite first to pick up the sugar, a bottle of lemon juice, and some boxes of fruit pectin. I had no idea what we were going to do with the pectin, but Gloria Jean said we needed it. She said everything else, including the mason jars, we could get at the Dollar General Store and that we should be giving Mr. Tucker as much business as possible since we were going to be negotiating a partnership with him shortly.

We put our groceries in the backseat of the LeSabre and walked across the parking lot to the Dollar General Store. Gloria Jean smiled when she saw Mr. Tucker and struck a pose kind of like the one in the photograph sitting on her television set.

"Llewellyn, dear, would you be so kind as to show us girls where the canning jars are? We are going to make us some strawberry jam this afternoon," said Gloria Jean, calling Mr. Tucker by his first name. Martha Ann and I tried not to laugh. We never thought of Mr. Tucker having a first name, let alone one like Llewellyn.

"Sure thing, Miss Gloria Jean, right over here," he said with an air of excitement, as if she'd agreed to go to a movie with him, not just walk to the other end of the store.

Mr. Tucker was a small man with no distinguishing features other than his thick, white hair that he cut real short like a soldier in the army. He got married for the first time last year, but Gloria Jean said he did that only because he was afraid of dying alone.

No man in his right mind, she said, would marry Blanche Baggett. She doesn't wear makeup, not even lipstick, and she weighs about three times as much as Mr. Tucker. Gloria Jean said it had been a miracle that she hadn't rolled over on him and smothered him to death. "Just a matter of time, girls, just a matter of time."

Mr. Tucker led us to the boxes of mason jars and Gloria Jean told him that we would need four dozen to start. "You know the preacher's daughters are looking to make a little money this summer," she said, continuing to explain the entire plan without pausing for him to interrupt. "I told them that I was certain you wouldn't mind them selling their jam here in the store."

"Uh, well, you know, Miss Gloria Jean, I'm not sure that the company will allow me . . . I mean, you know I would . . ."

Ignoring Mr. Tucker's hesitation, Gloria Jean proceeded, "I told them that you of all people would understand two enterprising girls wanting to make some money of their own. You being so kind and understanding and such a successful businessman and all."

Mr. Tucker stood there, shifting his weight back and forth from one foot to the other, staring at the floor. "Well, I'm sure I could make an exception for you, I mean for Reverend Cline's daughters, seeing how he's the preacher," Mr. Tucker finally confessed, looking up at Gloria Jean.

"You sweet thing," she said, winking at us so Mr. Tucker couldn't see. "Girls, didn't I tell you Mr. Tucker is about the sweetest man in town? It's just a shame Blanche got him to walk down that aisle before I did." Mr. Tucker blushed, now turning about as bright a shade of red as, well, one of my strawberries. "In fact, I bet he'd carry these dirty, old boxes out to the car for us. You know I just painted my nails and I sure would hate to chip them on one of these boxes."

Gloria Jean pulled a ten-dollar bill from her wallet and paid for the mason jars. She walked alongside Mr. Tucker, even resting her hand on his forearm as she led him to the LeSabre, ignoring me and Martha Ann altogether. He loaded the boxes just as she had asked, and I had a feeling I had already learned an awful lot about doing business that day.

We unpacked the jars and the groceries when we got back to Gloria Jean's house, and Martha Ann and I washed all the berries on one side of the sink while Gloria Jean washed the mason jars on the other. Using the back of a fork, my little sister and I crushed the berries against the side of the mixing bowl and then poured them into a big black kettle waiting for us on the stove. I added the pectin and Martha Ann added the lemon juice. Gloria Jean explained that the pectin and the juice would preserve the taste and color of the jam.

Then Gloria Jean turned on the gas under the black pot and told me and Martha Ann to stand back as she put a lit match to the burner. Martha Ann wouldn't take her eyes off the pot, waiting for the strawberry mixture to boil. Gloria Jean warned her that a watched pot of any kind never boils, but Martha Ann didn't dare blink. After it had bubbled and steamed for a minute or two, Gloria Jean added the sugar. Then we had to wait for it to boil again, but this time Gloria Jean kept scraping this pretty pink foam off the top. Martha Ann said it looked like pink clouds.

We had to wait even longer for our strawberries to cool down so that we could pour them into the mason jars. Gloria Jean fixed us grilled cheese sandwiches. She said eating would make the time pass more quickly, but even a warm grilled cheese sandwich couldn't take my mind off that pot. Finally, Gloria Jean handed us both a ladle and said we could start filling the jars as long as we were careful to leave a good quarter inch of space at the top of each one. I did most of the pouring, though, and then Martha Ann came behind me putting a metal lid on top of each jar. Then we went back and topped each one with a screw band that held the lid securely in place.

Gloria Jean said we did a real good job, but we weren't done yet. Then she put as many jars as she could at one time on a metal rack she had placed inside a large, stainless-steel pot. She filled the pot with water, making certain that the water covered all of the jars. Even when the water started boiling, Gloria Jean kept checking to make sure the jars were always covered with at least two inches of water. She said this was the most important step because we were killing all the germs that might otherwise make our customers sick. And that, she said, would not be good for business.

After about half an hour or so, we took the jars out of the water to cool once and for all. And there, sitting on the counter, was our first batch of jam. Gloria Jean said we were turning out to be real entrepreneurs just like our great-granddaddy, William Floyd, except that what we were doing was legal in all fifty states.

She pulled some paper out of a drawer and handed it to us. "These here are labels that you girls can decorate and then glue to the jars, right here, you see," she said, pointing to a smooth, rectangular space on each jar. "You're going to need to come up with a name for your jam."

Martha Ann and I looked at each other. We'd been so busy picking berries that we never gave a minute's thought to a name for our jam.

"Well, start coloring those labels, something will come to you."

We sat at Gloria Jean's kitchen table for an hour or more decorating labels and gluing them onto the jars. And she was right, the name just came to me. I called it *Preacher's Strawberry Jam,* in honor of our grandfather. I looked at Martha Ann, holding a jar of jam in my hands, and said, "You know, getting grounded may have been the best thing that ever happened to me."

"Honey, the Lord works in mysterious ways," added Gloria Jean with a smile on her face as she stood at the kitchen sink washing the big, black kettle.

By the end of the week, Mr. Tucker had sold every jar of jam we had given him, and he was asking for more. So Martha Ann and I happily spent the next month picking berries and making jam, and I think even Daddy realized that his punishment had turned into a lucrative opportunity. Ida Belle ordered a dozen jars to serve at church suppers. Lankford Bostleman said his aunt was wanting some for friends over in LaFayette. Even Mrs. Roberta Huckstep was seen picking up a jar or two. We had made almost two hundred jars when all was said and done. But our business came to an abrupt end one morning when I woke up with bright red blotches all over my body. I started screaming, thinking for sure I had scarlet fever. I had no idea what scarlet fever looked like, but since I was red, I figured I had to have it.

Daddy heard me crying and came rushing into my room. He took one look at me and picked me up in his arms and carried me out to the car. He sped into town, almost driving poor Brother Fulmer off the road. He thought I had scarlet fever, too, I knew he did.

But Doctor Brother Bowden took one look at me and started laughing. He said he and his wife had been enjoying my strawberry jam on their biscuits every morning, and he had a feeling that I had been eating my fair share of berries this summer. "I imagine quality control is an important part of the job," he said.

"Yes, sir. Kind of."

"Catherine Grace, I hate to tell you this but you have a severe case of strawberry rash, known to afflict ambitious young women who consume more strawberries than their growing bodies can handle. The cure is simple, no more strawberries, at least for a while."

It didn't take Daddy long after that to decide that it was time for my going-out-of-business sale. He said I had surely made enough money for one summer and that I should enjoy what little bit of vacation was left before school started. He also decided that I could go back to the Dairy Queen, probably figuring that Dilly Bars and daydreaming were a heck of a lot safer than strawberries.

After tending to all my financial obligations, which included reimbursing Gloria Jean her initial investment and paying Martha Ann the twenty-eight dollars and fifty cents in wages I owed her, I ended up with almost one hundred and forty dollars in the shoebox under my bed.

I agreed with my daddy. I didn't need to make any more jam this summer. I had learned my lesson, and I think he had learned one, too. Leaving this town was not going to be something I needed his permission to do. It was going to be my choice, and my journey had already begun.

CHAPTER FOUR

Preparing the Lord's Table for the Preacher and His Girlfriend

Sunday lunch was a sacred time at our house. It came with a certainty and sameness that was wonderfully comforting. Daddy would get up before daybreak and read over his sermon, spend a few quiet moments with the Lord, and then pull a chuck roast out of the refrigerator. He'd pat it with butter and brown it in a frying pan. The smell of the meat cooking was our wake-up call, an omen of sorts that this Sunday was going to be just like all the others that had come before it.

Any disruption to our Sunday routine, like when Buster Black finally died of old age and Daddy had to leave right after church to officiate at his burial behind Mr. Naylor's garage, always left me feeling kind of edgy, like something was seriously wrong with the world but nobody was going to dare tell me—the way I felt when Mama died.

But when things were as they should be, Daddy would lift the chuck roast out of the frying pan and put it in the Crock-Pot about ten minutes after seven. He bought that Crock-Pot at the Dollar General Store right after he and Mama got married. Mr. Tucker told Daddy that it was the newest concept in slow cooking and that every family needed one, and being a good husband, Daddy said he wasn't leaving the store without it. Ours was an awkward shade of green. Daddy called it avocado, which didn't mean much to me since I hadn't ever seen an avocado.

Daddy said the Crock-Pot must have been made by a churchgoing, Christian man because it was the only way a preacher could sermonize and cook all at the same time. Even when Mama was alive, Daddy always cooked Sunday lunch. He said the good Lord and a hardworking woman both needed a day off. He added four big potatoes, cut into chunks, one finely chopped onion, a bunch of baby carrots, and a bag of Green Giant frozen peas. Then he'd add a cup of water and one cube of beef bouillon, turn the Crock-Pot on high, and put on his Sunday suit. By the time we got home, the whole house smelled of perfectly prepared chuck roast. It was a warm, friendly smell, and I just wanted to wrap myself in it completely. I knew this was the same smell that my mama had come home to every Sunday after listening to her husband preach.

People were always begging us to come to their house

for Sunday lunch. Apparently it was something of an honor to have the preacher share a meal at your table. But Daddy always respectfully declined their invitations, even Doctor Brother Bowden's. He said it was our special family time and that only praying over some poor soul about to depart this world and burying one that already had would cause him to miss it. Or at least until Miss Raines came to town.

One Sunday, after Daddy had delivered a particularly loud, fist-pounding sermon about loving your neighbor as much as you love yourself, he came up to me and Martha Ann, and almost in a whisper, asked if either one of us would mind if Miss Raines joined us for lunch. We both looked at him, not knowing how to tell him that we minded a whole heck of a lot, and then said nothing. He asked again, and I finally mumbled some sort of reply, which he must have taken to mean that it was okay with Martha Ann and me, because the next thing I knew I was putting an extra placemat on the kitchen table.

Our Sunday routine was suddenly changing, and I couldn't do anything about it. Our sacred family time was being sacrificed for an appetizing, young Sunday-school teacher who was unusually talented with a felt board.

Daddy always sat at the head of the table, which long ago had been determined to be the end by the refrigerator because his arms were long enough to open the door without rising out of his seat. Martha Ann and I sat on either side of him, just like we'd always done. But today, Miss Raines sat on the other end, across from Daddy, probably where Mama used to sit. She'd look up at him with gooey eyes and call him by his first name: "Marshall, would you mind passing me the salt? Marshall, would you mind passing me the pepper?"

And Daddy would look at her and smile as if she had said something really profound. Sometimes I wondered if Daddy used to look at Mama the way he did Miss Raines. You could tell he thought she was real pretty, sitting there with her big, blue eyes and long blond hair.

I wanted to show her his crooked smile and the white hairs that were popping in around his ears. I wanted to tell her that he snored so loud at night sometimes I thought it was a train passing through town. But preachers seem to have a powerful hold over some women, at least that's what Gloria Jean said.

I think she was right. Women, and men for that matter, would do anything and everything for my daddy, long before he could even ask. Mrs. Blankenship dropped off five pounds of fresh butter from her husband's dairy farm on the first Monday of each month. In the summer, Brother Fulmer brought us the juiciest, sweetest watermelons from his own garden. He said he saved the very best for the preacher. And Ida Belle could hardly let a day go by without delivering some kind of tuna-noodle casserole or cold, fried chicken.

One time Gloria Jean was pulled over for speeding down Graysville Road. She was driving me and Martha Ann to a Saturday matinee over in Fort Oglethorpe. But when the sheriff walked up to the car and saw us two sitting in the backseat, he just told Gloria Jean to slow down. "Sure wouldn't want anything to happen to Reverend Cline's little girls."

It was as if a gift to my daddy was a gift to the Lord Himself, just as fine as any pot of frankincense or myrrh. Miss Raines was no better, except she seemed to know it was the preacher's daughters she needed to impress. She brought me and Martha Ann some kind of candy bar every single Sunday. I wanted to let her know right from the start that it was going to take a lot more than some chocolate and caramel to get me to change my mind about her dating my daddy, but, on the other hand, I hated to pass up a perfectly good Milky Way.

Miss Raines tried real hard to be our friend, even offering to play Monopoly with us on the living room floor. And once or twice, she stayed with me and Martha Ann when Gloria Jean was visiting Meeler down in Dalton and Daddy had to rush to the hospital to pray some poor soul back to health.

Personally, I never understood why Miss Raines was ever interested in an older man with two children and his own healthy crop of tomatoes. Surely she was going to want her own little babies and her own house and her own tomatoes growing right out her very own back door. Gloria Jean said pretty, young women always do.

But Miss Raines had Sunday lunch with us for the next five years. And sometimes Daddy took her to dinner or to a movie on a Friday night. One time I even saw him kiss her on the lips, with his mouth wide open. But he insisted she was just a good friend. That was kind of hard to believe since I never saw him kissing Brother Fulmer on the lips like that.

He said he had only one true love in his life and that was Lena Mae Cline and that nobody could replace her. But sometimes I thought Miss Raines sure was willing to give it a try. Everybody at church sure seemed to be hoping for a wedding. I saw all the blue-haired crones clucking among themselves whenever they spied Daddy and Miss Raines standing anywhere near each other.

"What could be more perfect," Roberta Huckstep said to Ida Belle one Sunday morning when she hadn't noticed I was sitting right behind her, "than our handsome preacher marrying our beautiful Sunday-school teacher? Besides, it's about time those girls got themselves a new mother and quit watching so much football and *Guiding Light,* if you know what I mean."

I didn't want a new mother. I already had one, and I hated Roberta Huckstep and the other blue-haired ladies at Cedar Grove Baptist Church who had apparently forgotten about Lena Mae Cline. Gloria Jean kept telling me not to worry. She said my daddy would never be able to bring himself to propose to another woman.

"Everybody needs a little adult companionship, girls, a little human contact, just look at me and Meeler. I love spending time with him, but I ain't going to marry him. It's the same with your daddy," Gloria Jean explained. "But if you ask me, I think he needs to let that poor girl get on with her life. He's still in love with your mama. He always will be. It's one of those haunting loves. No cure for that."

Maybe. But sometimes I just wanted to be certain. I just wanted Miss Raines to eat lunch at somebody else's house.

Then one Sunday morning, Miss Raines asked everybody in class if they had a favorite Bible verse. Ruthie Morgan raised her hand before anybody else had a chance and said, "Oh yes, Miss Raines, that would be John 3:16, 'For God so loved the world that He gave his only begotten Son, that whosoever believeth in Him shall not perish but have everlasting life.'"

"Oh Ruthie, that's an excellent choice, isn't it class?" Miss Raines responded, cooing like a dove sent from the heavens above. I just looked at Martha Ann and rolled my eyes. "Doesn't that make you all feel extra special knowing that God gave His only Son just for you, and you, and you," she continued, pointing to each and every one of us for added emphasis.

John 3:16 would be the obvious choice, especially for someone with a really brown nose and a perfectly pleated cotton skirt and matching blouse. But I had a better verse, one that I had been waiting for some time to share with Miss Raines, and now the ideal moment had finally arrived. I raised my hand, looking almost as eager and innocent as Ruthie Morgan, and said, "Miss Raines, I know one. I have a special verse."

"Yes, Catherine Grace Cline," she said, clearly annunciating the Cline as if to remind everyone I was the preacher's daughter and surely I knew some extra-special scripture. "Go right ahead."

"Yes, ma'am. It's from First Corinthians, chapter seven, verse number eight," I declared, standing in front of my chair so everyone could hear me. "Now to the unmarried and the widows I say: It is good for them to stay unmarried."

As soon as I heard myself say it, I regretted it, feeling oddly embarrassed and relieved all at the same time. I sat down in my chair. Feeling my cheeks turn red, I stared at the floor. I didn't mean to hurt Miss Raines, well, not that much. But I had to stand up for my mama because it sure seemed like nobody else was going to, not even my own daddy.

I knew I had hurt her. I could see it in her pretty blue eyes, which all of the sudden looked teary and sad. She glanced at me and forced a small, pitiful smile, probably wondering why she had wasted so much money buying me those candy bars.

"Thank you, Catherine, thank you for sharing."

After that, Miss Raines told us to quietly read from our Bibles until it was time to go hear the preacher. She sat at her desk, never once looking up to see if we were doing what we'd been told.

After the service, and after Daddy had said a few words to every member of the congregation, we began our long walk home. It wasn't really a long walk, just about the length, Daddy would say, of three football fields. But today, I felt like I was climbing a dang mountain—and pulling a bag of rocks behind me.

"Catherine Grace, I'm very impressed with your knowledge of the scripture," Daddy said before we had even left the parking lot. "I understand you were quoting from First Corinthians in Sunday school this morning. Sure does seem like an odd verse for you to have committed to memory, I mean at your age and all."

"I just remember it from a Sword Drill, I guess, that's all," I stammered, trying to come up with some reasonable explanation for my recitation.

"Well, it's my understanding that First Corinthians, chapter seven, verse eight, is your most favorite verse in the entire Bible," he countered, knowing he had me cornered like a cat toying with a mouse.

A moment or two of silence lingered between us while I tried to imagine myself any place but standing next to my daddy. Maybe, I hoped, this would be the end of this discussion if I could just keep my mouth shut. Maybe he just wanted to let me know that he knew. Maybe he figured I would feel so guilty about what I'd done that I would go to Miss Raines and apologize. He was probably right, but for now I wasn't saying another word. Nope, not one more word.

"Catherine Grace, I loved your mother more than any other woman in the world, and nothing's going to change that. But that doesn't mean that I can't enjoy spending time with somebody else, with somebody like Miss Raines," Daddy said. "And it doesn't mean there is any less room in my heart for you and Martha Ann. Do you understand all that?"

Sure, I thought to myself. Gloria Jean had already explained this powerful need adults have for one another's company. All I needed to say at that moment was "Yes, Daddy." Two simple words, that's it. But that's not what came out of my mouth.

"Everybody at church wants you to marry her. I hear all the old ladies talking. They think I don't, but I do. So does Martha Ann," I blurted, no more than sixty seconds after I'd sworn myself to silence. "Heck, even Ruthie Morgan thinks it's about time you two get married so I can get a mama who will teach me a thing or two about being a lady."

"Oh," Daddy said, like he was actually surprised people at Cedar Grove Baptist Church were gossiping behind his back about his marital intentions. "Well, girls," and he paused again, "I don't see us getting married. Well, at least not any time in the near future."

That was it. That was all he said. It was as if even my own daddy wasn't sure what to say next. And as we continued to walk toward the house, nobody dared to say another word. As soon as I opened the front door, I could smell the chuck roast simmering in the Crock-Pot, that wonderful, familiar aroma greeting me like a dear, concerned friend.

All three of us sat at the kitchen table for a long time, enjoying what we understood to be only a brief return to a much-loved routine. I knew that next Sunday Miss Raines would be back in her chair, staring adoringly at my daddy with those beautiful, blue eyes. Like I said, just seems preachers have a way of getting what they want. But for today, thankfully, it was just the three of us.

CHAPTER FIVE

Confessing My Sin with
a Teacup in My Hand

Daddy once told me that if you asked somebody where he was when he heard the news that President Kennedy had been shot, he could tell you right where he was standing. Daddy said the human mind can call up all sorts of details from the very moment of hearing something traumatic. He was right.

I was sitting in the third row, second seat from the left in home economics class when Mrs. Gulbenk announced that, with Mother's Day just around the corner, she wanted us girls to try something new this year. Instead of sewing the expected, ruffled gingham apron that everyone could give their mothers as a present, she wanted us to celebrate our mamas' steady love and devotion by honoring them with a special tea.

I was halfway looking forward to making that silly-looking apron, having always admired all the frilly aprons Ruthie Morgan's mama had hanging on a hook in her kitchen. I thought I might wear it on Thursday nights when I made meat loaf, something I had been doing since my thirteenth birthday and Ida Belle had given me the *Better Homes and Garden Cookbook*—a must, she said, for every kitchen. But a tea, I wasn't so sure about that. And the more she talked about it, the more uncomfortable I got.

Mrs. Gulbenk had gone to Memphis the summer before and her sister-in-law had taken her to the Peabody hotel for some kind of fancy tea party. She was so taken with all the beautifully decorated cakes and delicate, little sandwiches which had been served that she wanted to share the experience with us—broaden our horizons, was the way she put it.

I didn't mind the idea of broadening myself, but I surely couldn't see how sipping tea from a china cup was going to accomplish that. Heck, the woman had been to Graceland, but she didn't seem the least bit interested in broadening our musical horizons. Oh no, all she wanted to talk about were pretty pink petit fours and perfectly cut lemon wedges, not one word about Elvis and rock 'n' roll.

Ruthie Morgan and Shelley Hatfield, the first sophomores in Ringgold High's history to make the varsity cheerleading squad, were sitting in front of me, and I could tell they were grinning from ear to ear even though I couldn't see their faces. Their ponytails were swaying back and forth from left to right with such harmonious rhythm it was as if those girls were tapping their feet double time to the same silent beat.

"Mrs. Gulbenk," Ruthie Morgan interrupted before she could get her arm fully extended in the air. "My mama went to tea at the governor's house down in Atlanta once. I'm sure she'd be more than happy to help you, if you'd like her to."

Ruthie Morgan's father was a real live World War II hero. He ran away from home and lied about his age just so he could fight for his country. He was barely sixteen and serving in the South Pacific when a Japanese torpedo hit the tip of his submarine. Ruthie Morgan's dad pulled five other sailors to safety before they were surely going to be sucked out into the ocean. So whenever the state of Georgia wanted to honor its veterans, some government official called Ruthie Morgan's dad, and that's how Ruthie Morgan's mom ended up at the governor's house drinking tea.

"Oh Ruthie, dear, thank ya. That's a lovely idea. I never cease to be amazed at what your mama can do."

I had always liked Mrs. Gulbenk, despite her obsession with the tomato, until this very moment. I appreciated her teaching me to sew a button on a jacket and how to properly season a new cast-iron skillet. I never really figured either one was going to be particularly important to my personal survival, but somehow I just felt a little more womanly knowing how. But sitting in the third row behind Ruthie Morgan's ponytail, I suddenly hated her and this broadening notion of hers and Mother's Day and everything else that made me remember that I was the only girl in my entire class who didn't have a living and breathing mama. Besides, nobody with any sense drinks hot tea in May.

With all that hate swarming through my body, I barely heard Mrs. Gulbenk calling my name, "Catherine Grace, child, are ya in there?"

And in her well-intended effort to ease my discomfort, she only made it worse. "Catherine Grace, I'm gonna need one gul to help me pour the tea. It is a big responsibility, and I need someone with a mature demeana and a steady hand. I was wonderin' if you'd help? Of course, you should know, you won't be able to spend much time social-izin' with the otha guls."

The *other* girls in Mrs. Gulbenk's tenth-grade home eco-nomics class instantly turned to look at me with their sappy, sympathetic stares, letting me know that they had already deciphered what she was trying to say in polite code. Cath-erine Grace, since you don't have a mother, I have a very special job for you. That ought to make it all better, right dear? That ought to make that dull, aching pain you've gotten used to feeling in your heart soften a bit, right?

Lolly Dempsey was sitting next to me. She looked me in the eyes and mouthed two words, "I'm sorry."

"Me, too," I mouthed back.

I don't remember much more of that day except Mrs. Gulbenk's persistent rambling ringing in my ears. She kept talking in an unusually high, giddy tone that plainly revealed her excitement about her newly invented Mother-Daughter Tea. But every word fell into the next, and from the second seat in the third row, it all sounded like a lot of noise about nothing.

Lolly followed me out of the classroom as if to provide some sort of human shield between me and the other girls, you know, the girls with mothers. Lolly definitely had a mother, but mostly I think she wished she didn't. Her mama was almost fifty when Lolly was born. Mrs. Dempsey told me once that she was done taking care of babies when she got the news she was going to have another. It seemed like a mighty strange thing to be sharing with a child, but Lolly said her mama reminded her almost every day that she had been the product of a night of drunken thoughtlessness.

Lolly wasn't allowed to have many friends over to her house. Her mama said it was too much work, and taking care of Lolly was already work enough. She'd let me come now and again, but only because I was the preacher's daughter. You don't want the preacher thinking unkindly of you even if you don't attend church on a regular basis.

But I never cared to spend much time at the Dempseys' house. I didn't like the hateful way Lolly's mama talked to her. Sometimes I wasn't so sure if Mrs. Dempsey really knew how ugly she sounded. I think it had just become another one of her awful habits, kind of like those Virginia Slims she was always sticking between her lips. She would draw the smoke deep into her chest and just let it set there for a minute before blowing it out through her nose, sometimes right in Lolly's face. It was as if her mama blamed Lolly for simply being, and poor Lolly Dempsey knew from the very beginning what I had learned only at six—life's not fair.

Standing in front of our gray metal lockers, Lolly and I griped about Mrs. Gulbenk's new class assignment, trying to comfort each other by joking about how stupid a tea sounded and how making a quart of tomato aspic would be ten times better than this. We imitated Ruthie Morgan throwing her arm in the air and offering her mother up as some sort of statewide, recognized tea expert.

"Hey, you can bring my mom, Catherine Grace. I'm sure she'd rather go with you anyway," Lolly said with a look in her eyes that told me she wasn't kidding anymore.

"Thanks, but I'll be Mrs. Gulbenk's trusted little helper, the girl with the steady hand," I said, thinking as I looked back in Lolly's eyes, maybe it was better not having a mama than to have one who doesn't want you.

"Catherine Grace, seriously, I've got an idea. Why don't you bring Gloria Jean? You know she'd love to come. All you have to do is ask, and she'll be picking out the perfect shade of nail polish just for the occasion."

She was right. Gloria Jean would be thrilled to be my mother, even if it was only for one afternoon. She'd never had any children of her own, although she said she had come close once or twice. She said she had an angry uterus that just never took to growing a baby. But she loved every opportunity to dote on Martha Ann and me, even calling us the children she always dreamed of having.

Lolly was also right about the nail polish. But I already knew the shade she'd pick. Cherry Blossom Pink. Gloria Jean always said that Cherry Blossom Pink was just the right shade for bridal showers and ladies' luncheons, and I figured a tea fell somewhere between the two.

Most people in Ringgold didn't appreciate Gloria Jean's colorful sense of style. Gloria Jean called herself a liberated, modern woman who wasn't afraid to express her inner self. I knew that was talk she had picked up from one of those ladies' magazines she was always reading, and I also knew that the other women in town had less-flattering names for her.

When I was no more than seven or eight, Gloria Jean would take me to town while she did her weekly shopping. Everybody we passed on the sidewalk acted real friendly to her face. But I could tell that when she walked away, they were passing judgments. They'd lean into one another and whisper in each other's ears. I eventually figured out what they were saying. They thought her blue eye shadow was tacky and her red, silky blouse that pulled too tightly across her chest was whoreish. I knew they were wrong, and I tried to tell them by casting a scolding, evil stare in their direction. But they never paid any attention to a little girl.

I used to feel so hurt for Gloria Jean, even though she never seemed to notice. But as I got older, sometimes I found myself feeling more embarrassed than hurt. And then that left me feeling guilty and shallow. I just wasn't sure what to think anymore. One minute I'd be crying, the next I'd be laughing. Gloria Jean said it was nothing but *horrormones,* as she liked to call them, running wild throughout my body. But I wasn't so convinced that I could blame the way I was feeling on something I had never seen or heard of before.

But I did know one thing for certain, I wasn't feeling up to drawing any more attention to myself; being the only motherless child in class was bad enough without having to listen to all the talk about my special, colorful friend. No, I would just pour the tea and make myself feel better by spitting in Ruthie Morgan's cup.

For the next two weeks, Mrs. Gulbenk talked on and on about tea and tea parties. She said some English duchess back in the nineteenth century came up with the idea of serving tea in the afternoon so she could make it to dinner without fainting from hunger. We learned to make these tiny cucumber sandwiches, which were nothing more than two little round pieces of white bread with a slice of cucumber and some cream cheese between them. I didn't know about that English duchess, but even I knew it was going to take more than a piece of cucumber to quiet a growling stomach.

Mrs. Gulbenk insisted on serving her special tea. She said she found the recipe in the back of a *Good Housekeeping* magazine and that we should file this one away in our personal recipe boxes that we decoupaged last semester. She even wrote the mixture on the board so we could copy it onto one of those white index cards she kept stacked on the corner of her desk for us to use for jotting down a good recipe whenever one came our way.

> *½ cup Lipton Instant Tea*
> *1 large jar of Tang Drink Mix*
> *1 cup sugar*
> *1 tablespoon ground cinnamon*
> *½ tablespoon ground cloves*
> Add water to taste. Heat. Serve hot.

That was it. Her special tea. And since I was her special helper, I was the one entrusted with the responsibility of mixing the tea together in the school cafeteria. Mrs. Gulbenk insisted I make a batch a whole week before the party and then practice serving it to the class. I told her I didn't think that was necessary seeing how there were only six ingredients and one of them was water and I had been pouring iced tea into jelly jar glasses since I was no more than four years old.

"Catherine Grace, a good hostess always prepares new dishes for herself first, even tea, before serving it to her guests."

In that case, I asked if Lolly could help, pointing out that I might need an extra hand carrying the tea back to the classroom. Mrs. Gulbenk thought that was a smart idea, and Lolly and I were both relieved to get out of the room where all the other girls were giggling with excitement as they practiced decorating trays with miniature cakes and sandwiches and sprigs of parsley.

I had not mentioned this tea to anyone, not Daddy, not Gloria Jean, not even Martha Ann. I wanted to warn my little sister that in two years, she was going to be Miss Gulbenk's special helper at this sure-to-be-annual-mother-daughter event. But I didn't want to burden her with it. She hated these things as much as I did. So I kept it to myself.

Of course, what I wasn't expecting was for Miss Gulbenk to blab all about it to Gloria Jean. Other than just a polite hello, those two women have probably exchanged words a sum total of three times since the day I was born, and one of them was a week before the Mother-Daughter Tea.

"Catherine Grace," Gloria Jean announced one night when I had come over to watch *That Girl* on her new color television set. "I ran into Miss Gulbenk today at the post office. She told me all about the tea you girls are having at school, and she thought you might like it, sweetie, if I came, so you wouldn't be there without a mama and all. You know I'd love to. Just tell me when and where I need to be."

I mumbled something about needing to prepare the tea and how I'd be busy in the kitchen and not wanting to leave her sitting in the classroom with all those other mothers. "Really," I said, "I wouldn't want to bother you. I mean, you'd probably be bored stiff seeing how I'm Mrs. Gulbenk's special helper and all." I sat there listening to myself lying all the while acting as though I was only doing what was best for Gloria Jean.

Surely I had wounded her, too, just like I had Miss Raines, except that Gloria Jean was the closest thing I was ever going to have to a mama. And I just sat there on her soft velvet sofa staring at her television and stomping on her heart all at the same time. But she just smiled.

"Sure, honey. I understand. It does sound like you are gonna be pretty busy." She hugged me when I walked out the door, just like she always did. She even offered to let me borrow her brand-new bottle of Cherry Blossom Pink, the perfect shade, she thought, for a tea.

I was rotten, and so on the day of the historic, first-ever Ringgold High Mother-Daughter Tea, I found myself standing in the school cafeteria with my arm submerged in Mrs. Gulbenk's special tea feeling sad and lonely even though Lolly was standing right there beside me. She asked me if I was missing my mama, and I told her I wasn't sure who I was missing.

I sat like a perfect lady on the cushioned chair Miss Gulbenk had placed in front of the teapot. I even looked like a lady, wearing a green, cotton skirt and coordinating blouse with little pink and green flowers on it that Gloria Jean had specially bought for me at a store in Birmingham the week before, knowing good and well the other mamas had bought their daughters a special, new outfit just for the occasion. Gloria Jean said I needed to look better than everybody else seeing how I was serving the tea. It was the prettiest outfit in my closet.

I greeted every girl, including Ruthie Morgan, with a sweet, sugary smile. And I said a quiet, "Thank you," as every mama walked past me, gently patting me on the shoulder as if to let me know that they were so sorry that I was still a motherless child. They chatted among themselves and praised Mrs. Gulbenk endlessly for coming up with such a sophisticated idea in the first place. They all asked for the recipe for her special tea, and Mrs. Gulbenk promised to mimeograph copies and send them home with the girls.

After all the mamas had sipped their tea and nibbled on their cucumber sandwiches, they left. And as we all scurried about the room, cleaning up crumbs and paper napkins, Mrs. Gulbenk announced that the Mother-Daughter Tea had been such a wonderful success, she would surely be making it an annual event. Poor Martha Ann.

She told us that everything was beautiful and delicious and that we would all be gracious hostesses one day, and we should all go home feeling proud of our accomplishment. But I walked home feeling downright rotten. I might as well have come straight out and told Gloria Jean I was embarrassed to be seen with her. But it seemed no matter what I said or didn't say, she just kept on loving me as much as she ever had.

She baked her famous chocolate chip cookies the day

before the tea in case Mrs. Gulbenk needed extra. She even bought me a little silver charm that looked like a teapot to add to my charm bracelet because, she said, I needed to make a little noise when I tipped the pot. And she told me every single time I walked out of her front door that she loved me, whether I deserved it or not.

I guess I had been too afraid of being different, at least more than I already was. As much as I griped about everybody else's mama looking and acting so perfect, I figure that was what I really wanted, or thought I wanted. Funny thing, it took a silly cup of Mrs. Gulbenk's special tea for me to finally realize that being a perfect mama has nothing to do with the color of your lipstick or the way you wear your hair.

I knew I needed to make things right with Gloria Jean. So I hurriedly changed my clothes, leaving my skirt and blouse on my bed and grabbing some jeans that were crumpled on the floor. I walked out of my room, not really knowing what to say or do. I thought maybe I should take something with me, a sort of peace offering, but I wasn't really sure what would be appropriate for such an occasion, maybe a jar of marshmallow whip and a box of Ritz crackers. I headed across the front yard to Gloria Jean's, and I could see the light from the television flickering through her living room window.

"Gloria Jean, hey there, it's Catherine Grace," I called from the kitchen door. "Are you in there?" She didn't answer, so I walked toward the back of the house and called her name out loud.

"Hey there, honey," she answered, her voice sounding muffled and distant. "Come on in. I'm back here in my bedroom." When I walked in her room, I found her down on her knees with her head buried under her bed. She looked up when she heard me at the door. "What are you doing down there?" I asked, rather amazed to find Gloria Jean half buried under her mattresses like that.

"Heck, I'm looking for some old photographs, under the bed. I keep my life story right here so I can grab it in case I need to get out quick," Gloria Jean explained.

"Oh."

"I read it in *Better Homes and Gardens* years ago," she continued.

"Read what?" I asked, not knowing what she was talking about.

"I read that you should store your photos under the bed, in one place, for safekeeping." And without hesitating, Gloria Jean kept on talking, "So tell me, hon, how was the tea? Did you get everything mixed up all right?"

"Yeah," I said, not the least bit surprised that she was asking about my day. "I managed to smile at everybody, even Ruthie Morgan. But, uh . . ." I was having a hard time coming up with the right thing to say. On the walk over, I had begged the Lord to give me the words and now I was waiting for Him to put them in my mouth. It was helpful that her head was under the bed, where I couldn't see her eyes. I thanked the Lord for that.

"It was . . . it, well . . . it was just that I wasn't very

happy, Gloria Jean, and it had nothing to do with not liking tea. And it had nothing to do with not having my mama there."

"Oh," she said, pulling her head out from under her bed, holding a photograph of a girl in her hands. "Sweetie, I understand. I really do." And I knew she did.

"I know you're feeling all sorts of mixed-up things these days. It's part of figuring out who you really are. And I think mamas are important when it comes time to doing all that figuring. It's a hard job on your own. Know what I'm saying?" she asked, handing me the photograph in her hands. The girl looked familiar, but I didn't know her name.

"That's your mama, Catherine Grace. Lord, honey, she wasn't much older than you when that picture was taken." I had never seen my mama like this, leaning against the oak tree in the backyard wearing nothing but a bathing suit top and a pair of shorts. I mean she looked so young. I guess you never think of your own mama being a little girl.

"She had just found out she was going to have you when I snapped that picture. Mmm. Mmm. What a pretty thing she was." I looked even closer as if I was going to find some kind of explanation on this piece of Kodak paper. I mean, I knew my mama was only seventeen when I was born, but I always figured she looked older than this. You know, like the other mamas. I couldn't quit staring at the little girl in the picture.

"Listen," Gloria Jean said, drawing my attention back

to her, "some girls don't have the courage to be who they are truly meant to be. But you and me and your mama, we're just braver than most other folks, and don't you forget it. Now, why don't you open that marshmallow whip, and we'll see if we can't make this day a little bit better."

I never looked at Gloria Jean the same way again. Her brilliant, blue eyelids and her bold, red lips never looked more beautiful. In that moment, I knew I was brave and that I was destined to be a modern, colorful woman just like Gloria Jean Graves.

CHAPTER SIX

Waiting for My Moses Moment with Joseph Riding Shotgun

Daddy gave me my first set of luggage on my sixteenth birthday. He had all three pieces, which were the prettiest shade of baby blue I'd ever seen, propped up against the fireplace just like it was Christmas morning. A tag sewn inside one of them said they were made of 100 percent plastic vinyl, but they were streaked and veined to look like real leather. And I loved them. They were so beautiful sitting there, waiting for some unknown adventure.

Taped to the cosmetic bag was a Hallmark card that Daddy must have picked up at the Dollar General Store. A picture of a baby bird about to leap out of his mama's nest was on the front of the card along with this corny saying about needing to love someone enough to let him go because only then will the love come back to you. I got the point. Daddy was going to let me leave town on my eighteenth birthday without a fuss so I could get this big-city foolishness out of my system. But I'd fly back. He was counting on it, just like the little bird on the card.

When it came right down to it, I'm not sure my daddy was convinced I'd be brave enough to step out of his nest in the first place. Sometimes I wasn't so sure myself. In my most secret moments, I'd been known to do a little down-on-my-knees praying, begging the Lord to send me my very own savior, just like He'd done for the Israelites, except my Moses would take me by the hand and lead me right out of this town and into the Promised Land somewhere down in Fulton County. But with every "Amen" came the realization that God wasn't sending me an escort. Nope, this exodus was going to be up to me.

I had memorized every nitpicky detail of my long-awaited departure—down to the very minute the Greyhound Bus would be pulling out of the parking lot at the Dairy Queen. The bus schedule was taped to the back of my bedroom door. It was the last thing I stared at every night before closing my eyes. I had rehearsed my good-bye to Daddy and Martha Ann a thousand times, always reassuring my little sister that I'd be ready and waiting when it was her turn to leave the nest. And in my head, I sat on that old, sticky picnic table one last time, licking one more chocolate-covered Dilly Bar for old time's sake.

The one detail I hadn't planned on was Henry Morel Blankenship. Henry, or Hank, as everybody in town called him except his mother, was the captain of the Ringgold High School football team, leader of the Young Life Christian Fellowship, and president of the local chapter of the Future Farmers of America, all good reasons not to like him, in my opinion. I'd known Hank since, uh, forever. Of course, I'd known everybody in Ringgold since forever. There were only 1,923 of us, depending on who was coming and going from this world on any given day. But Hank and I had never bothered to get to know each other. We were more like two magnets that you try to force together but they just keep pushing themselves apart.

He was just too perfect. He was the cutest, smartest, most athletic boy in town. His daddy was a dairy farmer, and he must have made a better living than most of the other farmers in the county because Hank lived in a two-story, redbrick house with four white columns holding up the roof. There was even a fountain in the middle of the front yard that did nothing but spout water day and night.

But if that wasn't reason enough not to like him, he also had the most beautiful mama in town. When we were in grade school, she was always coming by our classroom to help our teacher cut odd little shapes out of colored construction paper and staple our artwork to the bulletin board. On his birthday, she would appear wearing a smoothly pressed dress with her warm golden hair pulled up in a neatly braided twist, and in her hands, she carried a platter of perfectly decorated cupcakes. My mama would have done that for me, I'd tell myself, only my cupcakes would have had chocolate frosting with pink sprinkles on top.

I told Martha Ann once that Hank was kind of like Joseph with his coat of many colors, which Miss Raines stuck up on the felt board. Joseph's father, Jacob, loved his son. In fact, he loved Joseph more than his other eleven boys. Joseph was handsome and perfect just like Hank. And when Jacob gave Joseph a rich, colorful coat, it made his other brothers so jealous that they threw him in a well and then sold him into slavery for no more than twenty lousy pieces of silver.

I never planned on throwing Hank in a well, but I can't say I never thought about it. It might have done him some good to sit down there for a while. He had the highest grade point average in Mr. Polter's algebra class, just two points better than my own. He was the town's essay-contest winner three years in a row. And he was always putting down my Bulldogs whenever he got the chance. A boy like that deserved to come down a notch or two.

But worse than any of that was his dogged determination to personally embarrass me at my daddy's own church. Hank Blankenship won the gold medal at Miss Raines's Bible Verse Sword Drill, every single year; and I know he did it just to make me, the preacher's daughter, look like a fool.

On the third Sunday in June, the day before the official start of Vacation Bible School, Miss Raines would have us move our chairs into a straight line stretching from one end of the classroom to the other. Each of us was assigned a chair where we would sit with a Bible resting carefully on our laps. Then Miss Raines would slowly and meticulously explain the rules of the Bible Verse Sword Drill, which we already knew by heart. And finally, when you couldn't stand the anticipation any longer, she would draw a small piece of paper from a basket and announce a chapter and a verse.

"Girls and boys, the first verse is E-PHE-SIANS FIF-TEEN-THIR-TY-SIX," she would say, annunciating ev-er-y syl-la-ble.

We would flip through the pages of our Bibles as fast as we could, racing to be the first to put our left index finger on the verse and our right hand high in the air signaling our success. The last person to find the verse was eliminated from the line, and the first one to go was usually Billy Thornton. Actually it was no big surprise when Billy was diagnosed with some sort of learning problem and sent to a special school down in Marietta. But for now, Billy, who was madly in love with Miss Raines, didn't seem to mind losing much because he still got his prize, standing next to his teacher and watching for hands, and Miss Raines's breasts, flying in the air.

One by one the others in the class would leave their Bibles in their chairs and take their place at the front of the room. And in the end, year after year, the glory of a first-place finish was always a race between Hank and me. And without fail, that boy would manage to find that last verse just a split second before I could get there. I'd have my finger moving down the page when I'd hear a shout from the other end of the room, "I've got it," and Hank would leave with another gold medal hanging around his neck.

By the time I turned sixteen, I had learned to tolerate his perfection, and he had learned to tolerate my surly indifference. "Gee, Catherine Grace," Ruthie Morgan would tell me, "with that pleasant attitude of yours, I'm sure the boys are just lining up to go out with you." Ruthie Morgan had always enjoyed pointing out my shortcomings, and now, all grown up, and dressed in a cute baby blue sweater set and freshly polished Papagallos, she seemed to have no visible imperfections of her own. She just made something of a hobby identifying mine.

Truth be told, most of the other girls were fairly certain I would be left a lonely, bitter spinster. But I think that had more to do with my refusal to attend Miss Lilly Martin's School of Etiquette and Social Graces held every Tuesday for two laborious hours in a house that reeked of mothballs and Glade room freshener.

Turned out, Lolly and me were the only girls in our graduating class at Ringgold High who did not also possess a diploma from Miss Lilly Martin's School of Etiquette and Social Graces. Lolly's mama said she wasn't going to spend one dime on teaching Lolly how to hold a knife and fork judging by the way she had gained weight. She said she had already figured out how to do that just fine. And Daddy said when it got right down to it, a man would rather have a wife who could talk football than etiquette. So I took my chances.

But my junior year, something strange and very unexpected happened. I saw Hank as if I were meeting him for the very first time. I was attending a Young Life meeting at church, something my daddy made me do regularly, since apparently being the preacher's daughter meant serving as his personal ambassador to all teenaged Christian functions. Anyway, we were singing the last verse of "Michael Row the Boat Ashore" when Daddy interrupted to ask the group if we would consider putting together a program for the Christmas Eve Cedar Grove Holiday Celebration. Of course, we had no choice but to say yes because when the preacher asked you to do something the answer was always *yes*.

Hank, not surprisingly, was excited about the chance to show off in front of the entire church. He looked up at my daddy and said something about it being an honor and that we would not let him or the good Lord down. Oh brother.

"Let's tell the story," he said with authority, like he had been thinking of this for a long time, "of the night Jesus was born. But let's tell it our way. In our version, Mary and Joseph will hitchhike all the way from some place like Louisville, wander along Highway 127, and then stumble into Ringgold sometime close to midnight. Worn out and dirty from their journey, they'll look for a place for Mary to have her baby. But will somebody in our small town, which, let's face it, was probably not all that different from Bethlehem, welcome a strange couple and embrace them in their time of need?"

I couldn't believe what I was hearing. The old blue-haired ladies might think this was blasphemy, but I thought it was brilliant. A bunch of teenagers were going to make their very own neighbors, their brethren in Christ, wonder if they would have been kind enough to give Mary a warm, safe place to birth our Savior and Redeemer, which I kind of doubted—remembering how Brother Hawkin's daughter had been hidden down in Texas for a good nine months while her good-for-nothing boyfriend strutted his butt around the county dating anybody with a skirt and drinking beers behind the high school on Saturday nights.

Anyway, I hated to admit it. I mean I *really* hated to admit it, but this was a great idea. And I felt like, for the first time, I wasn't the only one who was seeing the small-minded way of thinking here that people seemed to culti-vate just as mightily as their gossip and their vegetables. Even Mrs. Roberta Huckstep might be forced to consider if she was Christian enough to let some strange, young cou-ple rest their heads on one of her beds covered with those crisply starched, white cotton sheets that had a big pink *H* monogrammed on the edge.

Everybody was excited, patting Hank on the shoulders and chatting about the props and costumes and who should be Mary and who should be Joseph and if anybody in

town had a live baby we could borrow for the performance. Hank reminded us that we needed to be humble and
right-minded in making all these decisions. Then he closed
our meeting with a word of prayer just like he always did.

"Lord, thank you for bringing your children together
tonight for fellowship. We praise you for all you've given
us, and please guide us as we prepare for our Christmas
pageant. Touch Johnny Blanchard with your healing power
'cause his mama says he has mono, and uh, you better go
ahead and touch Lucy Mills while you're at it. And, one
more thing, we know you have the weight of the world on
your shoulders, but if you could lead the Ringgold Tigers
to victory Friday night, well, we'd love to win one before
the end of the season. In your name we pray, Amen."

I know the Lord works in mysterious ways. I'd seen it
for myself like when Daddy healed Ruthie Morgan's dying
grandmother simply by laying his hands on her head and
praying for one mighty long time. I couldn't make out a
single word he said, but the Lord must have heard him, because the very next morning, she was sitting up in bed eating scrambled eggs and fried ham.

But even that miracle couldn't prepare me for what
happened next. Shelley Hatfield, undeniably the most
beautiful girl in Ringgold, and undoubtedly the most obvious choice for Mary, said, "I think Catherine Grace Cline
should be Mary and, Hank, of course, you should be
Joseph."

I figured every girl in that room was hoping to be

Hank's Mary, especially Shelley Hatfield. I was planning on working behind the curtain, organizing props, turning on lights, anything but being Hank's fiancée knocked up by the Holy Spirit himself.

Martha Ann opened her mouth in disbelief. "You, Mary. Wait till Gloria Jean hears this," she said leaning into my ear.

Being the preacher's daughter had never really been an advantage, at least not as far as I could tell. My mama was gone and that stupid golden egg never did end up in my basket, and not one of those Sword Drill medals ever found its way around my neck. You'd think I'd have at least one pin for perfect attendance since my daddy had dragged me to church every single Sunday in those stupid, patent-leather Mary Janes. Nope, not that either, because I'd usually get some juicy head cold in the middle of February that would keep me in bed one Sunday out of the year. And now Mary, the one thing I *didn't* want, *didn't* need, was mine. Everyone else seemed equally amazed by Shelley's suggestion, and in the awkward moment of silence that followed, Hank searched my face looking for some sort of approval.

The very next day, I was standing in front of my locker putting away my composition notebook, when Joseph himself came up and grabbed me by the arm. "Catherine Grace, you know we need to start practicing as soon as possible. There's only four weeks before the holiday celebration, and I've got football practice almost every afternoon. So I was thinking maybe I could come over to your house on Saturday, and we could start figuring out what we're going to do."

"Fine, Hank, we'll work around your very busy schedule because I'm not really doing much of anything with my life, and I'm sure it is so time consuming trying to win one football game," I shot back, wondering myself why I was acting like such a sharp-tongued jerk.

"Catherine Grace, that is not what I meant, but if you're going to act like this, well, I might just leave your ass in that stable with the other donkeys, where apparently it belongs."

I stared at Hank in disbelief. I couldn't believe Mr. Perfect had said that to me, the preacher's daughter, of all people. Hank Blankenship was human after all. We both burst out laughing. And in that moment, I started looking at Hank differently. I had never noticed that he was a full head taller than me or that his arms were thick and rippling with muscles, or that his eyes were as blue as sapphires, or that Catherine Cline Blankenship had kind of a nice ring to it.

Oh, my God, I liked a boy, and not just any boy. I liked Henry Morel Blankenship. Gloria Jean said I had had an epiphany, an epiphany of the heart. Martha Ann loved the sound of that. "Oh, an epiphany of the heart," she echoed, "just like Romeo and Juliet, sort of, well, without the feuding families and the suicidal ending."

All I knew was that every time we practiced our lines, I

discovered something new and wonderful about him, like this sweet, tiny dimple on the left side of his mouth that grew deeper and deeper the more he smiled.

No, no way, I kept telling myself. I couldn't like him. And he certainly couldn't like me. But what if he did like me and we started dating and went steady and got engaged and then . . . married? I could end up living in Ringgold, raising his family, and growing his tomatoes. No, no, no. This was not part of the plan that I had rehearsed for the past sixteen years. I could not let some gorgeous, kind, generous, adorable, dimpled, football-playing Christian boy lead me astray.

Daddy announced our pageant from the pulpit every chance he got, and with so much advance publicity, the church was packed by curtain time. Most of the little kids had to sit on the floor just to make room for their parents. And though Hank and I had practiced our lines a thousand times, now waiting in the hallway, I started to sweat and feel kind of faint. I wasn't really scared about being in front of so many people; practically growing up behind the pulpit, I was used to that. But I had never been in front of so many people with such an important secret hidden in my heart.

I mean, would they be able to tell how I really felt? Would Miss Raines or Mrs. Roberta Huckstep or Ruthie Morgan or, worse yet, my own daddy know that secretly, deep down inside, I was falling in love with Hank? Would they be able to tell that Mary was having some very impure thoughts about Joseph? Leaning against the wall in the hallway outside the sanctuary, I slowly slid to the floor. I didn't even notice Hank standing in front of me, leaning over my body.

"Catherine . . . Catherine," he said ever so gently. "The shepherds are waiting. It's time to go on." But I just gazed at him standing there draped in an old green sheet that probably came from his mama's linen closet and said nothing.

"Catherine, hey, are you in there?" he asked, touching my cheek with his fingertips. "Come on, we gotta get you to the barn before the Christ child is born without us."

I looked up to see Hank holding out his hand. As I propped myself up against the wall, Hank leaned over me. He held my cheek in his hand and whispered in my ear, "I doubt the Virgin Mary looked as beautiful as you do tonight." And then he kissed me on the cheek.

When I walked into that sanctuary holding Hank's hand, I didn't look like some poor pregnant woman in the throes of labor who'd spent the last day or more riding in the back of a tractor-trailer. No, I looked like I had just won the monthly sweepstakes at the Shop Rite. And while the shepherds, or in Hank's version the farmhands, were announcing our Savior's birth, all I could think about was how much I wanted to wrap my arms around Joseph's waist, hold him tight against my chest, and French kiss him long and hard. That's right, I wanted to fall down in the hay and kiss him till my lips were sore. And I was pretty sure that was some kind of very special Christmas sin.

I said all my lines on cue and even managed to force a

tear when the baby Jesus, who would save all mankind from their sinning ways, was finally born. But by that time I figured the entire congregation could see that I was the first sinner who was going to need some saving.

Miss Raines rushed up to me after the performance and pulled me into her arms.

"Catherine, you were wonderful. You absolutely glowed tonight. I don't think I've ever seen you with such a smile on your face."

"Well, you know, it's, uh, well, the Christmas spirit and all."

"Whatever it was, sweetie, you were great," she said. And then in a hushed tone, she added, "I know that your mama is so proud of you tonight."

Oh my Lord. I was so in love with a boy that even my mama could see it from heaven. Oh God, maybe I really was glowing. I pulled my scarf farther down on my face and tried to act as though I had forgotten that Hank had kissed me on the cheek. But inside I felt like a bug flying to the light. I just couldn't resist his strong arms or his warm blue eyes. And he wasn't making it any easier for me, either. After the Christmas pageant, he walked me home with his arm around my shoulders, just to keep me warm, he said. At school on Monday, he found me in the cafeteria and squeezed his body in next to mine at the lunch table. And he started stopping by my house every day on his way home from school. True love was, as Gloria Jean had prophesized, more powerful than the both of us.

By Valentine's Day, it was official; we were going steady, something the other girls at Ringgold Senior High had a hard time accepting. The most popular boy in school had fallen for the sassy-mouthed girl who'd never had a boyfriend before in her life. Yep, that would be me.

I could tell by the way Ruthie Morgan and her friends whispered in one another's ears whenever Hank and I walked down the hall together that they were convinced that young Mr. Blankenship was wasting his time with the preacher's daughter. And I didn't know for sure, but sometimes I wondered if they were right. I wondered if Hank loved me because I was the one thing in his life that wasn't perfect.

But whatever his reasons, Hank wanted to be with me, all the time. And it wasn't long before we had developed a predictable yet wonderful routine of our own. We studied together every Monday night at Hank's house, where his mother would fix us spaghetti and a green salad tossed with Thousand Island dressing. On Wednesdays we went to the Young Life meetings at church, and before taking me home, Hank would drive me over to the Dairy Queen for some fries or a chocolate-dipped cone, knowing good and well I ate Dilly Bars only on Saturdays with Martha Ann. Then every Friday night he came to dinner at our house, something my daddy seemed to enjoy almost more than I did. They'd talk about sports and President Carter and just about everything in between. Daddy never acted like he regretted not having a son, but he sure did enjoy borrowing the Blankenships' once a week.

Sometimes when we were alone, I could barely keep myself from giving all I had to Hank Blankenship. Gloria Jean called it *the gift*. Daddy called it *the sin,* at least until your wedding night when it magically became *the gift*. The touch of Hank's hand on my breasts made me feel more like a woman than I figured any number of classes at Miss Lilly Martin's School of Etiquette and Social Graces ever could. There were times when we parked in his red truck down by Chickamauga Creek, when he'd unbutton my blouse and I'd toss his shirt on the floor, and I could feel his warm, smooth chest rubbing against my breasts. My entire body would flutter with excitement and I was pretty darn willing to give and sin all over Hank's beautiful, perfect body.

But not Hank. No, he said it wouldn't be right. Nothing beyond second base until there was a ring on my finger, especially with me being the preacher's daughter and all. Once again, being the preacher's daughter didn't seem to be working in my favor.

It shouldn't have been any big surprise that by the time graduation rolled around, people—not just our friends but Hank's mother, Gloria Jean, my own daddy, even me—started speculating about a possible Blankenship-Cline engagement. I mean, we had been dating for almost a year and a half and apparently that was almost as much of an official proposal as that ring on my finger Hank kept alluding to.

"Catherine, have you and Hank talked about your future, after graduation and all? I know you've been planning on leaving town, but I thought you might be rethinking that, you know since Hank's in your life now," Daddy said as we were standing in the kitchen one night cleaning the dinner dishes.

"Daddy, no boy is going to stand between me and my dreams. You ought to know that, believe it or not, not even Hank Blankenship. When this little birdie flies the coop, she's going to build her very own nest in a tree that's really big with lots of cool-looking branches," I said emphatically.

But inside, I was having doubts, big doubts about whether I'd be able to step out of the only nest I'd ever known. I loved Hank. I knew that. I couldn't imagine being without him. But I couldn't imagine living the rest of my life in Ringgold, even with Hank. I kept encouraging him to go to college, go to Georgia Tech, heck, I could learn to cope with a Yellow Jacket. He could be a veterinarian or a lawyer, anything but a dairy farmer. The biggest dream he had was going to the community college down in Dalton, studying a little agriculture, and coming back to Ringgold and working his daddy's farm.

I couldn't understand why he didn't want more. He wanted me. He told me that. But every time I asked myself if I wanted to grow his tomatoes, I felt sick to my stomach. Sometimes I wondered if my own mama ever felt sick to her stomach. Did she ever have thoughts of being something more? Was she afraid that Daddy was going to be the only true love of her life, and out of fear or stupidity, gave up her dreams and got married?

My head was spinning, something it had been doing an awful lot these past few months, but thankfully the only question Hank had on his mind was whether or not I was going to be his date for the Senior Prom.

Daddy asked Gloria Jean to drive me to Chattanooga and help me find a dress. I think even he was willing to admit that shopping for a formal gown was one of her God-given talents. So early one Saturday morning, Martha Ann and me piled into the front seat of the LeSabre and headed the twenty-something miles north to Chattanooga.

We got there an hour or so before the stores opened and decided to have breakfast at a cozy diner next to Loveman's department store. We sat in the last empty booth in the back of the diner and did what all the other women were doing, sipped coffee and hot chocolate and chatted about the day's possibilities. I kept thinking this would have been something Mama would have done with me, which made me feel excited and sad all at the same time, a kind of awkward, empty feeling that had become all too familiar.

As soon as the store opened, Gloria Jean took Martha Ann and me by the hands and walked us through the front doors and up a long flight of stairs. A white-haired woman wearing a navy blue dress and navy pumps appeared before us and offered to help, like a star guiding the way. Once she heard Gloria Jean say the word *prom,* she indicated she had heard enough and led us into a room that was filled with long, sequined dresses. She placed me in a fitting room and carried in seven gowns to try, each one a different color and fabric.

Another woman, dressed more like a waitress than a sales clerk, followed her into the fitting room, and without uttering a word insisted on helping me dress. I hadn't had anyone help me dress since I was a tiny girl. I didn't feel particularly comfortable with this stranger seeing me in my bra and panties, but she never gave me a chance to protest. As soon as I was zipped and buttoned into a gown, she would start drawing pins from a small red cushion strapped to her arm and placing them along the seams of the dress. When she was done, she positioned me directly in front of the mirror and stepped back so everyone, especially the woman in the navy suit, could see.

Martha Ann gasped, seeing each new gown on my body. "Oh, that one's it! Pick that one!"

But my favorite was made of pink moiré, with wide straps that stretched across my shoulders and crossed over my back. It was gathered at the waist and had a soft full skirt. Teeny pink beads were sewn all over the bodice. It was the most feminine thing I had ever seen. I had never loved a piece of fabric as much as I loved this dress. Gloria Jean agreed. This was the one. She talked to the saleswoman, and then explained to me that a few alterations would be made and that the department store would mail the dress to my house in a week or two.

With the color of the gown decided, we walked downstairs to the shoe department. I hadn't thought about shoes, but Gloria Jean told the sales clerk that I needed a pair of two-and-half-inch heels, closed toe, peau de soie, and that they must be dyed to match the dress that was upstairs in alterations. I didn't care what Daddy thought about Gloria Jean being married five times. When it came to formal wear, the woman knew what she was doing. While the sales clerk slipped different shoes on and off my feet, I just sat there and smiled. I had never owned a pair of heels, let alone pink ones, and I had never had a man put a pair of shoes on my feet before. I couldn't help but feel like Cinderella, squeezing my foot into the glass slipper until I looked down and noticed for the first time that my toes seemed exceptionally skinny and long.

Gloria Jean told me to stand up and try walking on the carpet. She took one look at me wobbling across the floor and said, "Honey, you are going to have to do some practicing in those shoes before the prom, or I think you'll come home in a cast." Martha Ann was laughing so hard, Gloria Jean had to tap her on the shoulder to remind her she was in a public place.

We left the shoes to be dyed and made arrangements for the department store to mail the shoes along with the dress when both were ready. It felt kind of funny to do all this shopping and then leave empty-handed. Gloria Jean must have thought so, too, because we were headed toward the front door when she suddenly stopped at the jewelry counter. She turned toward me, lifted my hair off my shoulders, and asked what kind of earrings I was thinking of wearing, knowing good and well I didn't have a clue what kind of earrings I was thinking of wearing.

"Sweetie, every girl needs to sparkle on her prom night. It's kind of like a dress rehearsal for your wedding day. I think this rhinestone pair is the perfect finishing touch, the pièce de résistance, as the French would say."

"I don't know, I've never worn anything so, so sparkly before," I said with some hesitation, not really knowing how Daddy would feel about his baby girl sparkling with a boy and all. But Martha Ann just kept staring at the light dancing off the earrings as if she were under some sort of magic spell. I could tell she loved them.

"My treat; this is a special, special night," Gloria Jean said, and I left Loveman's department store holding a shiny, black shopping bag.

The three of us walked out of the store and onto the sidewalk, where we stood for a moment breathing in the fresh air and soaking in the sunshine. I looked at my watch and couldn't believe it. We had been shopping for most of the day. I had never shopped for anything that long, and I was feeling tired and hungry from the effort.

"You see, girls, shopping is hard work, and there ain't a man on this earth that understands that," Gloria Jean announced. Sensing that Martha Ann and I were needing a rest, she asked if we wanted to go back to the diner for a grilled cheese sandwich and a Coca-Cola before heading back home.

Not many things in my life ever seemed to happen just like I wanted them to, but this . . . this was pretty near perfect.

When the morning of the prom finally dawned, Gloria Jean took control of my day like some kind of military drill sergeant. She drove me to the beauty parlor to have my hair done and told the stylist to pull it up in a twist because she wanted everyone to see the back of my dress and my rhinestone earrings. She wanted four curly tendrils hanging down my neck for dramatic effect. Only four, she was very clear about that. Then she told another woman to scrub my fingernails and paint them a soft shade of Baby Doll Pink, two coats of color and two coats of clear.

There were no grilled cheese sandwiches and Coca-Colas that day. Gloria Jean said only salad, carrot sticks, and lots of water. She read in one of her lady magazines that if you drink eight glasses of water in a day, you'll lose five pounds and your skin will glow. She wouldn't let me out of her sight for fear that Martha Ann would sneak me a Coke and some peanut butter crackers.

"Honey, you want to feel as light and airy as possible when you slip into that dress. I didn't eat for two days before I married Dwayne Dilbert. Heck, I fainted right before I walked down the aisle," she said, as though we should be impressed with her sudden lapse into unconsciousness. "All of that starving and for what? A good-for-nothing slouch. But Hank, honey, oh Hank's worth starving for."

She was right, because when I slipped into my dress, I felt more feminine than I'd ever felt in my life, if not a little light-headed. Gloria Jean zipped and buttoned me into place and Martha Ann shook the hem so the skirt would hang as full as possible. I stood in front of my mirror and stared at myself for five whole minutes. I wondered if I'd ever feel like this again, so I tried to memorize every detail of the moment. Then, yelling from behind my bedroom door, I told my daddy to close his eyes.

"No peeking, Daddy," I said as I cracked the door, "I mean it, no peeking." I crept out of my room and positioned myself directly in front of him. Gloria Jean and Martha Ann were trailing close behind, tending to my dress with every step. "Okay, now."

Daddy slowly and deliberately opened his eyes. He just stood there, staring, not saying a word, and trust me, preachers are never speechless. His expression grew big and then slowly softened. I think he even had tears in his eyes.

"C'mon, Daddy, what do you think?" I asked.

"Catherine Grace Cline, you are absolutely beautiful," he said, adding emphasis to every word. Daddy was always telling me and Martha Ann how pretty we were, but I had never heard him say it like that, so carefully. I could feel the tears welling up in my eyes. I couldn't cry, not now. Gloria Jean would kill me if all the makeup she spent the last two hours putting on my face started running off in a stream of teardrops. As I dabbed the corner of my eye with my fingertip, the doorbell rang, sparing me from any further embarrassment. It was Hank, and even though I was used to seeing him almost every day, tonight he looked particularly handsome, like some kind of movie star. He was wearing a brown tuxedo and a soft pink shirt he had picked out to match my dress. And in his hand, he was holding a corsage made of tiny pink sweetheart roses.

"Good evening, Mr. Cline, Martha Ann, Mrs. Graves," he said. Then he looked at me and, like Daddy, he just stared. "Catherine, you look amazing," he said, then he gave me a kiss on the cheek and slipped the corsage onto my wrist.

Daddy took at least a hundred pictures while Martha Ann stood there giggling and making funny faces. Then Gloria Jean, who had stayed to make sure that every hair on my head was cemented in place, took another hundred pictures with her own camera.

"Catherine Grace," she said as she put her Kodak Instamatic back in her pocket, "you look prettier than any bride ever could, and I've got the pictures to prove it." She gave me such a tight hug that I thought she was going to wrinkle the dress she had so meticulously pressed right before slipping it onto my body.

By the time Hank and I got to the school, the band was already playing, and it looked like the entire senior class was crowded onto the dance floor. The gym was decorated with balloons and crepe paper and tiny white lights. It didn't even look like the same place where I had spent so many hours doing sit-ups and pull-ups in the ridiculous hope of passing the Presidential Fitness Test. I had to hand it to Ruthie Morgan: all that time spent perfecting her home-making skills had really paid off as chairman of the decorating committee. This was the best that the Ringgold High gymnasium had ever looked.

Hank and I said a quick hello to Mrs. Gulbenk, who was guarding the punch her tenth-grade home economics class had made as a gift to the graduating seniors. "Are there any tomatoes in that punch bowl, Mrs. Gulbenk?" Hank said with such an adorable smile that she could only blush.

We joined our classmates out on the dance floor. The only time we took a break was so I could reapply my lipstick. Gloria Jean had given me very strict orders about when and how to reapply my lipstick, and I was not about to let her down. "Line, apply, pat. Line, apply, pat." I kept saying to myself for fear that if I did something out of order, I would come out of the bathroom looking more like a clown than a girl pretending she was Cinderella.

We were having so much fun that we almost forgot to have our official photo taken. Daddy and Gloria Jean had snapped plenty at home, but I wanted a photograph taken under the rainbow Ruthie Morgan had made with balloons and tissue-paper flowers. I grabbed Hank's hand and dragged him off the dance floor. We were making our way through the crowd toward the photographer when Trisha

Munger, senior class president, stepped onto the stage and tapped on the microphone.

"Welcome, Senior Class of 1972. It's that time we've all been waiting for, the announcement of this year's King and Queen of the Senior Prom. Are you ready, Ringgold Tigers?" she shouted, more as a cheer than a question.

I knew Hank would be crowned King of the Prom Court. Everyone knew that. And I never expected to be Queen; in fact, no one expected that. The queen was, as I predicted, Shelley Hatfield. Everyone let out a loud tiger roar, including me. It was hard for me not to like Shelley. If it hadn't been for her, Hank and I would never have gotten together in the first place. And even though she was captain of the cheerleading squad, she never acted better than anybody else. But when I saw the two of them standing on the stage, I realized how truly perfect they looked together. I had played with my Barbie dolls long enough to know that now I was looking at the real thing. Hank was Ken and Shelley was his Barbie. And in that moment, it hit me. Shelley was the kind of girl Hank needed.

He deserved a wife who would admire him, dote on him, and grow his tomatoes. The future wasn't just about my dreams; it was as much about his, too. His dreams were just as important as mine, even if I couldn't understand them. All of a sudden, my heart began to hurt.

The band started to play "How Can You Mend a Broken Heart?" and even though I knew the Bee Gees hadn't written that song with me in mind, it sure felt like they had.

I held Hank closer than ever, somehow knowing this would be the last time we would ever dance together. I pulled my mouth close to his ear and whispered, "You looked great up there, Hank . . . you and Shelley. You two look like you were made for each other."

"Catherine Grace, you are my girl, my only girl," he said softly.

His *only* girl, the *one,* the *one* and *only.* If that was true, I thought to myself, trying to absorb Hank's words while the music was pounding in my head, then I would have no choice but to marry him. Mrs. Hank Blankenship would be my destiny, my obligation. Truth be told, I had been worrying for a long time that Hank believed I was his one and only girl, but now I panicked.

"I don't know about that, Hank. I'm not sure there is an *only.* I mean Gloria Jean says that—"

"Don't tell me you believe anything that crazy old lady says," Hank interrupted, with a grin on his face. But I didn't think he was funny.

"Hank, she's not crazy," I snapped. "You don't know what you're talking about. Gloria Jean is an amazing woman who knows more about love than you'll ever be able to comprehend."

"Right."

I could tell by the way he said *right* that he was just humoring me, and I hated being humored. "Don't talk to me like that, Hank."

"Like what, Catherine? I didn't say anything."

"Oh yes you did. You said *right*. And you and I both know what that means."

"*Right* means you're right. Forget it."

But I couldn't forget it. Hank was loving the wrong girl, and I knew that now. "Just shut up, Hank. You know damn well that's not what you meant."

"Catherine, what has gotten into you?"

"Gotten into me? So you can look me in the eyes and tell me that Gloria Jean does in fact know a whole lot more about love than you, *perfect* Hank Blankenship?" My voice sounded sharp and hateful, and I knew, with every word I was pushing Hank further and further away. But it was for his own good. He needed to be set free.

"God bless it, Catherine. Look, the woman got left five times. I don't think any reasonable person would think she knows all there is to know about loving a man."

"Shut up, Hank. I mean it. Just shut up! No man ever left Gloria Jean," I shouted in his ear. People were starting to stare.

"Yeah right, Catherine. That's why she's sitting in that house all alone making herself up to look like some kind of two-bit tramp."

"Don't you talk about her like that. At least she's got the courage to live her life the way she wants to and doesn't just sit on some dairy farm making perfect little cupcakes for her perfect little boy."

"Catherine, you better shut your mouth before it gets you into trouble. Nobody talks about my mama like that, you understand, nobody," Hank ordered in this firm, unfamiliar tone. But I couldn't shut my mouth now. Down deep inside I knew I had been waiting for a moment like this, when I could prove to Hank he had fallen in love with the wrong girl.

"Nobody talks ugly about Gloria Jean. There were good reasons she got divorced, reasons I'd never expect you, some, some . . . small-town farmer boy to understand."

"Farmer boy! What the hell do you mean by that? Listen, you're no big, sophisticated city girl like you think you are. Face it, Catherine Grace, you're a country girl and you always will be! It's in your bones."

Now the tears were running down my face. I could feel them stinging my cheeks. I ran out of the gym. Hank ran after me. He grabbed my arm and turned me around so we were standing face-to-face. "Don't run out of here, Catherine Grace, like some spoiled little kid pitching a fit. Running away doesn't make it better, or haven't you figured that out yet, sitting on that picnic table licking your damn Dilly Bars?"

"Leave me alone, Hank." I pulled my arm from his grasp. "I'm not running away from anything. I'm running to something better, something you know nothing about. Now go on, go dance the last dance with Shelley."

I started running from the gym, not looking back to see

if Hank was coming after me. He wasn't, but I didn't care. He didn't have the right to say those things about Gloria Jean. She'd been like a mama to me. He didn't know anything about true love or reaching for the stars. He was just a stupid country boy who'd rather spend time milking cows and playing a losing game of football.

I walked home that night carrying my pink, peau de soie heels in my hand, wondering if fancy shoes like these were ever going to feel good on my feet. Something kept pulling me toward Chickamauga Creek. I don't know, maybe Mama was showing me the way.

As I crawled on my hands and knees down the grassy bank, I could see the light from the moon bouncing off the water. The reflection was so smooth and pretty, it was like it was begging me to come sit by its side. I lay down in the grass and stared up at the sky, looking at everything and nothing all at the same time. The only sounds I could hear were the water flowing over the rocks and a choir of crickets chirping in the background. Something was speaking to me down deep inside, and I don't know if it was the Lord finally taking the time to answer one of my prayers or my mama sending me a message from above. I stood up, took the corsage off my wrist, and tossed it into the creek, letting the water grab hold of another piece of my heart and wash it away like it had done so many years before.

Hank and I didn't talk much after graduation, and when we did, we just argued about stupid stuff like whether or not the Bulldogs were going to win the Southeastern Conference or the right way to lick a Dilly Bar. It was kind of like we were little kids again, just annoying each other whenever we could. Henry Morel Blankenship and I were done. I knew that. He belonged with a girl who wasn't dreaming of her exodus of biblical proportions.

CHAPTER SEVEN

Rolling Through the Red Sea
in a Greyhound Bus

My bedroom looked very different the morning of my eighteenth birthday. It looked lonely. I opened my eyes just as the sun started creeping through the window, and I stared at the white chest of drawers that had greeted me every morning since I could remember. Maybe it's stupid to think that a piece of furniture has feelings, but then again, I'm the same girl who kept my tattered old baby doll dressed in a sweater and knitted cap so she wouldn't get cold sitting on the top shelf of my closet. And this morning that chest of drawers was looking sad. All the photographs and trophies and silly knickknacks that had blanketed the top and told my life story better than any words ever could were gone, packed in brown cardboard boxes and neatly stacked in the cellar.

Even my pretty pink walls were bare. Mama picked this color after I was born, and I've never wanted to change it. Ruthie Morgan used to try to convince me that my walls should be painted some other color. "Pink's just not your color, Catherine Grace. You know as well as I do that there's not a speck of pink on the football field."

There was nothing she could say that was going to change my mind or the color on my walls. If I had, I would have lost another piece of my mama. And I wasn't letting go of any piece of her, pink or not.

Daddy insisted on replacing my tired, worn curtains a while back, but I threw such a fit that he spent a good seven weeks looking for the very same fabric, little bitty pink flowers on a white-and-pink-checked background. He finally found a few yards in some textile mill down in South Carolina. I told him there were a few things in life that should never ever be allowed to change, and my curtains were one of them.

So many other things were never going to stay the same, and this morning was one of them. I'd been praying for this day for as long as I could remember, and now that it was here, all I wanted to do was crawl under my covers and pretend it was any other day.

I couldn't help but think of Moses. He was certain the Lord had chosen the wrong man to lead His people out of slavery, and I wondered if I really had what it took to up and leave the only land I had ever known. But then I figured if Moses could question the Lord's intentions outright, surely it was natural for me to feel a little shaky about my pending exodus, now that the day had finally come.

I knew that this would be the last morning I would wake up in this bed as a Sunday-school-going, dishwashing, tomato-watering member of this family. I knew this would be the last morning I would wake up in the same bed where I had calculated God only knows how many algebra problems, the same bed I had hid under playing hide-and-seek with Martha Ann, and the same bed I had lain on and cried myself to sleep too many nights after Mama died. I wasn't sure how I was going to make it through the day considering I was having such a hard time just saying good-bye to my bed.

Normally, in the Cline house, on your birthday morning, Daddy would sneak into your room like some sort of undercover spy, stand over your bed, and start singing the Happy Birthday song just as loud as he possibly could. Last year on Martha Ann's birthday, Gloria Jean said that Daddy's cat-a-wallin', as she kindly called it, woke her up in such a panic that she almost fell right out of the bed.

"I damn near thought the early-morning freight train had jumped its track. Apparently the good Lord only thought it was necessary for one of your parents to carry a tune," she had said, laughing as she handed Martha Ann a box of perfumed body powder.

But today the house was unusually still. Everything about this birthday was going to be different, I could feel it.

The suitcases pushed into the corner of my room kept reminding me of that. I was trying to cram everything I owned into that luggage set Daddy had given me two years ago. Now I bet he was wishing he'd bought me that lilac cashmere sweater set I'd seen at Loveman's, the one just like Ruthie Morgan's, the one I'd been admiring since the first day she wore it.

I heard Daddy's bedroom door creaking in the distance and figured I might as well close my eyes so he could enjoy this birthday ritual one last time. He tried to sneak down the hallway, but the old floorboards under his feet were blowing his cover. My door opened slowly. I could feel the light from the hallway on my face, and I knew he was standing over my bed. I played possum, waiting for him to sing, but there was a long still silence instead. He knew this would be the last time he'd be singing the birthday song, waking Catherine Grace Cline from this very bed.

"Happy birthday to you," he began, speaking more than singing. "Happy birthday to you . . . Happy birthday, dear Catherine Grace . . . Happy birthday to you."

We both just stared at each other with tears puddling in our eyes. I lunged out of bed and threw myself in my daddy's arms.

"I love you, Catherine Grace. You know you will always be my little girl and this will always be your home," he whispered in my ear.

"I know, Daddy. I love you, too," I said, not wanting to let go.

This was going to be a long, hard day. I could feel it in my heart. Thankfully Martha Ann bounced through the door and announced that my birthday breakfast feast was cooking and I better get my lazy butt out of bed and make myself a little more presentable. Considering the fact that my birthday was about the only day of the year that Martha Ann ever cooked me anything, I did as I was told.

I put on my fuzzy chenille robe and matching slippers that Mrs. Blankenship had given me for graduation. She said that I would always be special to her even though Hank and I were no longer together. She said she was secretly hoping we would find our way back to each other someday. I wondered if Hank had ever told her what I said about her at the prom. I hoped she knew I didn't mean a word of it.

I splashed a little water on my face, pulled my hair back in a rubber band, and then walked into the kitchen to find the table covered with sausage and biscuits and gravy and scrambled eggs and pancakes and maple syrup. I sat down at my usual place at the table and noticed a plate of sliced, red tomatoes. "They're for good luck." Martha Ann chuckled.

"Very funny. What in the world got into you?" I said, ignoring her sense of humor. "I can't eat this much food."

"This may be the last home-cooked meal you get for a while, so you might as well have everything you like," Martha Ann said with a smile, knowing that I still didn't have a clue as to how I was going to make any money down in Atlanta. I had spent so many years planning my escape that I hadn't given quite enough thought to my long-term survival. I knew I wanted to work in retail. I wanted to be surrounded by all the pretty things I had admired as a little girl wandering through Davison's department store. And I knew I eventually wanted to go to college and maybe get myself a business degree. Gloria Jean said I was going to need that piece of paper to get ahead in this world.

But for now, I was certain I had enough *do re me* stuffed in my shoebox to last me at least a month or two, money I'd earned from making strawberry jam for the past five summers.

The three of us sat at the breakfast table for at least an hour. We'd eat, then get to feeling kind of full, so we'd wait for a while and talk and laugh, and then we'd start eating again. I didn't want to stop eating, not because I thought there was any truth in what Martha Ann had said, but because I knew that when I got up from the table, I was going to have to face this day head on. Finally, Martha Ann announced that she was going to wash the dishes. Apparently, she was the only brave one among us.

"Hey Catherine, have you talked to Gloria Jean this morning?" she asked as she stood at the kitchen sink with her hands elbow deep in soapy water. "She called late last night wanting to know when we were coming over. Said she had something special for you."

"No, but I've got a little more packing to do, so why don't we head over to her house in about an hour or so?" I replied. My daddy was still sitting at the table. He said he had some business to take care of over at the church and thought he'd be gone most of the morning. My daddy had never gone to church on my birthday, unless, of course, it fell on a Sunday. I honestly think sticking around the house was just too painful for him. I understood that. I was almost relieved to see him go.

After drying the dishes, Martha Ann came into my room and flopped her body across my bed. Any other day I wouldn't have minded, but I had spent a good twenty minutes meticulously folding the sheets and blanket so they were neat and tight. I wanted to leave my room looking extra nice for Daddy. But before I could start griping at her, she started to cry.

"Catherine Grace, I know this day has been part of your plan, I mean our plan, since forever. But all that talking, I just never counted on it being this sad," she said, her voice trembling as she talked.

"I know," I said, gently stroking the back of her head. "Just two more years, Sis, and we'll be together, living it up big, on our own. Just two more years."

I never was really sure if Martha Ann wanted to leave Ringgold as much as I did or if she just went along with the idea because she didn't know how to tell her big sister she wanted to stay home. But either way, sometimes I wondered if my leaving was going to be the hardest on her.

"You know," I said, trying to lighten the mood, "I can't fit all these romance novels that Gloria Jean has been smuggling to me for the past two years into my suitcase. It ain't

Shakespeare, but I think you're old enough now to handle these steamy love scenes. Just don't let Daddy catch you with them or we'll both be reading the Bible cover to cover."

Martha Ann wiped her tears on my bedspread, and then she seemed ready to change the subject. So we talked about clothes and hairstyles and her first heavy make-out session with Freddy Emerson behind the fence at the public swimming pool, something she didn't think I knew about. She wasn't sure if she should feel proud or ashamed, but I told her as long as he kept his hands out of her pants, she should walk around with a smile on her face. We laughed when we started wondering what would be the appropriate shade of nail polish for making out behind a recreational swimming facility. Martha Ann thought it should be Crimson Red. I said Pink Paradise.

All the time I kept folding and packing. Finally I looked at my little sister and announced, "It's done. It's all done." But before either one of us could start crying again, I suggested we walk on over to Gloria Jean's and then down to the Dairy Queen for one last, ceremonial Dilly Bar. We put on our new, hot pink flip-flops that Mr. Tucker had given us the day before as a going-away present. Then we left Daddy a note on the kitchen table and headed out the door. I knew this good-bye wasn't going to be easy, either.

Gloria Jean must have heard us coming down her gravel driveway because she was already standing on her front porch waving at us to hurry on inside. "Girls, you better get in here. I couldn't imagine Catherine Grace would leave this town without coming to see me one last time. I've even made you some chocolate chip cookies for the bus ride. I got some for you, too, Martha Ann," she said, talking so fast, something she does when she's trying to keep a feeling to herself. I knew she was going to miss me, probably almost as much as my own daddy.

"Get in here and tell me what you've decided to do when you get to Atlanta tonight. Oh Lord, child, I cannot believe this day is finally here. You got your jam money in a safe place? You know you can't carry that shoebox with you on the Greyhound. Any old fool will know what you got in there."

Martha Ann and I both felt like we had been swept up in a tornado and plunked down on Gloria Jean's bright blue velvet sofa where we had spent so many hours watching the *Guiding Light* and listening to her stories about love and romance.

She handed us both a plate of cookies and, as full as we were from breakfast, we still managed to eat every last one. Gloria Jean had always said it was these very cookies that had been responsible for attracting husbands numbers two and four; and someday, when we were ready for true and lasting love, she'd share the recipe with us. She almost gave it to me last spring, but something inside told her to wait a little longer. And she was right. It would have been a shame to have wasted Cupid's chocolate chip cookie recipe on Henry Morel Blankenship.

"Okay, Catherine Grace Cline, tell me. Are you ready? Are your bags packed?"

"Yes, ma'am. Somehow I've managed to fit everything I own into my luggage set. Kind of sad to think my entire life actually fits into three matching suitcases."

"Honey, you're life is just beginning. Today is the day. The adventure begins!" She was almost shouting at this point. "Remember, hon, what's really important in life is never gonna fit into those three suitcases anyway."

Boy, I was going to miss her.

"So the bus leaves at six o'clock sharp. Now tell me where you've decided to stay tonight."

"Well, I'm not getting to Atlanta until a little after eight. So Daddy arranged for some cousin of ours I've never laid eyes on before to pick me up at the bus station. She works in a bank downtown somewhere and she's going to let me stay with her for a while. She's getting married at the end of the month, so I have to be out of there by the twenty-fifth or so."

"Good. You got yourself a place to lay your head tonight. Now what about a job? Any last-minute news? Did you call my friend at J.C. Penney yet? If nothing else, she might know of some place you can live when it comes time to leave your cousin's."

"No, but I will. You know I'd still like to work at Davison's best of all, but any kind of ladies' shop, like Love-man's, would be great," I said. "So I thought I'd head over to Lenox Square mall first thing Monday morning and start filling out applications."

"Oh, honey, I'm gonna keep telling you what you already know. You will be wonderful in the world of fashion. You always look so cute even when you're in shorts and a T-shirt. You really do have that special something. I know you don't think you do, but you do, just like your mama," Gloria Jean said, complimenting me like I was her own flesh and blood.

"Catherine Grace, I've been saving something to give you. You know how much I loved your mama. When you were born, I used to go over and do a little cooking for her or rock you to sleep so she could get some rest. I'd sing 'Hush Little Baby,' not as pretty as your mama, but you'd fall right to sleep anyway. Worked like magic every time.

"Anyway, as a way of saying thanks, your mama painted this little box for me. She used to kid and tell me she made it to hold all my wedding rings," she laughed, handing me the box. "Look inside, she even lined it with red velvet and fancy gold trim." I held it for a long time, just feeling its weight in my hands. I opened the lid. The trim was straight and not a raw edge was showing.

"Now turn it over and look at what she wrote on the bottom of the box."

You welcomed my little Catherine Grace with love and joy.
I hope she celebrates life as you do.
Love, your friend, Lena Mae.

I couldn't believe that I was holding something so beautiful that my mama's very own hands had made, and I had that feeling, that really odd feeling deep down inside, that the message on the bottom of this box was meant as much for me as it had been for Gloria Jean. That familiar shiver ran down my back, Mama's way of letting me know she was floating nearby.

I hugged Gloria Jean and let my body rest in her arms before looking up to see that all three of us were sobbing like newborn babies. We sat there crying and hugging till finally Gloria Jean said, "Okay girls, enough of this carrying-on. You got an adventure waiting for you. Now, go on, get out of here. And don't worry about Martha Ann, I'll be looking after her."

"I love you, Gloria Jean," I said, and I wanted to keep saying it, over and over again.

"I know you do, hon," she said quietly. "Now go on, you must have a mountain of things to do before you get on that Greyhound."

Martha Ann and I walked down the driveway still sniffling and rubbing our noses with the backs of our arms. I held my box next to my heart, hoping Mama could see how pleased I was with her handiwork. Martha Ann asked if I wanted to stop by the house before walking to town so

I could put the box in my suitcase for safekeeping. I told her no. I wasn't ready to let go of it, not even for a minute.

We walked on to town, stopping on the sidewalk to talk to Mr. Tucker. I told him he had been partly responsible for this moment, letting me sell my jam in his store all these years. He asked me again when I was leaving, forgetting he had asked me the very same question only the day before. I said about six tonight and then told him how much Martha Ann and I loved our new flip-flops, shaking my left foot as I spoke. He told me he was going to miss me, and I said I was surely going to miss him, too. It was tiring, all this good-bying.

We even ran into Ruthie Morgan and Emma Sue Huck-step as they were making their way into the Dollar General Store, surely looking to buy themselves a new pair of hot pink flip-flops, having already seen ours. Ruthie reached out to give me the obligatory good-bye hug, but as I pressed my body against hers, I wondered if I hadn't been so busy hating her for the past eighteen years if we could have been friends. Leaving sure makes you rethink your friends and your enemies alike.

Emma Sue and I decided a polite smile would be suffi-cient.

Finally, we made it to the Dairy Queen, and fortunately nobody was there except Eddie Franklin, standing behind the counter as usual waiting to take our order. Eddie had worked at the Dairy Queen since he was no more than thirteen. He graduated from high school five or six years ago and now worked there full-time. No one can make a more perfect curlicue at the top of a soft ice cream cone than Eddie Franklin. Even when he dips the ice cream in the warm, melted chocolate, it holds its shape.

"Hey Catherine, Martha Ann, what can I get you girls?" he asked like he really had no clue what we were going to order.

"Same as usual Eddie, two Dilly Bars," I replied, putting eighty cents on the counter.

Lolly had said she was going to try to meet us here so we could see each other one last time before I left. I didn't normally encourage visitors while I was at the Dairy Queen, but today seemed worthy of making an exception to the rule. I figured Lolly's mama would probably come up with some stupid chore for her to do at the last minute just to keep her from coming to say good-bye. You'd have thought Lolly would have gotten herself out of town the minute she was handed her diploma, but for some reason she hadn't been able to go. I think that crazy mother of hers had convinced her she wasn't capable of much of anything, not even running away.

Martha Ann was sitting on the picnic table and staring blankly at the road in front of her. I handed her a Dilly Bar, and we sat there eating our ice cream and talking about life like we had a thousand times before, never once mentioning my leaving. We talked about the kids at school and Mrs. Gulbenk's tomato aspic and how it tasted like an unfortunate combination of Hunt's tomato paste and lime Jell-O.

And we talked about Miss Raines and her new boyfriend. She finally broke up with Daddy, saying it was time to get on with her life. After all that complaining I'd done when she first started coming over to the house, it turned out I really liked her. And I knew Daddy did, too. He obviously loved her but couldn't bring himself to commit to anything much more than Sunday lunch. I guess Gloria Jean was right. Miss Raines wanted to grow her own little crop of tomatoes while she still could.

Martha Ann asked me how I thought Daddy was going to handle my leaving.

"I don't know," I told her. "It's gonna be real hard, I'm sure, but, heck, I'm only gonna be a couple of hours down the road." But with Daddy it didn't seem to matter whether I was two hours or two days from home. I was gone.

"You know, Catherine Grace, I bet Daddy is not the only man who doesn't want you to leave town. Have you seen Hank lately? Ruthie Morgan said he'd been asking about you."

"No way. When she'd say that? She's lying. Anyway, Hank and I are history, you know that," I told her.

But I also knew that if I hadn't been so determined to leave town, Hank and I would have been engaged by now, spending these last days of summer picking out our wedding china and arguing with Ida Belle about the flavor of the wedding cake. Ida Belle would insist that it be almond, so I guessed it'd be almond.

I hadn't seen Hank in more than a month, which takes some doing in Ringgold. Somehow we had managed to successfully avoid each other all summer long, and I certainly wasn't expecting to run into him today.

"Come on, Martha Ann, it's getting kind of late. Daddy's probably back from the church wondering where we are." We slowly eased our bodies off the table and began walking on home. I couldn't help it. I just kept looking back at that picnic table till it was nothing more than a speck in the distance. When we got to the house, we found Daddy out back watering the flowers along the side of the garage. He looked up when he heard us coming. "So, Catherine Grace, you think your sister and I are going to be able to keep these zinnias and tomatoes from dying in this heat?"

"I don't know, Daddy," I said. "But I think it's a good thing you're a man of God because they're definitely going to need some saving if Martha Ann gets a hold of them."

"Hey," my little sister blurted, like she was actually offended. Truth be told, sometimes I thought Martha Ann killed Daddy's tomatoes on purpose just so she wouldn't have to take her turn watering.

"You know, sweetie, the mustard seeds that fell among the thorn bushes grew up nice and tall, but then the thorns choked them and their fruit never ripened. The seeds that fell in the good soil grew strong and bore many fruits."

"Daddy, c'mon," I said, a little irritated by this last-ditch effort to biblically guilt me into staying home.

If something was really heavy on my daddy's heart, then he started talking in parables, just like Jesus Christ Himself except in overalls. What Daddy was really saying was that Atlanta was going to be a difficult place to lead a good, healthy life. There may be too many temptations, too much money, too much fast living, too many smooth-talking men. I could only hope.

But here in Ringgold, where the soil is rich and healthy and temptations are few and far between, I could grow a strong, healthy family and be bored out of my mind.

"Well, at least I always knew you were going to leave . . . not like your mama."

"Daddy, I'm not dying. I'm just going less than a hundred miles from here. You're going to see me again," I said, even more irritated that he was talking about Mama like that, like she died on purpose. I guess his heart had finally caught up with his mouth.

"I'm sorry, sweetie. I didn't mean that the way it came out. It's just harder than I thought," he said, staring at the ground. "Maybe we oughta get your bags in the car. Your bus is going to be here soon, and I know you need to be getting on your way." I walked into my room and saw my suitcases against the wall, just where I had left them. I couldn't bear to look at my room anymore; the emptiness was hurting too much. I never for a minute would have believed a dream could be this painful.

Somehow I managed to drag all three of my bags to the front door, carrying the smallest one across my shoulder and pulling the other two behind me. If my house had any feelings at all, I sure hoped it understood why I left without saying good-bye.

Daddy put my luggage in the backseat of the Oldsmobile. Then the three of us climbed into the front, not wanting to be separated for a minute more than we had to be. Martha Ann called shotgun, but that was fine with me; I wanted to be nestled in between the two people I loved most in this world.

We pulled into the parking lot next to the Dairy Queen, surprised to find the bus already there, the driver standing by the door licking a chocolate-dipped ice cream cone, obviously the handiwork of Eddie Franklin.

Daddy pulled the bags from the back and handed the two biggest ones to the bus driver. He handed me the small cosmetic bag where I had packed Gloria Jean's chocolate chip cookies, her brand new copy of *Vogue* magazine that she had given me even before reading it herself, and, wrapped in an old soft hand towel, my mama's box.

"We're running right on time, little lady, and I intend to keep it that way," the driver said rather firmly. It was kind of hard to take him too seriously, though, since he had a big chocolate stain on the pocket of his white uniform shirt. "I'm going to finish this ice cream, and then we're off. So say your good-byes and find your seat."

"Yes, sir." I was panicked and relieved to know that

after eighteen years of waiting, my moment was finally here. In my dream, I had planned on having a few more minutes with Daddy and Martha Ann, but I guess by now I'd said all that needed to be said.

"I love you," I mumbled, afraid if I said it too clearly or too loudly then I'd start crying again. I wrapped my arms around them both and lowered my head between their bodies.

"I love you, too. I'll be right here waiting on you," Daddy said, sounding calmer than he had all day.

I turned to Martha Ann and she held me tight. "I don't know if I can do this without you," she said.

"Yes, you can," I told her, whispering in her ear. I felt so guilty leaving her behind. Maybe she really did need me to stay. I wondered if this was how Mama felt when she got to heaven, happy to be there but sorry she had to go. God, I wished Gloria Jean were here, pushing me onto that bus. She would tell me that I had to go, that Martha Ann was going to be just fine, that she had some dreaming of her own she needed to do.

"I'm not going to be far," I said, and kissed her on the cheek, stepping onto the Greyhound without looking back.

As soon as I was situated in my seat, the driver climbed onto the bus and started the engine. It was all happening much faster than I had imagined. But I think the good Lord knew that I, unlike Moses, needed my exodus to be short and sweet. I just kept staring out the window, looking straight ahead, not looking back.

The driver yanked the door shut, revved the engine, and then steered the bus onto the main highway. He was barely out of the parking lot when a red pickup truck came barreling down the other side of the road, forcing the bus driver to swerve his Greyhound off onto the dirt shoulder. "Holy crap," the driver shouted. But I knew that truck. I came out of my seat and pushed my way to the other side of the bus, leaning over some poor old man. It was Hank. He sped into the parking lot and jumped out of the front of his pickup. He stood there staring at the bus, looking as stunned as my daddy and Martha Ann. I didn't know what to do so I fell back in my seat and closed my eyes.

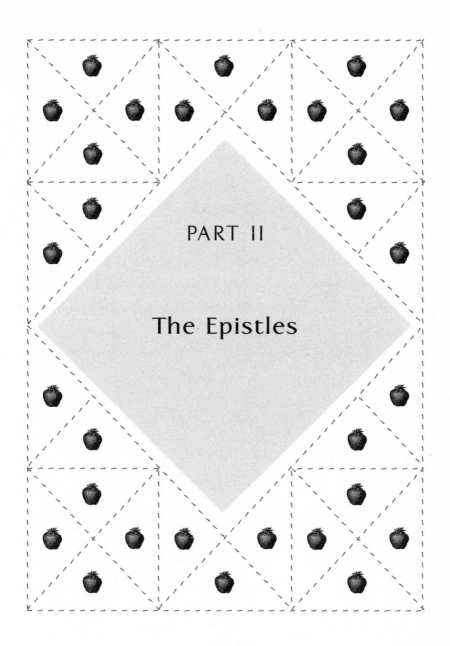

PART II

The Epistles

always figured my Moses was going to be a strong, handsome man capable of parting an ocean with one hand, not some bald-headed bus driver with blobs of chocolate dripping down his shirt. But I guess there's no sense in questioning God's choice in saviors when you're making your way to the Promised Land.

Laura Lynn Cline picked me up at the Greyhound station just like she told Daddy she would. She had written my name on a piece of white cardboard and was holding it out in front of her chest so I'd know who she was. What a sad thing, I thought, needing a sign to find a girl who's got some of the very same blood running through her veins as is running through mine.

Turns out, I didn't need any old piece of cardboard. Laura Lynn was staring at me with those same steely blue eyes that can belong only to a Cline. Daddy said her great-granddaddy Merrill Otis and our great-granddaddy were brothers, but Laura Lynn said her mama told her that after William Floyd found the Lord, he never had much to do with his brother. They just figured William Floyd was too busy doing God's work to keep up with his family, especially considering Merrill Otis was a whiskey-drinking Methodist and all.

Laura Lynn had moved to Atlanta three or four years ago and was some kind of loan officer at the Peachtree Savings and Trust. I really didn't know what she did but she wore the same dark navy suit to work every single day. To tell the truth, I'd never seen a girl dress more like a man than she did, and except for that string of pearls hanging around her neck, you'd hardly know there was a woman inside that get-up. Laura Lynn said that's what all the professional women in Atlanta wear these days, and if I ever wanted to make something of myself, I better understand real quick that it's a man's world out there.

Actually my cousin didn't seem to like men much, except for Royce that is. She had gotten engaged back in the spring sometime, and her pending nuptials and her fiancé, Royce Randolph Duncan, III, were all she knew to talk about. She always said his name real slow like I was supposed to be impressed. So I called him Roy whenever Laura Lynn was around just to see her squint her little eyes and puff those cheeks out like some kind of African blowfish I'd seen in an old *National Geographic*.

Laura Lynn said that she and Royce were getting married at his mother's house over in Buckhead, some rich, fancy neighborhood in town. Since she and Royce didn't go to church much, she thought it more appropriate to get married in a house not belonging to the Lord. She also said that someday they would be the ones living in the big house in Buckhead.

They even went and hired themselves a caterer for the wedding reception. Of course, when I asked what a caterer was, Laura Lynn just rolled her eyes like I should know better. Ida Belle would absolutely die if a bride at Cedar Grove paid somebody else to make her ham biscuits and Cheddar cheese straws. But Laura Lynn said that anyone who's anybody in Atlanta would know to hire a caterer.

Truth be told, I figured Laura Lynn would be more like me—and not just because we turned up sharing the same last name. I thought she came to Atlanta to do something that she couldn't do back in Martin, Tennessee. But instead she seemed to be like all the other girls back home, just waiting for the world, or a boy named Royce, to take care of her.

But one thing was for darn sure. I decided real quick that hanging around two people in love was about as awkward as watching Brother Fulmer's horse when he's put out to stud. Gloria Jean was right—there's no sin in loving somebody, but you sure don't need an audience. And Royce was stuck to Laura Lynn's lips like a magnet. Unfortunately, her apartment was real tiny, and there weren't many places for me to go unnoticed. So I spent a lot of time out on the balcony, but I really didn't mind. In fact, I liked it out there, especially late at night when all the lights in the city were turned on bright and twinkling all around me. Heck, I felt like I was standing smack dab in the middle of a birthday cake with all its candles ablaze.

I could see Laura Lynn's bank building from up there, and I couldn't help but wonder what all those women in their dark navy suits did behind those glass walls all day long cooped up like a bunch of chickens in a henhouse. On top of the building stood this giant orange ball that turned 'round and 'round day and night. I reckon it was supposed to be some kind of oversized Georgia peach.

A little bit farther down were two big yellow arches that glowed in the dark like the Star of David lighting the way for all those weary shepherds apparently hungering for a burger and an order of fries. McDonald's was open twenty-four hours a day, and that's the God's honest truth. I'd figured only hospitals and police stations were open all night long, and I certainly couldn't imagine Eddie Franklin staying up until three in the morning to make banana splits and chocolate-dip cones for anybody, not even his own mama. One time I made Royce walk me over there after midnight for no good reason other than I wanted to order something in the dead of night. I got a Quarter Pounder with cheese, French fries, and a large Coca-Cola and sat there under those golden arches until one in the morning.

And lucky for me, Lenox Square mall was only four

blocks from Laura Lynn's apartment. She was real anxious
for me to get over there and start "knocking on some
doors," so to speak. I told her that it made me a little nervous walking there seeing how I had to cross a road that
looked more like an interstate than a city street. She told
me I was being ridiculous, that I had two good eyes and
two good legs, so use them. Personally speaking, though, I
always considered it somewhat of an accomplishment making it to the other side in one piece.

I'd been to the mall only once before, with Daddy and
Martha Ann, and that was a long, long time ago. And
other than the toy department at Davison's and that Barbie
doll dressed in her white winter coat, I really didn't remember much. All these years later, I couldn't help but wonder
if that Barbie doll was still hanging around, maybe sporting
a little cotton sundress and a wide-brimmed hat.

But when I got there, what I found looked more like a
city than a shopping mall. There were so many places to
eat and spend your money, I figured you could be lost for
weeks and come out none the worse for wear. One store
sold nothing but women's handbags and another one sold
nothing but women's underwear—all sorts of silk panties
and lacy bras—things I was not sure should be displayed
for everybody to see. But I decided right at that very moment that when I got my first paycheck, I was marching
into that store and buying myself a pair of pink panties
with little pink roses embroidered all over them. Somehow
knowing that Ruthie Morgan would trade her best cashmere

sweater set for a pair of those panties would make it worth it, no matter what they cost!

I must have filled out at least a dozen applications and, even though my feet were hurting from walking so much, I headed on over to Penney's to introduce myself to that old friend of Gloria Jean's. I had made a solemn promise that I'd look her up as soon as I got to town, and there's no going back on a solemn promise, especially one involving Gloria Jean Graves.

A tall, slender woman with bright blue eye shadow was standing behind the jewelry counter, and I knew without even asking her name that she was the woman I was looking for. She said she didn't know about any jobs at Penney's that would be good for a girl like me, but she did know a sweet, old lady, a Miss Myrtie Mabie, who might have a room to rent, something I could afford.

She handed me a small piece of paper with Miss Mabie's phone number on it and suggested I call her, not too early and not too late, seeing how she was nearing eighty. And seeing how I was sleeping on some crummy old couch Laura Lynn bought at the Goodwill store, which had such a stale smoky smell about it that it left me feeling like I'd been puffing on Mrs. Dempsey's Virginia Slims, I was real eager to call this Miss Mabie.

Living with Laura Lynn wasn't all bad, don't get me wrong. But I must admit that my favorite time of day was right after she left for work. As soon as the door slammed shut, I fixed myself a bowl of cereal and turned on the television. Daddy never let Martha Ann and me watch too much TV, said it wasn't good for our brains. But here, I just couldn't get enough of it, especially the Action News on WSB-TV.

Every morning, this nice-looking man, much younger than Daddy's Walter Cronkite, talked about all the bad things that had happened in Atlanta while I was sleeping—all the things I imagined Daddy hoped I would never hear or see. Truth be told, probably not a single night went by when somebody wasn't getting robbed or shot, but the man's voice was so warm and soothing that it just never sounded all that bad.

Today the worst thing he had to say was that the temperature was going to be close to one hundred and five, again, some kind of late-summer heat wave pushing east from the Great Plains. I'd never sweated more like a stuck pig in my life. Laura Lynn said it was all the asphalt and concrete, something about an urban jungle. So I decided today was as good as any to sit by the telephone, in the air-conditioning, in front of the TV, and wait for somebody to call and give me a job.

And sure enough, someone did. A man, a senior manager I think he said, from Davison's department store phoned a little before noon and wanted me, Catherine Grace Cline, to come in for an interview. He said he was looking for an energetic young woman to join a new department that was scheduled to open early next week. He said he had read my application carefully and was very impressed with my entrepreneurial spirit. It was possible I might have made my jam-making business sound a little grander than it really was. But either way, he figured I must be a real go-getter, just the kind of person he wanted representing Davison's department store.

My nerves started twitching right there on the telephone, but I kept telling myself that any girl who can sell strawberry jam can surely sell pretty clothes and high-heeled shoes. Then I started blabbing, telling him all about my daddy and the time he brought me to the store to see Santa Claus and how I had dreamed of working there myself someday. He said he looked forward to meeting someone who loved Davison's as much as he did and that I should meet him at the back door, by the loading dock, the very next morning at nine o'clock sharp.

I spent the rest of the day trying to decide what to wear, finally choosing my Villager set that Gloria Jean had bought me a couple years ago for the Mother-Daughter Tea. Laura Lynn said it didn't look very professional, not being navy and all, but she guessed it would be okay for retail work. I was really growing to dislike that girl.

The next morning I woke up extra early, not even needing to set my alarm clock. I wanted to spend a little time in the bathroom before Laura Lynn started shooing me out of her way, leaving me to brush my teeth in the kitchen sink and fix my hair staring into the side of the toaster. The man on the television said it had been a real

quiet night in Atlanta, and I took that to be an omen of
sorts that something good was coming my way.

Mr. Wallis was standing by the back door, waiting for
me when I got there. Thankfully, I was five minutes early
'cause I noticed he glanced down at his watch and noted
the time. Mr. Charles Humphrey Wallis turned out to be a
very soft gentleman even though his voice had sounded big
and strong on the telephone. He was short and thin and
had thick, gray hair parted neatly on the side and coated
with some kind of oil that made it shine real bright in the
sunlight. A little blue handkerchief was tucked inside his
suit pocket and gold buttons were fastened to his shirt cuffs.
He was dressed more like the governor than any other man
I had ever met before in my life.

We walked from one end of the store to the other, and
even though I kept step with Mr. Wallis, I couldn't keep
my eyes from darting every which way. I started wondering how many people it would take to buy up all the
dresses and jewelry and perfume that were on display,
more than everybody in Ringgold, that's for sure. Mr. Wallis didn't seem to notice any of it. I wondered if that would
happen to me after a while.

He led me into a small but comfortable-looking office
directly behind the women's shoe department. He sat behind the desk and I sat in front of it, and we talked back
and forth for almost an hour. He asked me all sorts of
questions about Ringgold—about school and making jam

and the like. He even asked me about Daddy and Martha Ann. Next thing I knew, I had myself a job, although I wasn't going to be selling cosmetics or fancy dresses. Turns out, I had gourmet food experience and would be working in Davison's new specialty foods department, selling expensive crackers and olives and candies and . . . yes . . . jams.

But Mr. Wallis said that if I did a real good job, the store's executives might even consider me for the management-training program. "Because Davison's is all about opportunity." That's exactly what he said.

Mr. Wallis started as a sales clerk just like me, and he told me that if I worked hard, someday I might be sitting right where he was. I wasn't sure if perched behind a stack of women's shoes was exactly what he meant, but I smiled and told him I sure hoped he was right.

Laura Lynn was almost happier than I was to hear about my new job. She had already figured that with a paycheck or two in my pocket, I could be looking for a place of my own and she and Royce could get back to loving each other full-time. Heck, Royce almost picked me up off the floor when he heard the news. Those two will most surely be birthing a baby by their first wedding anniversary, if not sooner.

But after Laura Lynn went to bed, I got down on my knees and thanked the Lord for Mr. Wallis and my new job. If I was going to be the best sales clerk Davison's had ever had, I figured I was going to need the Almighty on my side. To tell the truth, talking to the Lord was coming a whole lot easier these days—what with Him finally listening and all.

Of course, Daddy always taught me to pray for my enemies first, but I skipped right over Laura Lynn and the like and started thinking on Daddy and Martha Ann and Gloria Jean. I wondered if they were missing me as much as I was missing them. I hadn't heard from Daddy yet, even though I had already written him two long letters. I reckoned the church was keeping him pretty busy, especially with Homecoming just around the corner. And I was sure Roberta Huckstep was buzzing about his ear, reminding him how little Emma Sue would never think of leaving her family like I'd up and done.

After saying all that, I just lay there and wondered about Hank. I saved him for last, so I could take my time thinking about his blue eyes and his strong arms and the way he'd whisper in my ear, causing my insides to tingle. I saw his red pickup pull into the parking lot at the Dairy Queen as my bus was pulling out. A part of me had wanted to yell at that driver to stop and let me get off. But I just closed my eyes instead. And now when I couldn't think about Hank Blankenship anymore, I just closed my eyes and went to sleep.

September 19, 1975

Dear Catherine Grace,

I was so excited to finally get a letter. Mr. Winfield brought it right to the door. He said he knew I'd been waiting on pins and needles to hear from you and that the U.S. Postal Service wanted to do whatever it could for Reverend Cline's baby girl. Ha, the U.S. Postal Service being Mr. Winfield and his wife!

You have no idea how much I've been missing you, but I am absolutely thrilled to hear about your new job—although you have to admit that it's a little ironic that you had to go all the way to Atlanta to sell strawberry jam! No kidding, we're all real proud of you. Gloria Jean says sales are sales and you obviously have a natural-born talent for it. Daddy even smiled when he heard the news.

As exciting as it must be in Atlanta, rest assured that it is just that quiet here. And who would have thought this place could get any worse? Thank goodness Gloria Jean has been coming by to check on us, because if she didn't, I don't think this house would have seen a smile lately. She said to tell you that she's waiting for a letter of her own!

I know you'd like to hear that Daddy is doing fine, but I have to be honest with you, Catherine Grace, he's not. He's sad, really sad. He misses you terribly. And most days, he acts as though you've up and died. He spends most of his time at the church reading the Bible and doing God only knows what. And when he comes home, he never has much to say. He watches the news, shakes his head as if to remind me that the world is a bad place, and then goes to bed.

Last Sunday, he woke up acting more like his old self. He even put a pot roast in the Crock-Pot. I had hoped Miss Raines might be coming over for lunch just like she used to. But she didn't. In fact, Daddy hardly spoke to her after the service. And oh my, the sermon, let's just say he spent more than an hour preaching the parable of the Prodigal Son—sounding very much like the wounded father. I think he just wanted to remind the congregation that his precious, wayward daughter would be coming home as soon as she figures out what a big mistake she's gone and made. (Although he may have to rethink this, seeing how the Prodigal Son never landed a job at Davison's department store!)

And just so you know, according to Daddy's version of the story, I'm the loyal, devoted child who stayed home to water all these stupid tomatoes. And of course I'll also be the one stuck cleaning the house and helping Ida Belle cook for the big party he's going to have in celebration of your grand return!

Laura Lynn sounds nice enough, but you're right, it is really strange to think about the family we have and don't know anything about. But I guess lucky for you a Cline turned up in Atlanta even if she wasn't what you were hoping for.

OK, now you need to sit down, Catherine Grace, because if you don't, you are going to hit the floor laughing. At the Tigers' first home game, little Miss Emma Sue was making her official debut as a Ringgold varsity cheerleader. Yuk! Anyway, her entire family was there, sitting in the bleachers, waving signs that read, "Go Tiger Sue," and taking at least a million pictures.

During halftime the cheerleading squad ran out onto the field for their big cheer, and Walter Pigeon lifted Emma Sue up over his head. She was standing on Walter's shoulders, grinning so big, so impressed with herself. Anyway, she was supposed to fall into Walter's arms, but somebody blew a horn and distracted poor Walter Pigeon and Emma Sue fell right on the ground!!!

She cracked her cute little tailbone! In two places! And now she has to sit on this piece of foam that looks like a giant doughnut. She carries it around with her everywhere she goes. If she's not sitting on it, she's wearing it around her wrist like a bracelet! I have never laughed so hard in my entire life. Mrs. Roberta Huckstep hasn't been in church for two weeks. I think the entire family is suffering from terminal humiliation, at least

that's what Gloria Jean called it. I love it—
terminal humiliation!

Of course, we lost the game, but nobody cared.
Robbie Preston is the only quarterback I know of
who can't throw a football. And you know as
well as I do that we can't beat Lafayette just
running the ball up and down the field.

By the way, the new English teacher from
Murfreesboro never showed up. Apparently she
got caught in a compromising situation with the
principal at her old school. Needless to say,
she was asked not to come to Ringgold High. So
Mr. Boyce, a retired English teacher from some
boys' school in Chattanooga, was hired at the last
minute. At first I thought he was going to be a
downright, total bore. But he's wonderful. He
actually believes that there are other great
American writers besides Mrs. Tyne's beloved
William Faulkner!

He told me I'm one of the most promising
students he's ever had, and as much as I love
words, I ought to think about being an English
teacher or a newspaper writer or maybe

somebody kind of like Mary Tyler Moore. How about that?! Maybe I could work for the paper in Atlanta, and then we could live together. Wouldn't that be great!

Of course, we might have to wait till poor Daddy has completely lost his mind or is dead and buried cause I'm not sure he'll ever be able to stand both of his baby girls leaving town. Just kidding! I think!

Lots and lots of hugs and kisses,
Martha Ann

Turns out the nice old lady with the room to rent lived in a big beautiful house right smack dab in the middle of Buckhead. Laura Lynn couldn't stand it that I, Catherine Grace Cline, made it to the fancy neighborhood before she did. She was so mad, she could have spit but instead she dropped me off at the end of Miss Mabie's driveway, leaving me to lug my bags to the house all on my own. I was huffing and puffing something awful by the time I made my way to the front steps.

Miss Mabie was standing just outside her door when I got there, looking real tiny and small next to the huge, square white columns stretched across the front of her house. She had a rather nice figure for a woman her age, and her hair was snow white and cut in a short, stylish bob. She looked very sophisticated and elegant till you got down to her feet and saw her brown, clunky orthopedic shoes. She told me later that she was a vain woman from the tip of her head all the way down to her ankles—but that's where her vanity turned to comfort.

"Child, are you Catherine Grace Cline?" she asked, pointing her little crooked finger right at me.

"Yes, ma'am, I am."

"Child, you walk all the way here?"

"No, ma'am, my cousin dropped me off at the end of your driveway."

"Hmm." Then she looked me over long and hard. "Well, your cousin's either got no manners at all or she doesn't like you too much. Which is it?"

"I think a bit of both to tell the truth."

"Damn it. Well, I've either got me the best tenant I've ever had or I need to go and lock the silver closet. Come on and get in here and let's find out which it is."

She yelled for Flora to come and take my bags, and almost instantly a large black woman appeared from behind a white swinging door. Miss Mabie didn't introduce us, but Flora flashed a quick smile and then headed up the stairs carrying all three of my bags in her hands.

Miss Mabie turned her back to me and walked away, obviously intending for me to follow. She stopped in the kitchen and pointed to the kitchen table, directing me to take a seat. She fixed me a glass of iced tea, all the while explaining the rules of the house. No smoking and no loud music. Rent was due the first of the month. Local calls could be made from the phone in the kitchen. And any gentleman callers were welcome as long as they didn't smoke or play loud music.

Then without me even asking, Miss Mabie told me that she ran away from home when she was no more than sixteen, catching a ride with some insurance salesman passing through Georgia on his way to New York City. She said she used to model for a store called Bloomingdale's and even danced on Broadway! She said Gene Kelley was a very good friend and she emphasized the *very*. And she said she used to be tall till life and old age beat her down.

I didn't understand her ever wanting to leave New York City, but she said she loved the South and since her daddy left her with more money than she knew what to do with, she figured she'd come home and spend the rest of her years sipping gin and tonics and swatting flies. She told everyone in town that she had been married twice and widowed twice. She said that Atlanta society preferred to think that she had known the love of a man only within the sacramental confines of matrimonial bliss. "Marriage would be wonderful, dear," she reassured me, "if it weren't so everyday."

Miss Mabie's house was like a giant jewelry box filled with treasures she'd found all over the world, like that huge blue-and-white jar that always sat in the middle of the dining room table. Miss Mabie said it was an ancient Chinese vase and that it was older than Ringgold. Flora kept it filled with fresh flowers every single day.

My room probably wasn't much bigger than our toolshed back home, but I loved it. It was painted a soft shade of yellow and had a large picture window that looked out on the backyard. And right outside my window was one of the prettiest magnolia trees I'd ever seen. Sometimes, when I was lying in my bed, I actually felt like that little baby bird Daddy was always talking about. And there I was, safe and sound, settled in my nest way up high in my beautiful magnolia tree.

Miss Mabie said she loved knowing somebody else was in the house with her, especially the daughter of a preacher. Flora was always there, too, but she was the biggest scaredy cat I'd ever seen. When it was storming and lightning one night, Flora cried so hard, Miss Mabie had to let her come in bed with her just to quiet her down.

I liked to sit in the kitchen and talk to Flora while she worked. She was a large-boned woman, but the graceful way she moved her body around the kitchen was something beautiful to watch. She was a lot like Ida Belle, actually, but with skin as dark as night. She'd been cooking Miss Mabie's meals since she was fourteen years old. Flora said her own mama died shortly after giving birth, and she said her daddy never did get used to looking at her. Her daddy worked for Miss Mabie's daddy and so they met when Miss Mabie was home visiting. He told her he had a girl, didn't know what to do with her. Miss Mabie said she did. Flora said Miss Mabie was the only mama she'd ever had. She also said she was the craziest white woman she'd ever known.

"Oh precious Jesus," she told me one afternoon while she was rolling out dough for the evening's biscuits, "she took me shoppin' for some new clothes as soon as I started workin' for her. She said there was no lookin' like a street chil' in her house. You shoulda been there. She tol' all a those clerks that I was her baby niece visitin' from South Carolina. I think she done it for fun, jus' to watch 'em all squirm like some little earthworm after the rain. But Miss Mabie spent so much money in that sto' they jus' had to smile."

Flora thought it was very funny that I was selling fancy foods and didn't know how to do much of anything in the kitchen but make strawberry jam and Thursday-night meat-loaf. I told her I also knew how to make Mrs. Gulbenk's special tea, but she said that didn't count.

Most nights Miss Mabie asked me to join her for dinner, unless she was too tired, and then Flora served her in her room. We always sat on opposite ends of the big, long table in the dining room. Miss Mabie was a little hard of hearing, so talking at the table was more like a shouting match on a school playground than the exchange of some polite conversation. Flora always sat in the kitchen by herself, except for Christmas, Thanksgiving, and Easter. I felt kind of funny about that, but I didn't dare ask Miss Mabie how come.

Most days I just couldn't stop pinching myself. I had paid Miss Mabie my first month's rent, had bought myself a pretty pair of panties, and still put one hundred and fifty-three dollars in the bank. I was waking up in a world that I had only dreamed about, except in this dream there was a magnolia tree outside my window. And even though I found myself wondering what Daddy and Martha Ann were doing, I just couldn't imagine being anyplace else.

October 25, 1975

Dear Catherine Grace,

I am so excited for you. First your job, now Miss Mabie. She sounds wonderful, Flora too. I agree, the Lord is listening to you now!

Daddy said that maybe I could come down and see you sometime in January, after the Christmas-shopping rush. I can't wait to see your new room, Miss Mabie's fancy house, and Davison's. Sounds like you're living more like a princess than a preacher's daughter!

We were all sorry you couldn't come home for the Cedar Grove Homecoming. I really missed you, but I understand that working retail means giving up some of your weekends. It was a lot of fun, though, more fun than I ever expected it to be. The youth group played bingo with the Euzelian class, and for the first time ever, the youth group won. Of course, all we won was another bingo party hosted by the Euzelians. Ha!

Ida Belle outdid herself in the kitchen, of course. She fried seven hundred and twenty-five pieces of chicken and baked more than four hundred and fifty brownies. She wanted to be sure everyone, including Brother Fulmer, left with a full stomach.

The best part though was playing musical chairs. Everybody played—Lolly, Miss Raines, Ida Belle, even Emma Sue, although she's still carrying that stupid doughnut pillow around, which slowed the game down a bit. Mrs. Huckstep says her little Emma Sue has a very delicate bone structure and the healing process is taking longer than expected. Naturally.

Anyway, Mrs. Huckstep couldn't bear the thought of losing even a child's game, so she would linger around a chair just waiting for Mrs. Gilbert to lift her fingers off those piano keys. Heck, that woman practically knocked me over trying to plant her big butt on my chair. But I squeezed in right under her. It was actually pretty funny!

OK. I know I haven't mentioned Hank. I guess to

be perfectly honest with you I was avoiding the subject because I really didn't know how to tell you this. He is dating somebody else. They've been going together for about a month now. He said they'd been friends forever and then one day they just saw each other in a different way. I am so, so sorry.

But here's the really bad news. It's Ruthie Morgan. I'm sorry, so, so sorry. I couldn't believe it either. But I have to say Catherine Grace, Ruthie has been a lot nicer these past few weeks—maybe Hank's rubbing off on her—he certainly has enough goodness to spare and still nobody would think any less of him. But I know that's got to hurt.

Listen, please don't waste one minute of your time thinking about Hank Blankenship. I know you're going to meet somebody a lot more exciting than Mr. Ringgold. Besides, you need a man who's much more worldly and cosmopolitan than the son of a dairy farmer!

When you come home for Thanksgiving, we can stay up all night counting all the things we hate about Ruthie Morgan, starting with her collection of cashmere sweaters! I cannot wait till you come home. I've been missing you so much lately.

Oh yeah, thanks for the jar of raspberry jam. You were right, there is a little hint of lemon in it. I like it, but it does seem kind of silly for Davison's to sell jam made all the way over in England when the very same thing is made right here in Georgia. On the other hand, I guess the kinds of people shopping at Davison's aren't the same ones looking for the weekly specials at the Dollar General Store. Oh well, what do I know about retail!

Love You Lots,
Martha Ann

ank and Ruthie Morgan. Well, how about that. I guess I wasn't surprised Hank was dating again. Boys his age like to have a girl they can call their own, at least that's what Gloria Jean always said. And maybe when you're eighteen and you plan on running your daddy's dairy farm, there's nothing else to do but marry some pretty girl and start having babies. But Ruthie Morgan, damn-it-to-tarnation, I had to wonder if he chose her just to get under my skin like a tiny little chigger that leaves you itching and scratching for days.

But I didn't care. Really. I didn't.

Lolly wrote me a real long letter. She felt I needed to hear the news from my best friend. She said Hank and Ruthie were always together, hugging and kissing on each other, even in plain daylight at the Dairy Queen. I could not believe Mrs. Morgan would let pure, precious Ruthie get away with that kind of behavior, in public and all. Maybe it's not so trampy when your potential son-in-law can keep you knee-deep in butter and milk for the rest of your life.

But I didn't care. Really. I didn't.

Then Hank wrote me a letter. He thought it only right that he let me know that he and Ruthie were going steady. He said he hadn't planned on falling in love with her, and he figured it must be hard for me knowing how I feel about her and all. But he said if I ever took the time to get to know her, I'd fall in love with her, too.

I almost threw up. I knew he'd fall in love, but why her? Why Ruthie Morgan? She always had everything,

everything I didn't—pretty clothes, pretty hair, and a mama and daddy who were home every day just waiting for her to waltz through the door. I know life's not fair, Daddy said it all the time. But for some people, it just seemed to be so much better.

I kept telling myself that I didn't care. Really. But I did.

I cared that Hank was in love, and not with me. I cared that at night, when everything was quiet and I started thinking about him, my heart would start hurting so much that I was afraid that there was nothing in this world that would ever make it stop.

And I cared that Daddy and Martha Ann were probably going to think that I didn't care about anybody but myself when they found out I couldn't come home for Thanksgiving. I cared all right. I cared about a lot of things.

Mr. Wallis never said flat out that I couldn't go home, but he sure said enough that made it hard to think that I could. He said the day after Thanksgiving was the store's busiest day of the year, and he suspected it would be the biggest day yet for the new gourmet foods department. Then he said I was the best junior sales clerk he ever had and that you couldn't get ahead in the world of retail without making some sacrifices. And if that wasn't enough, he said he would be naming an assistant manager before the end of the year. He said my name had come up in conversation, and even though I wasn't sure what that meant, he said it was a very good sign.

I finally found the courage to write Daddy and tell him

the truth. That may have been one of the hardest things
I've ever done in my life, almost as hard as leaving him in
the first place. Miss Mabie said that Martha Ann and
Daddy were welcome to come to Atlanta for Thanksgiving.
She said she had plenty of room and plenty of turkey. I told
Daddy he was welcome to come, but I knew better than
anybody that a preacher during the holidays was in more
demand than a sales clerk at Davison's department store.

Daddy wrote me back right away. He said Martha Ann
was very upset with me. He said that of course time heals
all wounds, like that would really make me feel any better.
Funny how preachers can deliver all these sermons on forgiveness and then faster than saying "Amen" can make you
feel guiltier than dirt.

Miss Mabie could see the sadness filling my eyes. She
told me she had been away from her daddy more Thanks-
givings than she should count. She said she knew exactly
what I was feeling and that's why she told Flora to make
her famous bourbon pecan pie. She said after just one bite I
wouldn't be missing my family quite so much. Then she
walked into the kitchen and told Flora she better make two.

Thanksgiving at Miss Mabie's turned out to be a very
formal, fancy affair unlike anything I'd ever seen. Even
though it was only the three of us, the table was perfectly
set with the prettiest china, crystal, and silver. The dishes
were creamy white with Miss Mabie's monogram in the
center, written in a deep, brilliant blue. And I could even
see myself in the silver spoon and knife resting by my

plate, although Miss Mabie was quick to point out that the knife and spoon were for eating, not for self-admiration.

And Flora, well, she done outdid herself. She cooked all week long and in the end there was turkey, sweet potatoes, green beans and stuffing, rolls and cranberry sauce enough to feed an army. And Miss Mabie was right about Flora's pie. One minute I was feeling awful sad and homesick, out of place at this fancy table, and the next minute I couldn't stop giggling. Everything turned funny; even the marshmallows on the sweet potatoes were looking pretty silly to me.

I fell asleep after dinner, which was just as well, better than sitting in my room wondering what Martha Ann and Daddy and Gloria Jean were doing. The next morning I didn't have time to think of anybody. Mr. Wallis wasn't lying. The day after Thanksgiving was the busiest day I'd ever seen at Davison's department store. I stood on my feet for twelve hours, barely having time to stop and pee!

You'd have thought Christmas was the very next day the way everybody was reaching and grabbing for things. I even sold ten tiny cans of smoked trout, although I'm still not real sure what you do with it. I told Mr. Wallis I'd probably caught my weight in trout, but I'd never seen it all brown and dried-out looking and costing six dollars and ninety-five cents a can. Mr. Wallis said it was a delicacy, and I should sell it with a smile. So I did. In fact, Mr. Wallis gave me a twenty-dollar bonus for selling more trout and jam and olives than any other sales clerk in our department.

After work, Babs Young asked me if I wanted to drive out to the Varsity and get a hamburger or chilidog or something. Mr. Wallis had hired Babs the same day he hired me, but we had never done much of anything together except inventory the new shipment of marmalades that had come all the way from England. I told her that I had always wanted to go to the Varsity since I was a little girl and that I had asked Laura Lynn to take me but she was always too busy. Babs just waved at me to quit talking and follow her to the parking lot.

Turns out her real name is Barbara, but she said she hated the way it made her sound like an old woman, so she called herself Babs instead. She grew up in Atlanta and after work she usually met up with some of her old high school friends. I didn't know where they were tonight, and I didn't care.

The Varsity turned out to be the biggest hamburger stand I'd ever seen in my life, probably longer than a football field if I had to measure it. But the burgers and milkshakes weren't the best part. After we finished eating, we just drove around town, with the windows down, singing real loud with the radio. We were freezing, which only made us sing louder. People were looking and laughing. It was so much fun being with somebody my own age. But it left me missing Lolly something awful, left me missing somebody who knew my whole story. Sometimes, I was realizing, dreams left you feeling kind of lonely.

December 1, 1975

Dear Catherine Grace,

God only knows how much Daddy and I missed you Thanksgiving Day. Daddy was really upset, not acting himself at all. But your not being here was not the only reason for his state of irritated distraction. I really don't know how to tell you this Catherine Grace, BUT, Miss Raines is pregnant. Yes, PREGNANT!

She said she has known for several months but had been too afraid to mention it to anyone at Cedar Grove, seeing how she's not married yet. I thought she was putting on a little weight, but I never dreamed she was carrying a baby. And not only is she pregnant, but she's engaged, too. Her fiancé, I think his name is Donald Semple, lives down in Summerville. She said he's a manager at some feed store down there. They plan to marry by the first of the year, and then she's moving to Summerville to live with her beloved Donald. That's what she called him, her beloved Donald.

She came over to the house the day before Thanksgiving. She said she wanted to tell Daddy in person. She was crying a lot, and her eyes were real red and swollen. But I swear I heard her tell Daddy that she would always love him, and she hoped he wasn't too disappointed in her.

Daddy had no idea that I was listening from behind my bedroom door. I think the news stunned him so that he forgot I was in the house. Daddy's voice was so soft and low, it was hard to make out much of what he was saying. But I did hear him tell her that if she needed anything, anything at all, just to ask.

He told me later that night that he had something very confidential he needed to tell me. He said he wanted me to hear the news from him and not from Emma Sue Huckstep. Miss Raines was going to have a baby, for sure. But it wasn't contagious, and he didn't want me treating her like she had the plague or something. She's already feeling awkward enough and doesn't need any disapproving stares from a teenaged girl.

Daddy said she was afraid she might lose her teaching job, and even though she'd be moving soon, she needed to work as long as she could. He said he was going over to the school first thing in the morning and talk to the principal himself. He said he was a real understanding man with a forgiving heart, but the parents were already talking about her not being a good example for the children. He figured saving her job might take a little divine intervention.

And, of course, there is plenty of talk already swirling about town. I'm almost surprised you haven't felt the meanness floating in the wind down in Atlanta. Emma Sue said her grandmother thinks Miss Raines was so upset over losing Daddy that she went positively wild and gave herself to the first man she met. She doesn't even think Miss Raines knows the baby's daddy's name and that she's just trying to figure out a way to save face.

Honestly, Catherine Grace, it doesn't upset me that she's gone and gotten herself pregnant before she got herself married. Heck, this Donald Semple isn't married either but nobody's pointing a finger at him. But I thought she was still in love with Daddy. Gloria Jean said that a broken heart could make you do some pretty stupid things. I guess making this baby is one of those stupid things.

I can't wait to see you. I miss you. I'm counting the days till Christmas.

Love,
Martha Ann

December 7, 1975

Dear Catherine Grace,

   Got your letter, and I don't think Miss Raines's condition is anything to joke about. And she certainly cannot explain the baby's conception on a felt board like you suggested. Very funny Catherine Grace.

   Listen to me, this is serious, and I don't think you really understand that, not being here and all. I mean things have settled down a bit. Parents have quit showing up at the school every day waiting in line to talk to the principal. And most of the kids have come back to her Sunday-school class.

   But Daddy is acting very strange, and Miss Raines has been coming by the house almost every day to talk to him. She told me the other night that she's sorry to keep bothering us but that she finds the company of her preacher particularly comforting right now at this very trying time. Trying. Not joyful. Trying.

And Daddy tends to her like she was having his baby. Catherine Grace, don't you get it? Miss Raines _is_ having Daddy's baby! I am absolutely certain of it!!! That's why nobody's ever met Donald Semple. There is no Donald Semple. There is only our Daddy.

Please come home. I need you.

Love,
Martha Ann

December 15, 1975

Catherine Grace,

I don't sound a thing like Mrs. Huckstep! And I can't believe you would even say that. You're not here, remember, and you have no idea what it's like to watch Daddy and Miss Raines together. It's not some crazy, made-up idea of mine. It's the truth. But stick your big head in the sand for all I care.

You didn't say one word about coming home for Christmas. Maybe you think your needing to be here, at home, with your family, is another one of my crazy ideas!!!

Martha Ann

My daddy was not having anybody's baby. That idea was nothing more than the nonsensical jabbering of a bunch of overwrought, emotional women—including my very own sister! Daddy might still have feelings for Miss Raines, but he was not her baby's daddy. Lord, I only hoped Martha Ann was not spreading this crazy idea of hers around town any more than she already had. And I only hoped she remembered what happened when she told Ruthie Morgan that Gloria Jean had gone to some *specialist* in Dalton to have a *cyst* removed. The next thing you knew, Gloria Jean's *sister* was in Dalton tending to the *special* needs of some doctor.

Daddy loved Miss Raines, we all knew that, but apparently not enough to marry her and certainly not enough to have her baby. He would have done it the right way. He would have started with a ring, not a pacifier.

I told Miss Mabie and Flora all about Miss Raines. I told them how she used to love my daddy but now she was marrying a man named Donald. I told them how she'd gone and gotten herself pregnant before she got herself married. And I told them how my little sister was convinced there was no man named Donald and that she was having my daddy's baby instead.

Flora said that a true man of God would never give in to the desires of the flesh like that. Miss Mabie told Flora to open her eyes, that a true man of God was no different than any other man when it came to satisfying his most basic need.

Miss Mabie said that when she lived in New York City, she knew a Broadway director who had donated his sexual time and energy to three women, leaving them each with a baby to raise. As far as she was concerned, anything was possible when it came to men and their paternal output. I was pretty certain she was talking about sex, but I'd never heard it put quite like that. But that director was not my daddy. Flora just shook her head and kept saying, "Lord have mercy. Say it ain't so. Lord have mercy."

And now, given the very delicate nature of Miss Raines's condition, Martha Ann was never going to forgive me for not coming home for Christmas. Just like Thanksgiving, Mr. Wallis did remember telling me that I could have an extra day during the Christmas holiday since my family didn't live here in town. And just like Thanksgiving, he said that I was welcome to take it. But he also told me that he and all of the other managers and manager trainees would be back in the store first thing on the twenty-sixth, and he would prefer that I wait till the first of the year.

Although Mr. Wallis never talked about his personal life, I was more certain than ever that he had never had a wife or children. All he ever said was that his family was right here at Davison's. Seemed kind of like a funny place to call home.

But one thing was for darn certain: My sister was not going to understand anything other than my being home in Ringgold, Georgia, on Christmas morning. But I couldn't afford to be anywhere but here in Atlanta, especially considering the fact that I was the only soon-to-be manager trainee at Davison's who didn't wear a coat and tie. Mr. Wallis told me just the other day that pending a positive performance evaluation, I would be officially approved for the management-trainee program. He said it was about time there was a manager at Davison's wearing high heels.

I was on my way. I just felt it in my bones. I felt it in my heart. I really believed that my being here, working at Davison's, living with Miss Mabie—it was all part of a greater plan. I just wished my family understood that.

When I was little, I never thought God was listening to me. I never thought He got it, how badly I wanted this. Turns out, the Lord was listening all along, and when the Lord is showing you the door, Daddy always said you better walk through it.

Next Christmas, things would be different.

December 23, 1975

Dear Catherine Grace,

I never thought your dream would mean giving up your family. Hope you have a Merry Christmas with Miss Mabie and Flora.

Martha Ann

Telegram

DATE: JANUARY 3, 1976
RECIPIENT: CATHERINE GRACE CLINE
            C/O MISS MYRTIE MABIE
SENDER: MARTHA ANN CLINE

DADDY DIED. COME HOME.

SF-1301 (R5-69)

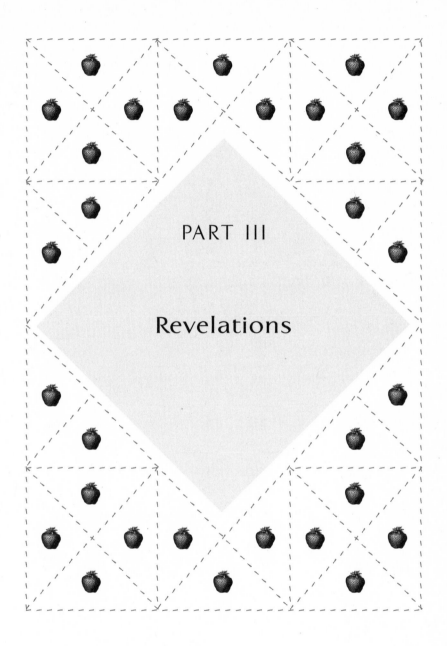

PART III

Revelations

CHAPTER EIGHT

Leaving the Promised Land with
a Blue Vinyl Suitcase

Flora handed me the telegram. She didn't know what it said, but I guess she figured it had to be bad if somebody had taken the time to send a message by Western Union. Thank God she was standing there beside me because I fell right into her strong, black arms.

The next thing I remember is hearing her deep, gentle voice telling me to let the sadness pour out of my body. "Oh Lord, child, just let it out. Just let it out," she kept chanting, all the time holding me tight, pressing my head against her bosom.

My daddy was dead, and unlike a six-year-old girl, I knew what dead meant. I knew I was never again going to hear his voice calling me to the breakfast table or call out the high-school football scores. I was never going to see his body sway behind the pulpit or his strong hands tenderly handle the vines of a young tomato plant. He was gone, and he had left this world just as suddenly as my mama, not even bothering to tell me good-bye. Nestled in Flora's arms, I felt terribly alone. I cried and cried right there on the living room floor until my entire body began to ache, and then I cried some more.

Miss Mabie sat in a chair, wringing her hands. She looked awkward amid all the crying and left Flora to comfort and soothe my trembling body. I held my head up long enough to tell Miss Mabie that I needed to go to Ringgold as soon as I could. Martha Ann needed me, I said, and I needed Martha Ann. I needed to be in my own house, crying into my own pillow. I needed Gloria Jean. And I needed my daddy. "Miss Mabie," I softly pleaded, "if you or Flora could just get me to the Greyhound station, I sure would appreciate it." I needed to go home.

But instead I found myself sitting on my bed in Miss Mabie's house, staring out the picture window while Flora scurried about the room packing all my belongings into my set of blue vinyl suitcases, the ones, I told her, that my daddy had given me for my sixteenth birthday.

Miss Mabie said she and Flora both were going to personally deliver me to Ringgold. She said I was in a fragile state and shouldn't be traveling on my own. Then she told Flora that when she finished packing my bags to come and find her, that she was going down to the kitchen to make some sandwiches for the trip, and she wanted Flora to give her a hand. She said we needed to get on the road just as soon as we could. She didn't want Flora driving after dark.

Flora kept moving about my room, stopping only to mumble a short *yes ma'am* to let Miss Mabie know she would meet her in the kitchen as soon as the packing was done. I just kept staring at the magnolia tree. It had always looked so grand and magnificent, but today it was mocking me, reminding me that I was the one who had up and left my daddy's nest. I closed my eyes and saw my daddy sitting in his worn, brown reclining chair, holding his Bible, begging the Lord to bring his baby girl home. Now I was on my way.

Flora zipped my suitcases closed, and then she sat down on the bed next to me, taking my hands into hers. "Miss Catherine Grace, I'm gonna go downstairs and git you somethin' to eat. I've never known Miss Mabie to make much of anythin' in the kitchen 'cept maybe pour herself a glass of milk, and she don't even do that without makin' a mess. But you gonna need to eat. You gotta keep up your strength," Flora said, squeezing my hands to let me know she understood what it took to bury someone you love.

"Miss Catherine Grace," she said, as she raised her body off the bed, "you know this ain't your fault. It was jus' your daddy's time. God got himself a reason. We jus' gots to accept it, baby."

Flora sounded so certain that for a moment I wanted to believe her. But I knew she was wrong. God didn't do this.

Not this. He took my mama, I was sure of that, but He didn't take my daddy. I had done that all by myself, without any help from above. I hurt my daddy's heart so badly, it just stopped beating.

Miss Mabie wrapped three tuna fish sandwiches in wax paper and put them in a brown paper bag along with some apples and oatmeal cookies and three Coca-Colas, more than enough food for the three of us considering we were only going a couple of hours up the road. After Miss Mabie walked out to the garage, I saw Flora unwrap each one of the sandwiches, checking to make sure they were good enough to eat. She added some lettuce and a dash of salt and then rewrapped the sandwiches and packed them away in the brown paper bag.

Flora took me by the arm and led me out to Miss Mabie's black sedan, opening the rear door and guiding me into the backseat. She lifted my suitcases into the trunk, thinking I might want to stretch out and shut my eyes for a bit. Then she slammed the door closed and slid behind the steering wheel. Miss Mabie sat in the front next to Flora. I could barely see Miss Mabie's white head bobbing above the seat, but I could hear her raspy, old voice telling me to lean on the Lord. But all I could do was lean my head on the car window and stare at the bare, dead-looking trees blur one into the next as we sped along the highway.

In the reflection of the glass, I could see Martha Ann, sitting at the kitchen table, all alone, waiting for me to come home. She had been waiting a long time. She said the pot roast was getting cold. I told her I was on my way. But she said it was too late.

Then I heard Miss Mabie calling my name, telling me to open my eyes. I had fallen into a dream, and I wanted her to hush so I could drift back to my place at the table. Daddy would be there, waiting for me.

"Catherine Grace, child, Catherine Grace," Miss Mabie said, her voice determined and insistent, bringing me back to the sadness I had managed to escape for a while. "Sweetie, we are almost to Ringgold, and Flora needs some directions to your house."

I raised my head above the seat and peered out the windshield. The sky was spitting just a few drops of rain, but Flora switched on the windshield wipers anyway, causing them to screech as they moved back and forth across the glass. The rain was making her skittish, and Miss Mabie had to keep telling Flora that she needed to calm down and open her eyes before we ran off the road. I told Flora to turn right and left and then left again. Still feeling fairly foggy brained, I wasn't sure if I was sending her in the right direction or not. But when I looked up, there was my house, my white, wooden house with the big front porch. It looked brokenhearted, too.

Cars were parked in the driveway and up and down both sides of the gravel road. Apparently everyone in Ringgold was either inside my house or standing on the porch. As the preacher's daughter, I had been around death enough to know that they had come as much to express their sympathies as they had to support one another during their time of great loss.

"Lord child," said Flora, "your daddy musta been a great man, a true servant of the Lord, jus' look at all these people who comin' to pay their respects."

But I wanted them to go away, just like when Mama died.

Brother Fulmer, dressed in his usual denim overalls and white cotton shirt, was leaning against the house, not saying a word to the people gathered around him. He was dabbing his eyes with a handkerchief when he heard Flora pull into the driveway. He raised his head and stared at Miss Mabie's black sedan. I'm sure he was wondering who these two, strange women were, one black and one white, and why they had come to Reverend Cline's house.

"Flora," Miss Mabie said, "you grab Catherine's bags and help her into the house. I'm going to walk on ahead and introduce ourselves."

Carrying all three suitcases in her hands, Flora did as she was told. She led the way to my own front door, the crowd parting in front of her as if she were navigating the Red Sea. Out of the corner of my eye, I could see their sad, curious stares.

Flora set the bags down on the porch and stepped aside. I stood frozen in the open doorway, not sure whether to take the next step or sink to my knees. From out of the confusion swelling inside my house, Gloria Jean rushed toward me and snatched me up in her arms.

"Oh baby, I am so sorry," she said. "I am so, so sorry."

With the sound of her voice, the pain started pouring out of my body again. "I did this," I sobbed, confessing my sin. "I left him. He didn't want me to go. My leaving, it, it was too much for him. I killed him, Gloria Jean. I broke his heart."

But Gloria Jean told me to hush.

"Stop that right now, Catherine Grace. I don't want to hear that kind of talk out of your mouth again. This had nothing to do with you. Blame the Lord if you want, He's the one who decides who's coming and going, but you had nothing to do with it," she said in a firm, unwavering tone, pushing me back from her chest so she could look me directly in the eyes.

"You understand me," she added, more as a command than a question. I wanted to believe her, but forgiveness wasn't as simple a thing as the Bible or Gloria Jean would have you believe.

Then she walked me into the house, holding my body next to hers. Ida Belle and Roberta Huckstep were passing plates of ham biscuits. Mrs. Huckstep nodded as I passed, for once uncertain of what to say. Ida Belle gave me a hug and a hot ham biscuit neatly wrapped in a paper napkin. She said I needed to keep up my strength. I figured she'd already been talking to Flora.

Gloria Jean kept moving me through the room, not letting anyone pull me into a conversation. But suddenly I felt somebody tugging at my hand. It was Lolly. She hugged me tight around the neck and said she was sorry about my daddy. She said her own mama cried when she heard about Reverend Cline dying so sudden and all. Lolly said there was so much she wanted to tell me, and she hoped we'd get a chance to talk while I was in town. I told her I was glad she was here. When I was in Atlanta, I honestly hadn't thought of Lolly much since I'd gone to the Varsity with Babs. I guess I was too busy thinking about myself, but now, looking at her face, I wanted to drag her into my bedroom and tell her everything that was racing through my head—everything about Daddy, Miss Raines, Martha Ann, Mr. Wallis—just everything.

Miss Raines was sitting on a chair in the far corner of the room. Her long, blond hair was pulled back tight in a pony-tail, and her beautiful blue eyes looked red and swollen. She was alone, weeping gently into a worn-out Kleenex she held up to her face. Until now, I had forgotten about my Sunday-school teacher and her delicate condition. Martha Ann was wrong about her and Daddy. She must have been spending too much time listening to Emma Sue and her grandmama's web of lies and gossip. Daddy was a true man of God, just like Flora said. He loved Miss Raines. I knew that. And I also knew he would have never taken a woman into his bed without a wedding ring on her finger. But I couldn't think about that right now.

Gloria Jean led me to Martha Ann's bedroom and opened the door. The light was low, but I could see my little sister, lying on the bed with a pillow over her head.

"She hasn't come out of here since this morning. Maybe you can get her to talk. At least get her to take that pillow off her head before she suffocates."

I stepped quietly into her room, not sure if she was sleeping or just hiding in her own body.

"Martha Ann, it's me . . . Catherine Grace," I said gently as I moved closer to the bed. She sighed, letting me know she wasn't asleep. "I'm sorry. I'm sorry I wasn't here with you." But Martha Ann remained motionless, refusing to acknowledge my presence.

"Martha Ann," I said again, this time sitting down on the bed next to her, stroking her head just like I did when she was little and had a hard time calming down at night. "I know you can hear me, whether you want to or not, so I'm just going to keep talking," I said, pausing for a minute while I tried to straighten out my thoughts. "I never meant to hurt you or Daddy. I just wanted something of my own and I guess I thought that . . .

"Well, I guess I figured, way down deep, Daddy understood. I mean when he gave me the luggage, I always thought it was his way of . . . Oh God, I don't know. But I do know that I wouldn't have left if I thought for one minute I could have done something, anything to keep Daddy from dying."

I knew my thoughts were pained and twisted, but I couldn't help believing that I was at least partly to blame for me and my sister being left alone, without a mama or a daddy. If she never spoke to me again, I would accept that as part of some deserved punishment I must endure for the rest of my life. But then she moved. Martha Ann moved her right foot just a tiny little bit, but it was enough to let me know she was willing to talk. I lifted the pillow off her face and saw the tears running down her cheeks. I started crying too, and without saying another word, we held on to each other, painfully aware that we were all alone in Ringgold, Georgia.

I woke up the next morning in Martha Ann's bed and found my house feeling more like its old self. Everyone had left, except for Gloria Jean, Miss Mabie, and Flora. Gloria Jean had convinced them to stay a few days, and Flora was already at the stove cooking bacon and scrambling a dozen eggs. And Miss Mabie and Gloria Jean were sitting around the breakfast table chatting like old friends.

"Well, honey," Gloria Jean said as soon as she saw me walk through the kitchen door, "you are looking much better this morning. I was pretty worried about you and your sister last night. Sit down." She motioned for me to take a seat next to her.

"Your dear Miss Mabie and I have been getting to know one another. Turns out, she and I come from the same part of Alabama, right outside Birmingham. We figure there's a good chance we may be kinfolk. Heck, we figure there's a good chance we even loved some of the same kinfolk, the Birmingham Hixson boys," she said with a laugh, nodding at Miss Mabie as though they had a closely guarded secret. "How do you like that!"

I couldn't help but laugh a little, too. It felt good. I took my seat at the table between Miss Mabie and Gloria Jean, and all of the sudden I started thinking about what color nail polish Gloria Jean would find appropriate for a funeral, probably some deep, dark shade of red, like Ruby River Night. And then I felt guilty, wondering why I was thinking about something as silly as nail polish the day after my daddy died.

Flora put a plate in front of me and told me to eat up. "I know," I told her. "I'm going to need my strength." But I had to wonder how much strength it was going to take to bury my daddy. I doubted there was enough bacon and biscuits to give me what I needed.

Gloria Jean said that the funeral home director down in Dalton suggested that both the service and the reception afterward be held at the church since Daddy was sure to draw a big crowd. The fellowship hall could hold at least five hundred. Since there wasn't a funeral parlor in Ringgold, visitations should probably be held at the house, where the family would be most comfortable. Besides, Gloria Jean and Brother Fulmer were afraid that the drive back and forth to Dalton might be hard on the Euzelians. "And Lord knows those blue-haired women will want to keep a prayer vigil going for the next few days."

Then Gloria Jean turned to me and asked what day I wanted to have the service. She said we couldn't wait too long, but anytime before the end of the week would probably be fine.

"And, sweetie, you need to be thinking about who you'd like to give your daddy's eulogy. I'm sure Brother Fulmer or Brother Blankenship would be honored to do it or, if you'd prefer, we could get that preacher over in LaFayette that your daddy liked so much, if you'd rather have a certified man of God overseeing everything."

Whatever, I thought to myself, but nothing came out of my mouth.

"I'm going to head down to Dalton later this morning and pick out a casket. Now, you don't need to go with me, unless you just want to," Gloria Jean continued.

All these decisions needed to be made, I understood that, but I kept thinking I shouldn't be the one to make them—in my house, I felt like such a little girl. "No, I think I'll stay here with Martha Ann. Just be sure it's real pretty, something simple but pretty," I said. Daddy never put on fancy airs when he was alive, and he certainly wouldn't want to in his grave.

But before leaving, Gloria Jean said she and Flora were going to walk down to the church. Ida Belle had called an hour ago and said that the florist had already delivered more than fifty arrangements, just this morning, and that before long no one was going to be able to find her among all the gladiolas and red carnations. Gloria Jean said she actually heard for the very first time a tinge of panic in Ida Belle's voice, and Flora thought she might be able to help.

Gloria Jean hadn't stepped foot inside Cedar Grove Baptist Church for years, not since Mama died, and now she was on her way to help make sure things looked pretty for my daddy's funeral. I never really knew what had kept her from going to church, but whatever it was, I guess daddy's dying left her feeling a bit more forgiving.

Anyway, Gloria Jean thought I might like to go with her and spend a few quiet moments in the church before everyone in town started coming to pay their respects. Miss Mabie said she'd stay at the house in case Martha Ann woke up. She promised she'd call as soon as Martha Ann got out of bed.

"Flora," she called as we were walking out the door, "don't stay down at that church too long 'cause we got to get this house in order 'fore the mourners start showing up in droves."

Flora just waved her hand like she was hearing what she already knew. She insisted on driving Miss Mabie's sedan the half mile or so down to Cedar Grove. I told her we could walk, that's what we always did. But she said it was too cold for her to do that what with the arthritis in her knees acting up. Daddy drove the Oldsmobile to church only when it was thundering and lightning. He said walking with the Lord helped prepare him for the morning. It felt wrong to be driving.

Climbing out of the backseat of Miss Mabie's sedan, I thought I saw Daddy standing on the top step, holding his arms open wide, waiting to welcome me home. I gasped, and looked again, but he was gone. "Come back, Daddy, please come back," I cried to myself where nobody could hear. Three generations of Cline men had welcomed the faithful and prayed for the lost right there on those steps. Now the steps were bare, and I wondered who was going to shepherd Ringgold's orphaned flock.

I mounted the stairs with Flora standing steady behind me, and then I slowly walked down the red-carpeted aisle toward the cedar pulpit that my great-granddaddy had made with his own two hands. I savored every step, thinking of all the times Daddy had pounded his fist on top of that pulpit, drawing my attention back to the sermon. I wondered if he knew all the times that Martha Ann and I were playing tic-tac-toe while he was working up a sweat trying to save another soul. I wondered if now that he was in heaven he knew about all the little secrets his girls held tightly on the back pew.

Flora found Ida Belle in the kitchen, already boiling water for the deviled eggs she planned on making later that afternoon. Ida Belle never liked people in her kitchen offering to help. "The helping hand strikes again," she'd say, shooing some well-intentioned old lady out of her way. But Ida Belle didn't seem the least bit bothered by Flora's presence. In fact, she seemed to appreciate another woman who knew her way around a kitchen as well as Flora did, even if her hands were dark brown.

Gloria Jean and I made ourselves comfortable on the soft, plush rug in Daddy's office. She said she couldn't remember when she had gotten down on the floor for any man, but I told her it just didn't feel right to sit anyplace else. Brother Fulmer said Daddy died working at his desk, preparing Sunday's sermon. Daddy always said the good Lord would take him in his boots, so to speak, and apparently He honored his word. Now all I knew was that his chair seemed like some piece of holy ground, and I didn't feel worthy enough to touch it.

We read some of Daddy's old sermons and flipped through the pages of his Bible, looking for favorite verses he had marked with a pencil. Just touching the pages I knew my daddy had touched a thousand times felt comforting, almost like we were reaching out to each other. I told Gloria Jean I thought we should read from Galatians and Second Timothy. We both agreed that the choir had to sing "The Old Rugged Cross" and "Just As I Am." And that was all I knew to do.

Gloria Jean wondered if Brother Fulmer should deliver the eulogy, since he was so devoted to my daddy. But all I could see was Brother Fulmer standing on the front porch, wiping tears from his eyes. "No," I said, "let's get the preacher from LaFayette. The church needs to grieve."

"I think your daddy would be very proud of you, Catherine Grace," Gloria Jean responded, as if I had said something thoughtful and wise. "Listen, hon, I'm going on. Now don't stay here too long. You need to go on home and get some rest. You hear me?"

"Don't worry, I will," I said automatically, already feeling anxious about leaving Martha Ann back at the house.

Gloria Jean got up off the floor, which took a little doing, and then hugged me good-bye and walked back into the sanctuary. The church doors blew shut behind her, rattling even the walls in Daddy's office. But in the quiet that followed, I lay down on the floor, and with Daddy's worn, tattered Bible placed across my chest, I stared out the window, wondering if Daddy was riding on one of those clouds floating by in the sky, wondering if he had found Mama. Closing my eyes, I started singing softly to myself.

> *Just as I am, Thou wilt receive.*
> *Wilt welcome, pardon, cleanse, relieve.*
> *Because Thy promise I believe,*
> *O Lamb of God, I come! I come! O Lamb of God, I come!*

I rocked myself back and forth and continued to sing, lulling my body into a comfortable place it hadn't known the last couple of days. Suddenly I felt someone watching over me, listening to me, and I wondered for a moment if maybe my daddy had come to check on his little Catherine Grace. Flora said that when you pass to the other side, sometimes you stop and spend a few days saying all your earthly good-byes before you go and take your place in heaven once and for all. I even felt a shiver run down my spine, a sure-enough sign, Flora said, that a spirit had come to pay a visit. My spine never did tingle after Mama died, although sometimes I pretended it did.

I figured this was as good a time as any to tell Daddy

how bad I felt about leaving town. I was truly, truly sorry I broke his heart. I just couldn't seem to help wanting something else. And though I hated to make him feel bad on his first full day as an angel, I desperately wanted to ask him about Miss Raines and why he kept his love for her a secret from Martha Ann and me. I mean, seeing her last night, with those teary eyes of hers, left me feeling certain that what she and Daddy had must have been a true, abiding love. But I still didn't believe that she was carrying his baby. Lord, what was Daddy planning to do, ship her down to Texas like they did the poor Hawkins' girl and just pretend that nothing ever happened? But when I opened my eyes, all I saw was a white puffy cloud hanging outside the window.

Flora and Gloria Jean said it was the Lord who called my daddy home. Now I knew it was not right to question the Lord's intentions, although, truth be told, questioning His master plan had become something of a habit of mine. And looking up at that cloud, I had to wonder if He had really thought this one through. There sure were a lot of mixed-up, hurt feelings down here, and I couldn't help but think that maybe my daddy's earthly departure had been prematurely miscalculated. Being nicknamed the Almighty would lead one to think that the Heavenly Father is incapable of such a scheduling error, but with so many lives to follow, I think a miscalculation is a reasonable conclusion. I mean, it sure would explain a lot of misfortunes in this world, like little babies dying of a high fever, or a daddy falling over at his desk, or a mama floating down a river.

The heavy, wooden door at the front of the church suddenly slammed shut again, bringing my attention back to the world around me. I expected to hear somebody walking down the aisle toward my daddy's office or back toward fellowship hall. But I never heard any footsteps. I didn't feel any shivers down my spine, either. No, it felt more like a real-live person was haunting me this time. I jumped up off the floor and was about to hightail it out of my daddy's office when I ran into a large, strong body.

"Good Lord, Ida Belle," I shrieked, "you practically scared the pee out of me."

"I'm sorry, darling. I was just getting a little worried about you. I heard the door, but when I didn't see nobody, I thought I better come check on you."

"You heard it, too?" I asked, sounding a little anxious.

"I heard the door, if that's what you mean. Lord, every time it slams shut it shakes the whole building from top to bottom."

"I know. But Gloria Jean shut the door behind her when she left. I heard it close."

"Oh, baby, I bet that florist sneaked in here with another arrangement and was too scared to show his face. He probably didn't get the door shut tight, and then a big old gust of wind come along and slammed it closed. That's all," she explained and then stared at me with a small, sweet smile on her face, checking to see if I had been calmed by her explanation. "Oh, baby, were you thinking that your—"

"No," I said before she could finish. I didn't want Gloria Jean or Ida Belle or anybody else believing I was seeing ghosts or even looking for them, for that matter, but I sure as heck didn't want to believe it was the florist, either.

"Your daddy will come along to you soon enough, maybe in your dreams tonight," she said, seeing the disappointment in my eyes. "The dearly departed always have a way of checking on us, especially when they have to leave so sudden like poor Brother Cline did. Sometimes we know it, and sometimes we don't. But I do know one thing for darn sure: Your daddy loved you very much, and he would not leave this world without making sure you was okay."

My eyes were filling with tears again. "Yeah, that's what Flora said."

"Well, you'd be wise to listen to Flora, 'cause I tell you any woman who can roll a biscuit as light and feathery as she can knows what she's talking about. That's right."

I desperately wanted to believe her, and standing there in that dirty white apron of hers, Ida Belle seemed almost official, like what she was saying had to be right. But I knew it didn't always happen that way. Mama never came to me. God knows I begged her to. But she just walked out of this world and never looked back, no good-byes, no nothing.

The clock on my daddy's desk told me that I had been lying on that floor for more than two hours. I imagined by now Flora was back home frying chicken and cooking a pot of green beans, and if I didn't get there soon, she'd have my sister sitting at that table and be feeding her like a little baby.

I hugged Ida Belle good-bye and realized that in all the years I had known this woman, we had never really talked about much more than Wednesday-night suppers. Dying has a funny way of making you see people, the living and the dead, a little differently. Maybe that's just part of the grieving, or maybe the dead stand there and open our eyes a bit wider. Either way, I left the church feeling like a young girl again, my daddy walking next to me, holding my hand, just like he used to do.

As I got closer to the house, I saw five or six cars parked in the driveway. People were already coming to pay their respects, again. I guess they figured that crowding into my house and making small talk and eating chocolate layer cake was going to make me and Martha Ann feel better. I'm sure Miss Mabie was enjoying hosting the party. After all, she was a professional socialite of sorts. But the thought of facing all those people was making my stomach ache.

I glanced over at Gloria Jean's house, hoping to see the LeSabre parked in the driveway. Nothing was there but a hungry, old squirrel tiptoeing over the gravel and nibbling on some scrap of food that somebody must have dropped from another ham platter intended as a gift to the grieving family. Well, the Lord certainly giveth and taketh away, I thought to myself while watching that squirrel guarding his newly found treasure. Then I wondered why such odd thoughts kept popping about in my head at a time like this, leaving me to feel like a big pot of corn kernels sitting on a red-hot stove.

Lord, surely Gloria Jean would be back from Dalton any minute now. I'd never picked out a casket myself, but I couldn't imagine it was a real time-consuming purchase. Suddenly I was feeling kind of desperate to see her.

As I turned back toward my house, I heard a creaking noise coming from Gloria Jean's porch. I knew that sound. I'd heard it a hundred times before, that worn-out metal glider of hers moving back and forth, desperately screaming out for a shot of WD-40. Thing is, there wasn't enough wind blowing to cause that rusty old thing to move on its own. And even though it wasn't night yet, the sun had already found a place to hide, making it hard for me to see anything other than that damned squirrel feasting on a dirty old piece of meat.

I looked a little closer and saw something in the gray darkness that had been looming over my head since the day daddy died. It looked like a woman, a skinny little thing at that. But when I looked again, she was gone. I'd been spooked enough for one day, that's for sure. And there probably wasn't a jackrabbit in this county that could have hightailed it to my house any faster than I did.

Gloria Jean was walking through the front door up

ahead of me, and I ran past all the men gathered on the porch, once again ignoring their attempts to tell me how much they had loved Brother Cline. And though I was certain Mrs. Huckstep would not approve of me running through a wake of any kind, homespun or not, I needed to tell Gloria Jean that she had company. I needed, truth be told, to be next to her.

"Hey there, hon," she said, pulling me into her arms and giving me a tight squeeze. "How ya doing?" she asked but never waited for an answer. "Lord child, you are going to be so pleased with your daddy's casket. It is downright beau-ti-ful. It's a shame we have to put something so good-looking six feet down in the ground where nothing but some old earth worms can admire it."

"Gloria Jean," I said with a slight, cautious smile, "only you would think of a casket as a fashion statement."

"Well, honey, you need to go out in style, that's for darn sure. I even picked one out for myself while I was there. Blue velvet interior. Thought it'd feel like home."

"Hey," I said, almost frantic to change the subject, "there's a woman on your front porch. She was sitting there real quiet just before you got home. Then she just up and disappeared."

Gloria Jean looked at me with that worried expression of motherly concern painted all over her face. "Honey, you feeling okay?" she asked, once again not waiting for an answer. "I talked to Ida Belle. She said you got a little spooked today down at the church. You know that's natu-ral, sweetie, what with the kind of sadness you're feeling right now. I shouldn't have ever left you there alone."

Gloria Jean lifted her arm and wrapped it around my shoulders again. She was right about one thing. She shouldn't have left me. I needed her. But I wasn't imagin-ing anything, either. I was right about that.

"This is different. I'm telling you the God's honest truth. There's a squirrel in your driveway and a woman on your porch!" My voice now sounded insistent and mad. She pushed me back a bit so she could look me straight in the eyes.

"Okay, okay, I believe you," she said, sounding honest and concerned. "I guess I better go check on my two guests then before they rob me blind, stealing all my nuts and fancy jewelry." She laughed softly at herself and then hugged me once more before heading back out the door. "Now don't run off. Wait for me right here."

I followed Gloria Jean toward the door and I would have run after her but I got caught in a small band of Euzelians who were starting to swarm in my living room again. Thankfully Mrs. Blankenship emerged from the middle of the hive and took my hands in hers and led me safely into the kitchen. I couldn't help but notice how soft and comforting her touch felt. She told me she was here for me, day or night, and to let her know if there was anything she could do to help in this trying time. She still looked so perfect with her blond hair rolled into its usual braided twist on the back of her head. I had always loved looking at Mrs. Blankenship. She said Hank would be stopping by later, and then she went to pour me a glass of iced tea.

Mr. and Mrs. Tucker were standing side by side just inside the kitchen door. He was holding his arm around her waist, or as much of it as he could. They actually looked like they belonged together even though she was at least twice his size. He offered to personally deliver anything from the store that we might need. All I had to do was call. Mrs. Tucker asked if I had tried her hash potato casserole. I'd be sure to, I told her.

Uncertain of where to be, I found myself wandering back into the living room. Martha Ann was sitting on the sofa talking to, of all people, Emma Sue Huckstep, who, I noticed, was still preening on her doughnut-shaped pillow. "Hey there, Emma Sue," I said, trying to hide the smile that I knew was growing on my face as I watched the little princess position herself more comfortably on her specially ordered throne. "Gee, I heard about your cheerleading accident, Emma Sue. Boy, I bet that hurt."

"Well, it did, to tell you the truth, but Doctor Bowden said I'll be back to cheering in a couple more weeks, in time for the basketball play-offs."

"Yeah, I'm sure the team misses that winning spirit of yours. And, hey, be sure and tell Walter to hang on to you the next time." And with that said, I realized I had nothing more to say to Emma Sue. I turned to Martha Ann to see if I could get a sense of how she was feeling. She actually looked as though she was enjoying her conversation, that in some way it was making this day a bit more normal for her.

"I'm sure you two have a lot to talk about. Don't let me get in the way," I said, unable to refrain from adding just a tinge of sarcasm to my voice, which Martha Ann clearly did not appreciate.

I was headed toward the kitchen when Gloria Jean came scurrying back through the front door, her face looking like she had seen a ghost of her own. And before I could ask what was wrong, she told me to come with her. I did as I was told, but on the way to her house, Gloria Jean suddenly turned and stared right at me. She looked so serious and somehow I knew that look was all about me.

"Honey, sometimes people do things that they wish they hadn't. And sometimes people do things that they wish they hadn't but the thing is so big they just don't know how to make it right. You know what I mean?"

No, I didn't, but I nodded like I did. For once, Gloria Jean really didn't seem to be making any sense at all, and that made me more uncomfortable than anything she was saying, or trying to say.

"Look, I know you've had a whole lot to deal with the last couple of days, more than any girl your age should have to face. But I've got some news for you that is either going to knock you flat down or is going to bring you some comfort, but only you are going to be able to decide that."

"Something bad has happened, Gloria Jean, I know it. It's that friend of yours, what's she done to you?"

Gloria Jean held my shoulders in her hands. "Sweetie, she didn't hurt me, or at least she didn't mean to. Now you have to be strong," and she paused for a moment to see if her words were making any difference, "for Martha Ann and for your daddy. Promise me?"

"Shit, Gloria Jean, you're scaring me. And I've had enough of that today."

Gloria Jean grabbed my hand, squeezing it with her fingers till it almost hurt. She dragged me into the living room and in front of a woman who promptly jumped up from the blue velvet sofa. The stranger stood real still, almost seeming afraid to move any closer, like a lizard under a cat's watchful eye.

"Catherine Grace, my friend here came to town when she heard the news about your daddy."

"Oh, you knew my daddy?" I asked the woman. She nodded. "Are you here for the funeral?"

But again, the woman only nodded. Finally, Gloria Jean answered for her. "Yes, yes, she did know your daddy, many, many years ago. But, honey, it's actually you she's come to see."

I stared at the woman and speculated about the right thing to say to a stranger who seems to know more about you than you'd care for her to know.

"I'm very sorry, Catherine Grace, about your daddy,

I mean," she stammered breathlessly. "I know this must be a hard time for you. It's just that, well, I've waited," and she stopped, as if searching for the right words was exhausting her.

"Hey, I don't mean to sound rude or nothing, but I'm feeling kind of funny here. I mean you knowing my name and all, and I don't know anything about you, not even what to call you. Gloria Jean?" I was looking for help, and yet Gloria Jean could only look at the woman as if asking for permission to make an introduction. She seemed so pale and sickly that I wondered if she was going to faint right in front of me.

"Gloria Jean, your friend don't look so well," I whispered to her. "And this is really creeping me out. I want to go home."

"Catherine Grace," Gloria Jean said, waiting no longer for a cue, "this is—" And then the woman interrupted her.

"No, Gloria Jean, let me do this," she said with some unexpected strength. Then she steadied herself by holding on to the arm of the sofa, took a deep breath, and finally said what she'd come to say.

"Catherine Grace, I'm your mother. I'm Lena Mae." She lowered her head, afraid to look me in the eyes.

I heard what this woman said. I mean, I heard the words, but I couldn't understand what was coming out of her mouth. "Lady, you are out of your mind, or incredibly mean, or both. I don't know who the hell you are or what kind of sick joke you're pulling. Damn it, Gloria Jean! Why did you let this nutcase in your house?" I found myself shouting, my own voice echoing in my ears.

"Catherine Grace, I know this must be a terrible shock," Gloria Jean said, "but listen to me. You've waited years to see your mama, and here she is. I know the timing might be bad but Lena Mae thought now she might have a chance to see you, to explain, maybe even to help."

"What? Help?" I still couldn't make sense of what anybody was saying to me. I just heard words, words, more words but nothing was meaning anything. I tried to run out the door, but Gloria Jean stepped in my way and held me in her arms.

"Your daddy," the woman started talking again, "your daddy said that if I left town, I couldn't come back. He wouldn't have it. I didn't want to leave you like that. You have to believe me," she said, talking real fast now, like a little girl who has waited too long to tell the truth. "I just couldn't stay, Catherine Grace. But then I couldn't come back. I didn't know—"

"You're a liar! An evil, wretched, devil liar! My daddy would never keep me from my mama," I screamed so loudly even the crowd next door surely heard me.

"I know. You're right. I'm sorry. All I meant was that he had a hard time letting go. . . . I mean, when Martha Ann came along . . . I just . . . I just didn't know what else to do." She stumbled, and it looked like talking and standing might yet prove too much for her frail body.

"What have you done to Martha Ann?" I screamed, tears streaming down my face.

"Nothing. I haven't seen Martha Ann. I promise. I came to the church earlier thinking I might be able to see you girls, but I got scared and left. I haven't seen her. I promise. I know this is hard. I do. But the minute I heard that Marshall had passed, I knew this was my chance to finally see you. I have missed you girls so much. I guess I should have given you more time," she said.

"Time! More time! What about the last twelve years of my life?" I sobbed, somehow knowing and yet refusing to believe that this woman was my mama. "My mama drowned when I was six. My mama loved me."

"I still love you, Catherine. I have never stopped loving you."

"No! No, no! My mama wouldn't have run away from home like some stupid little kid."

"Dear God, I'm so sorry," the woman said, her voice shaking and full of tears. "I was a *stupid* kid, Catherine Grace. I was so young, and I just figured you girls would forget about me after a while. Marshall said you would."

"Forget? You are out of your mind!" Everything she said was terrifying me. I had memorized every detail of my mama's beautiful face, her brown eyes, her delicate nose, her kind smile. The woman in the photograph sitting on my dresser would never believe that her babies could simply forget that they're the only ones who didn't have a mama to bake them a birthday cake, or make them clothes for their Barbie dolls, or iron their Sunday dresses.

"I am so sorry," the woman repeated, like this time it might have some meaning. She just kept babbling about being so young, too young to be a good mother and having dreams and I don't know what all. All I knew was that there was nothing she could say that was going to make me accept that she was my mother.

"Get out! Just get out! " I shouted, starting to feel light-headed.

"I'm sorry. I'm very sorry," the woman whispered as much to herself as to me. And without even the courage to look me in the eyes, she made one last declaration. "I have loved you every day of your life. You need to know that."

I turned to Gloria Jean and begged her to make this woman leave.

But Gloria Jean just stood there, motionless.

"Gloria Jean," I pleaded, "please."

"I can't, honey."

"Why not?" I asked, feeling the room spinning around me.

"Because she is your mother."

CHAPTER NINE

Standing at the Pearly Gates
Begging for Forgiveness

Martha Ann was pressing a cold washcloth on my forehead. A drop of water trickled down the side of my face and settled in my ear. Gloria Jean was gently slapping my hand. "Catherine Grace, wake up, honey. You need to open your eyes."

I found myself lying in my own bed, hoping for that first innocent moment of wakefulness that the woman claiming to be my mother had been nothing but a bad dream.

"Gloria Jean," I asked, "that woman, who came to see you, she's gone, right?"

But Gloria Jean took a deep breath, her body's way of telling me that she wasn't particularly comfortable with what she had to say. So I closed my eyes again, longing to drift back into that world of never-ending darkness. Lena Mae, she said, was still in Ringgold. Apparently, after Dr. Bowden gave me some pills to make me sleep, she decided to stay the night and was now sitting at the kitchen table drinking a cup of coffee, talking to Miss Mabie. She was real worried about me.

"When you fainted, you need to know that it was your mama who helped me get you into your bed, well, your mama and Flora. She just wants to make sure you're okay before she leaves town. She knows you're not ready for anything more right now."

I looked at Gloria Jean and couldn't help but laugh out loud. The woman who left me crying myself to sleep when I was six years old was suddenly worried about me.

Propping myself up on my elbows, and speaking slowly and deliberately so no one would misunderstand what I was saying, I told Gloria Jean to get the woman with the long brown hair, sitting at the kitchen table drinking coffee, worrying about the little girl she abandoned, out of my house.

Martha Ann took the cloth off my forehead and knelt down beside me so we were staring at each other eye to eye. She hadn't said much since I had come home, but now her face was full of words.

"Catherine Grace, Mama coming here is a gift from God, and she is not leaving," Martha Ann announced in an abrupt, firm tone. "Yesterday, we were not much better off than two little orphans, and today we've got a mama.

Maybe I should be mad. Maybe I will be mad. But right now, today, I am so happy to have a mother, even one that's left and come back."

And then, putting her hand over mine, Martha Ann spoke in a softer voice, "You need to hear her out, Catherine Grace, and then if you want to be mad at somebody, fine, but maybe you need to consider being mad at Daddy, too."

"Daddy didn't leave us!"

"No, but maybe he didn't give Mama much of a choice. You need to talk to her."

I just stared at my little sister. I couldn't make sense of anything anybody was saying anymore, but somehow I knew I was going to have to come face-to-face with the woman sitting at the kitchen table. But be mad at Daddy? No. I just couldn't believe that my own daddy had known all these years that Mama was alive. What kind of daddy, what kind of man of God, would let his babies suffer like that? My head was spinning. I kept closing my eyes, hoping it would make the confusion go away. But it didn't help.

"Listen, honey," Gloria Jean repeated, "your mama loves you, and she has had to live with what she has done every single day since she left you girls. Your daddy was a good man, nobody's denying that, but he had a hard time accepting that somebody could love him and still want something more. I'm just not sure she really thought she had much of a choice. She just didn't have the courage that you do."

"What kind of monster do you think Daddy was?" I yelled, surprising myself.

"He wasn't a monster, honey. He was human. And I just think you need to understand this about your daddy. He could see marriage working only one way. I'm not sure he could admit to himself, let alone to anybody else in this town, that his young, beautiful wife was dreaming of something even bigger than the great Reverend Cline. She had a gift, Catherine, you know that. But you know all this already. You know what it means to love somebody but still want something more. And you know your daddy."

"You knew," I said, again surprising myself with the sharp tone of my voice. "You knew all these years that my mama was alive but didn't say anything. What? You just thought you'd keep this little secret to yourself? Is that it? You couldn't have any children of your own, Gloria Jean, so you kept your mouth shut so you could step right in and be our mama," I shouted, attacking the one woman who had never abandoned me.

Before I could even look for the hurt in her eyes, I started begging for forgiveness. "I'm sorry, Gloria Jean. I am so sorry. I didn't mean it." I didn't mean it, but I desperately wanted somebody to hurt as much as I did.

Gloria Jean took me into her arms like she had done so many times before. "Baby, I didn't know she was alive. I had always thought something wasn't right. I had hoped. But I didn't know, and I certainly couldn't say anything to you without knowing for sure," she said, patting my back in a familiar rhythm. "And you're not the only one who's feeling hurt right now. She was my best friend. Oh hell, honey, she was nothing more than a child, a child with little babies of her own."

I sat in my bed with my eyes wide open and wondered what this woman sitting at the kitchen table could say to me that would undo all the damage that had been done. I could already smell the bacon frying on the stove, and I knew that before long Flora was going to start chirping her morning trill about me keeping up my strength. But I wasn't stepping foot in that kitchen until I made sure my daddy was dead.

I jumped out of bed and started searching for my brown penny loafers.

"Honey, where are you going?" Gloria Jean asked.

"To church," I said.

"Now?"

"Yes, now. I have to see my daddy. I have to make sure that my daddy is lying in that casket. I have to make sure he's dead, dead, dead and that nobody is playing another cruel joke on me." I had to make sure he hadn't decided to go and make a better life for himself in Little Rock or Knoxville. Maybe he was already there waiting for Miss Raines to join him. Nope, I wasn't taking any chances, not this time.

Gloria Jean and Martha Ann both stood by my bedroom door, unable to think of the words to stop me. Maybe, Gloria Jean suggested, it would be better if I waited until she was certain that the funeral home had delivered Daddy, and she had a chance to make sure he was properly situated and all.

I told her I didn't care if he was situated or not. I would sit on the steps of that church and wait for him if I had to. I never saw my mama's face after she died, and I wasn't going to make that mistake again.

After grabbing my coat from the hall closet, I stopped at the kitchen door just long enough to catch a glimpse of Lena Mae Cline. She looked up at me as I hesitated in the hallway. She had so much hope in her eyes—hope that I'd say something, anything. But I turned away, making it clear I wasn't ready to listen to her sad story.

I pushed the storm door open and let it slam behind me. I jumped off the porch and headed for Cedar Grove. But before I got there, I could hear the sound of cars in the distance churning up the gravel on the road. I looked up to see a black car pull into the church parking lot with a black hearse following close behind. Hidden within the cloud of dust that was hovering above the road, I could see a group of men, all dressed in dark suits and dark overcoats, step out of the car and move toward the back of the hearse.

One man, wearing a black hat, opened the back door and then directed the others to stand in two lines facing each other. They all bowed their heads, as if they were saying a prayer, and then the man in the hat directed the others to pull the brown, wooden casket out of the hearse. Running toward the church, I began yelling at the men in the dark suits.

"Hey, stop right there," I cried. "Stop! Stop right there!"

All seven of them looked up at once, shocked, scanning the parking lot for the person they could only hear. The man with the hat yelled back, telling me that whoever I was, I needed to leave, that this was a solemn moment.

"Don't tell me what this is or isn't," I shouted back, now standing clearly in the parking lot next to the men holding my daddy's casket. "That is my daddy in there, and you're going to open that box right now and let me get a good look at his face," I continued with a harsh determination. The men looked shocked and confused. I could tell they were waiting for some concerned relative to appear and carry me away. But nobody came. Finally, the man in charge cleared his throat.

"Miss, we are real sorry for your loss," he said as the others stood silently, bearing the weight of the casket. "You are obviously upset, and I understand your wanting to see your daddy, but the parking lot is not the appropriate place for a viewing. You need to go on home like I said and come back later, with your mama."

I didn't have a mama, I told him, and at that very moment, I wasn't really concerned with what was or was not the proper etiquette of the dead. So I walked toward the men, and without waiting for an invitation, squeezed my body between them. And right then and there, in the parking lot of Cedar Grove Baptist Church, I lifted the lid of my daddy's casket.

Resting his head on a white satin pillow, my daddy was just lying there, quiet and peaceful, far away from all the trouble and sadness he left behind. He was so still. He didn't look like the man who used to carry me in his arms. There was makeup on his face, and it made him look like one of those mannequins in the men's department at Davison's. I touched his hand, but it was cold and hard. I yanked my hand away and tried to catch my breath. My daddy was dead, that's for sure, but I didn't have any tears to offer him. I wanted answers. I wanted an explanation, and Daddy wasn't speaking up.

"Everybody seems to think that you had something to do with Mama's leaving," I told him. "I missed her so much. Nobody knew that any better than you. And now I think I might be needing to hate you, but you've gone and up and died and I can't even do that. What kind of man runs away, Daddy? Huh? Tell me that."

"Miss," the man interrupted, "I'm not so sure you should be yelling at the dead out here in the parking lot. I understand you've got some things you need to say, but I'd feel better about it if we could at least get your daddy in the church safe and sound."

"Fine," I replied. "Take him on into the house of the Lord. He'll know what to do." I couldn't help but wonder if the minute he arrived at those Pearly Gates, he hadn't gotten down on his knees before Peter himself and started begging for forgiveness.

I closed the lid and politely told the strange men in the black suits that I appreciated their time, and then I started my walk back home. I'd barely gotten one foot in front of the other when I looked up and saw Miss Raines standing at the end of the driveway.

"Well, hello," I said abruptly, "I guess you heard all of that."

"Yes, Catherine Grace. But I didn't mean to," she said, casting those pretty eyes of hers to the side so she wouldn't have to look me in the face.

"So I hear you're expecting," I said, hardly waiting for her response.

"Yes. Yes, I am."

"How about that! What a wonderful surprise. You must be thrilled," I replied with a big, sarcastic smile stretching clean across my face. "Listen here, Miss Raines, nothing really is as it should be right now, and I don't have the patience or energy to beat around the bush. Is my daddy the daddy of your baby? Tell me. Yes or no?"

A long silence said what Miss Raines could not.

"Well, how about that! Apparently my daddy did whatever the hell he felt like doing, all in the name of the Lord."

"Catherine Grace, nobody needs to know."

"It's a little late for that, Miss Raines, or did you forget you are living in Ringgold, Georgia. I bet the entire Cedar

Grove congregation knew you were having that baby before you did."

"It doesn't really matter what they think, I guess. I'm leaving town just as soon as I can. Nobody is going to want me here reminding them that Reverend Cline has . . . has . . ." She couldn't bring herself to say it, has gone and knocked up the Sunday-school teacher. That's right, my daddy, the great man of God, has gone and fornicated the Sunday school teacher. Adulterous fornication, that's it. Wonder how Martha Ann would like the sound of that— adulterous fornication. I knew Roberta Huckstep would love to let those words slide off her tongue.

"Listen, Catherine Grace, I promise I won't cause any problems for you or Martha Ann. Your daddy was a good man. He even arranged for me to stay with a wonderful family down in Summerville," Miss Raines tried to explain.

"Oh good. Because it's so comforting for me to know that Daddy arranged to hide you away with some good Christian family. That does make it so much better, don't you think, Miss Raines?"

"Catherine Grace, he was only thinking about my reputation, and yours and Martha Ann's. He couldn't marry me and . . ." She started muttering.

"Excuse me. He couldn't what? He couldn't marry you?" My voice was loud and shrill and I could see Miss Raines started to tremble right there in front of me. "You knew, didn't you? You knew he was still married to my mama?"

"No. I mean yes. I mean, he only told me after I found out I was expecting, Catherine," she said, as if that made good sense.

I stared at Miss Raines, and then at the men carrying my daddy's casket through the front doors of the church. I knew that was my daddy inside that box, I saw him with my own eyes. But it sure didn't seem like the same man who had taught me about football and pot roast and eternal salvation. And I wasn't so sure I was going to hang around town and act like he was the great man of God he had led me, and everybody else, to believe he was. I wasn't sure I had the strength for that.

CHAPTER TEN

Bearing the Sins of My
Mama and Daddy

I left Miss Raines crying in the parking lot and headed back to my house under a sky that felt dark and dreary even though the sun had finally found its way from behind the clouds. My mama and daddy had certainly left me a mess to sort out, and I couldn't think of a single verse of scripture that was going to comfort me as I came to terms with an adulterating daddy, a resurrected mama, and an expectant mistress with an imaginary fiancé.

One thing was for certain, I was going to pack my blue vinyl suitcases, and then I was heading back to Atlanta, whether Miss Mabie and Flora took me or not. And as much as those two seemed to be enjoying the gracious hospitality here in Ringgold, I thought I might very well be traveling alone. But I didn't care, my head hadn't stopped spinning since I'd come home, and I needed to get back to the city where I could think straight.

As I walked past Ruthie Morgan's house, something red caught my eye. And there, in the dead of winter, I looked up to see three terra-cotta pots sitting on the front porch, each one filled with a large, blooming geranium. I knew they were made of plastic, nothing could be that perfect, not even at Ruthie Morgan's house. I wondered if she was out with Hank, snuggled up close to his body in the front seat of his red truck. Maybe I needed some plastic plants on my front porch so I could pretend, at least for a day or two, that everything was perfect.

Instead, my house was looking pretty pitiful, smoke pouring out of its single brick chimney, a dead poinsettia left sitting by the front door—an appropriate welcome to the Cline house.

Everyone was probably still sitting around the kitchen table, drinking coffee and reassuring Lena Mae that her oldest daughter would find it in her heart to forgive her. Not yet. No, I wasn't ready to start forgiving anybody. I walked right past my house and into town. I walked past the Shop Rite and the Dollar General Store, where I could see Mr. Tucker stacking jars of Vaseline on the end of aisle eight. I kept my head down, hoping he wouldn't notice me and want to stop and speak. I walked past the high school, where a couple of boys were bundled up in jackets running around the field, tossing a football. I walked past the Dairy Queen and could see Eddie Franklin's red hair popping up behind the ice cream machine. I imagine he practiced making chocolate-dipped cones all winter long just to keep his form at its best.

I walked past the Old Mill, and then turned right, and headed straight for Lolly Dempsey's house. When I lived here, I rarely went to Lolly's house, and yet today I was desperate to get there. I was desperate to find something normal, even if it was a house full of anger and stale cigarette smoke. A tattered paper sign taped to the Dempsey's doorbell said it was broken. That bell had been broken for years, ever since Lolly and I accidentally tripped on some wires up in the attic.

We were playing with a Ouija board we had bought at the Dollar General Store, both of us too afraid to admit that we had it, for fear that my daddy or her mama would think we were playing some game with the devil. Mr. Dempsey decided that a rat ate through the wire, and we never had the nerve to tell him any different.

I pounded my fist on the door and then waited a moment for Mrs. Demspey to start yelling, just like she always did. "Lolly! Lolly! Get the damn door, I'm watching my programs."

Lolly acted like she never heard her mother screaming across their tiny, two-bedroom house. It was Lolly's one little act of defiance, one that always seemed lost on her mother. I waited a minute more, then Mrs. Dempsey cracked the door just enough for me to see her standing there in her bathrobe, a lit cigarette dangling from her mouth. It was good to see her.

"Lord, Catherine Grace, what the hell are you doing here?" she asked, opening the door all the way into the living room. I didn't even bother trying to explain because I knew Mrs. Dempsey wasn't really interested in anything I had to say. "Sorry to hear about your daddy. Tough break," she added, making that the most she'd ever said to me. I guess dying really does bring out the best in people.

Lolly suddenly appeared behind her mother, almost pushing her aside to make room for herself. "Catherine Grace," she shouted, grabbing my hand and practically dragging me inside the house. "I was so afraid I wasn't going to get to see you," she said as she hugged me tight around the neck, again. "Come on, let's go to my room and talk. You want a Coca-Cola or something, some hot Dr Pepper?"

"No thanks, I'm good. I just wanted to see how you were doing, before I headed back to Atlanta."

"So you're going back right after the funeral? I was kind of hoping you were going to stay for awhile."

"No, I'm leaving tonight."

"Catherine Grace, are you kidding me? Tonight? The funeral is not till tomorrow. What's going on?"

I told her straight-out that my mother was still alive, and I said it with such a matter-of-fact calmness that I think it took Lolly a minute to comprehend what I had said.

"Yep, looks like she ran away from home," I repeated, just to be certain that she had heard me right.

Lolly's mouth fell open, and I threw myself across her bed. "Now that my daddy's dead, she's shown up to let me know that she loves me. You know my mama has an absolutely beautiful singing voice. I mean it would have been a sin if she had kept that gift to herself. So she went and followed her big dream, and I think that took her right back to Willacoochee. And the best part, my daddy knew she was alive, sharing her gift with a bunch of drunken men in some no-good, sleazy honky-tonk. But Martha Ann, she doesn't really care what he did or what she did. She's just so happy to have a mother, any mother, heck, she'd probably take yours," I said, without thinking about Lolly's feelings.

"I'm sorry, Lolly," I said. Somehow I'd always found some rotten comfort in thinking that no matter how unfair my life seemed, it was always better than Lolly's. But now I wasn't so sure. Mrs. Dempsey might not like Lolly, but at least she never abandoned her.

Lolly asked me about Miss Raines's baby, if what Emma Sue had been saying about town was really the gospel truth. I told her, yep, my dead daddy was going to have a baby. Lolly's mouth fell right open, but then she started talking in her kind, smooth voice, trying to reassure me that my life was not as tragic as it sounded. As the sound of Lolly's voice filled my head, my eyes were drawn to a small crystal vase sitting on the table next to her bed.

I picked it up and turned it over and over in my hands. I had never seen anything so beautiful in Lolly's house.

"Where'd this come from?" I asked, interrupting her good-hearted effort.

"How about that?" she said with a smile on her face. "My mama gave that to me for my eighteenth birthday."

I couldn't believe something so fine had come from Mrs. Dempsey. She didn't seem capable of giving anything of any beauty to anyone. I kept turning it over in my hands, trying to absorb the unexpectedness of her gesture.

"Catherine Grace, have you talked to your mama?"

"A little bit. No, not really," I said. I told Lolly there was nothing much to talk about. I didn't believe there was any good reason for leaving your children and letting them think that you're dead. But what I didn't tell Lolly was that I was really afraid that the woman sitting at my kitchen table was going to tell me that she left because she just hadn't wanted to be a mama, that she wanted something else more than her girls.

"All I'm saying, Catherine, is that you of all people ought to understand what a powerful hold a dream can have on a person."

"Damn it, Lolly. Why does everybody keep telling me I should understand? I didn't float down some river leaving two little babies behind thinking I was dead."

"No. No, you didn't. But if you had been walking around in your mama's shoes, you might have wanted to float away, too," Lolly said as she moved next to me on the bed. She wrapped me in her arms and we sat there for a long time before she said another word.

"Catherine, your daddy always said that the Lord plants a small seed of goodness in each and every one of us. Sometimes that seed grows into a mighty tree, and sometimes it struggles to take hold at all. It's up to us to help the Lord nurture the good in ourselves and the people around us."

"Yeah, well, he said a lot of things that weren't true."

"Maybe. But you know there's some good in all of us," Lolly said, taking the vase into her hands. "You just got to be willing to look harder in some than others."

I fell back on Lolly's bed. Her room was so wonderfully still and quiet. I closed my eyes, trying to absorb the peacefulness through every part of my body. Then Lolly touched my hand. "Catherine Grace, I really don't know which is worse, having a mama who leaves you thinking that she loved you or having a mama who lets you know almost every day of your life that she wished you'd never been born. I just think you need to hear her out."

I pulled my body up and rested my head on Lolly's shoulder.

"Just hold on to the good," she said, still holding the vase in her hands. "Remember, Hank found the goodness buried way down deep in Ruthie Morgan." Lolly laughed, trying to lighten the mood.

"Yeah, I guess poor Hank had to water and fertilize that scrawny little vine every day to get it to take root."

"Yeah, but I think Ruthie may be heading into a hot, dry summer," Lolly said, smiling, waiting for me to beg her for more information. I tried to act like I didn't care, but Lolly knew better.

She slowly unfolded the details of her information like she was unwrapping a beautiful package, trying hard not to rip the paper as she went. Lolly said that before I had come home from Atlanta, Hank and Ruthie had been over to my house to pay their respects to Martha Ann. Hank had asked Lolly if I was home yet, and apparently Ruthie thought he had kept an awfully close eye on the front door.

I told Lolly that didn't mean anything. Hank was just being Hank.

"Maybe. But I walked out behind them. I just wanted to get a little fresh air, so I stood out in the driveway away from the crowd that had gathered on the porch. Anyway, they started arguing about something."

"About what?"

"I don't know for sure, but I think Ruthie was mad that Hank kept looking at that door, obviously waiting to see you. But I did hear this. Ruthie said something about Miss Raines's illegitimate baby, as she called it, and then she said something about it explaining the way you turned out."

"Huh? Like what? What'd she mean by that?"

"Who knows, who cares? That's not the point. Hank was so mad he walked her straight to her front door and left her there, not even waiting to see that she got inside," Lolly said triumphantly.

My heart suddenly felt a little lighter, and yet I hated to credit Hank Blankenship with that. "Well, I guess that's a tiny bright spot in an otherwise crummy day."

"Tiny bright spot! Damn it, girl, are you blind? Don't you get it, Catherine Grace? Hank still loves you."

CHAPTER ELEVEN

Finding Salvation at the
Dairy Queen

M rs. Dempsey was sitting on the sofa watching *The Price Is Right* when I walked back into the living room. A fresh cigarette was clenched between her lips, and she was maneuvering a lit match toward its tip. I said a quick good-bye, barely raising my head as I walked toward the door. I'd learned through the years not to expect any conversation from Mrs. Dempsey, especially when she was watching one of her programs. She never offered much more than a grunt and a wave of the hand, and even the effort of doing that seemed to annoy her most days.

Today wasn't any different. But as I opened the front door, I glanced back at her, and even though the room was filling with smoke, I could see that her eyes were saying something I had never noticed before. They were wounded and dull. She looked like an animal that's hurting but can't tell you where.

When I was little, I couldn't imagine Mrs. Dempsey not loving Lolly. I couldn't imagine any mama not loving her baby. Truth be told, it scared me, but not for Lolly. I figured if Mrs. Dempsey could hate her own daughter, then maybe it was possible that my own mama hated me. I mean, if she had loved me, really, truly loved me, then she would have been more careful in that creek and not gone and gotten herself killed. That's what I used to think, but now not even that crazy talk makes any sense anymore.

Turns out, Mrs. Dempsey does love Lolly. I mean, she sure doesn't love her right, but in some small or strange way, that woman sitting on that faded old sofa loves her daughter enough to save what little money she has to buy her something as beautiful as that crystal vase.

Daddy said you can see the devil in people's eyes, but maybe the devil is nothing more than the sadness they carry around inside of them, bottled up so tight that it comes out as pure ugliness, like it does with Mrs. Dempsey. And maybe my own mama was too filled with sadness to love Martha Ann and me right. Maybe she wanted to be up on some stage so badly that she couldn't figure out a way to make herself happy without it. And maybe that's the way it is sometimes, that there are some mamas so filled with sorrow that it's better that they leave the mothering to somebody else. I needed to see my mama's eyes.

"Three hundred and forty-five dollars," Mrs. Dempsey shouted, bringing my attention back to the *Price Is Right* and the new Maytag washing machine that the beautiful woman on the television was caressing with her hands.

Out of nowhere, a smile came over my face, and I stepped onto the front stoop and into the chill of that January day. The sky was growing darker. It felt like it might snow. I started walking toward home but stopped and watched a wave of dark, heavy clouds settle in over Taylor's Ridge. As I stood there, something down the road caught my eye, a light blinking on and then off, and then on, warming up an unusually bleak, wintry day. It was the red-and-white sign at the Dairy Queen. I felt like it was calling me, begging me to follow its light right to the counter where Eddie Franklin was waiting for Catherine Grace Cline to come and place her order.

"Hey there, stranger," Eddie said with that warm, expectant smile on his face that in my eighteen years on this earth had become wonderfully familiar. "Kind of thought I might be seeing you today. Sorry to hear about your daddy," he said as he shook his head to add a little more emphasis to what he was saying. "Reverend Cline sure was a great man, yes sir, a great man of God, and this town is really going to miss him something bad."

"Yeah, great man of God," I repeated, with a slow, flat voice, not even trying to disguise my sadness, "really great." Eddie Franklin obviously hadn't heard that the great man of God had been an even greater liar, bearing false witness all about town or at least in the bedroom of one special member of Cedar Grove's devoted congregation.

"So what can I get for you, Catherine Grace?"

"Oh, I don't know, Eddie. Maybe I'll have a Dilly Bar." I acted as though I had to give it a bit of thought, pretending that it didn't bother me that Eddie was still asking me the one question I was absolutely certain he knew the answer to.

"I guess now that you're living in Atlanta, you haven't had much need for a Dilly Bar, huh?" he asked.

I hadn't really thought about it till now but Eddie was right. I hadn't been to any Dairy Queen in months. I didn't even know where one was, and for some reason, I guess I felt like I'd be cheating on Eddie Franklin if I told him about my trip to the Varsity or my midnight run to McDonald's.

All those years growing up in Ringgold and hardly a Saturday had gone by when I hadn't been standing right here right before Eddie Franklin, offering up part of my allowance just as faithfully as I had those two shiny quarters I tossed in the offering plate on Sunday mornings. I stood real still for a moment, letting the days since I left town pass before my eyes as if I were watching them on the giant movie screen at the Tivoli up in Chattanooga, hoping, I guess, to see how this story was going to end. All of a sudden I came to the part where I was standing in this very parking lot, next to a Greyhound bus, saying my last good-byes to my daddy. That seemed like a lifetime ago now, and my daddy seemed so far away.

I dabbed a few tears on my coat sleeve and looked down at the ground. "How ya been, Eddie?" I said real quickly, not nearly as interested in his answer as I was in changing the subject. Somehow it didn't seem proper to do my grieving standing at the counter at the Dairy Queen. And I surely wasn't in the mood for Eddie to try to make me feel better by saying something stupid like "the good Lord sure must have needed your daddy or heaven's shining even brighter now that your daddy's gone home." I'd heard all that talk when my mama pretended to die, and it didn't make me feel any better then either. Thankfully, Eddie just answered my question.

"Real good, to tell you the truth," he said kindly, pretending not to notice that my eyes were starting to puddle. "We haven't had much cold weather till now and that's been real good for business. You know some Dairy Queens just close up altogether in the winter, Catherine Grace, just lock the doors till the first sign of spring. I can't imagine that. Heck, I've sold more dip cones from Thanksgiving to Christmas than I ever have before. Seventy-three, to be exact."

Eddie could probably tell from my blank expression that I wasn't sure that that was intended to be an impressive number. "Oh come on, girl, that may not seem like much to you, not being in the ice cream business and all, but it makes me happy to know some people never lose their appetite for a chocolate-dipped ice cream cone, no matter how cold it is outside," he said, again flashing that calm smile of his that made me think he was telling me more than he was saying.

"But enough about me. How's Atlanta? Guess it's a lot more exciting than Ringgold."

"Oh, I don't know about that. Seems there's plenty going on here."

Eddie lifted the lid to the deep freeze and then lowered his entire upper body into the frozen chest, searching for a freshly made box of Dilly Bars, the one ice cream treat Eddie Franklin created well before his customers ever ordered it. He said it took time and concentration to make a perfectly round ice cream confection that would satisfy his customers' high standards.

"Lord, you got that right." Eddie kept on talking, reporting all the goings-on in town, not even noticing if I was really interested or not.

"Mrs. Gulbenk had some more bout of pneumonia last month. We were all real worried it might be her last Christmas on this earth. Now stop me if Martha Ann has already told you this. But then that sweet old lady made some sort of potion out of a can of stewed tomatoes and a jar of horseradish and she was right back on her feet helping Miss Ida Belle serve New Year's Eve supper at the fellowship hall. She even had this idea to put real sparklers in the flower arrangements. They looked great until some kid took a match to one of them and nearly caught the entire table on fire. Ida Belle warned that she better not find out who put a big brown mark on her best white cloth. They'd be shucking corn all summer long!

"And Mrs. Huckstep, oh my, you wouldn't believe what that woman is up to now, Catherine Grace. She's planning the town's first debutant ball. Tell you the truth, I'm not really sure what that is but she said Emma Sue needed to be officially presented to society, and she could do that only at a debutant ball. And I'm not really sure what society she's talking about neither, but I am pretty certain she don't mean me. I think Emma Sue may end up being the town's first and only debutant unless Ruthie Morgan can convince Mrs. Huckstep that she's not too old for a formal presentation."

There was so much power and confidence in Eddie's voice that I could hear every syllable even with his head buried deep inside the freezer. He has always acted so sure of himself, never seeming regretful or bored with the life he had chosen. Sometimes I wondered if making those dip cones so perfect was harder than it looked.

"Oh, heck girl, I'm sure I'm just boring you." He reappeared, holding a Dilly Bar in his right hand, his fingertips turning red from the cold. He presented it to me with a *da da da dum* as if I'd won it at the clown toss at the state fair. I put my forty cents on the counter and turned to walk away when I heard Eddie calling me back.

"You know, Catherine Grace, I've seen you eat at least a thousand of those Dilly Bars right there on top of that picnic table. And I've watched you stare up at Taylor's Ridge for hours, straining so hard sometimes it looked like you were actually trying to move that dadgum mountain with some kind of superhuman powers, like Wonder Woman. But I, uh . . ." And Eddie, who had never been at a loss for words in his life, paused for a moment. He looked me straight in the eyes as if he were desperately trying to figure out the best way to finish what he had started. All of a sudden his eyes grew deep and bold, and it felt like he was the one with the superhuman powers.

"What is it, Eddie? My Dilly Bar's going to melt." Of course, we both knew that wasn't true since I was standing there with snowflakes in my hair. But I could feel my heart starting to beat a little faster just anticipating what was about to come out of Eddie Franklin's mouth.

"Well, it's just that I find it kind of funny that you've been so busy looking at that mountain that you've never seen what was right here under your nose."

"Eddie," I said impatiently, my voice growing as chilly as the night air, "I don't care that Emma Sue is going to be a stupid debutant."

"No, I'm sure you don't care, Catherine Grace. That's my point. But I guess finding out the Sunday-school teacher is having your dead daddy's baby is something worth caring about. Not to mention your mama coming back to life and all. And it just seems that—"

"Eddie Franklin," I stopped him with the right amount of indignation in my voice to hide my hopeless resignation. I guess it was ridiculous to think that just this one time I could keep my business a secret, but apparently everybody in Ringgold, even Eddie, already knew that my daddy was a fake, nothing more than a cheating liar, a cheating, lying, adulterating man of God. But some things are just too big to hide, and Miss Raines's growing belly and my mama's sudden resurrection were two very big things.

"You better hush," I warned him, but he didn't seem the least bit scared. "And wipe that stupid grin off your face. There's nothing about this situation that's the least bit funny."

"Oh come on, Catherine Grace. What'd you expect? No one's a stranger here, and nobody's laughing, either. To tell the truth, and I'd put my hand on the Good Book to prove it to you, everybody's real worried about you, even Emma Sue."

"I don't need Emma Sue Huckstep to be the least bit worried about me. I'm just fine. Better than fine, I'm good. I'm real, real good," I said, raising my voice like a mama about to scold her child. My head started spinning again. I had too many thoughts coursing through my brain, and I needed to put them in some kind of basic order before my head spontaneously combusted. I read in one of those newspapers stacked by the checkout at the Dollar General Store that your body can actually explode with no warning at all. And figuring the way my day was going, I thought it was quite possible my head was about to blow like a stick of dynamite.

"Eddie Franklin," I shouted as I turned to walk away,

"just for the record, you don't know a damn thing about me. Oh, yeah, you may know that my daddy was a first-rate sinner and that my mama floated right out of my life 'cause she had something more pressing to do than taking care of me and Martha Ann. But you don't know one thing about me, Catherine Grace Cline, or what I need or what I should do or what I'm thinking about on top of that picnic table. All you know is that I like Dilly Bars. So just stick to your ice cream and maybe you'll sell a hundred of those damned things before the end of the month."

I sounded so mean and hateful. It was like I was throwing knives right out of my mouth and straight into Eddie's heart.

"Just 'cause I like serving ice cream, Miss Cline, don't make me stupid. Or are you too smart to figure that out, too?" Eddie said. The smile drained from his face.

"God Almighty, Eddie, I don't think you're stupid," I shot back, knowing good and well that up until this moment that's exactly what I had thought. I had never given Eddie Franklin the chance to be anything more than a country boy with a knack for soft serve.

"Right, sure, well, you've never been very good at hiding what you're thinking so just go sit your big-city butt on top of that picnic table and eat your Dilly Bar, like every other time, not thinking about anything or anybody but yourself, especially not Hank or Gloria Jean or your dearly departed daddy, who, yeah, turns out was a sinner just like every one of us, or even your poor mama or any of the other people who'd do damn near anything for you. Listen," and Eddie's voice was suddenly soft again, "I know your heart is hurting bad, but maybe this time, while you're sitting up there, you can takes your eyes off that mountain for a minute and take a good, hard look at yourself."

I wanted to scream at Eddie. I wanted to tell him that I hated him and I hated that mountain. But more than anything else, I wanted to tell him that right now I hated my mama and I hated my daddy. I hated the way they both left me here. But nothing came out of my mouth. All I saw was a redheaded boy who had never gotten much more from me than an off-handed thank-you. I held on tight to my Dilly Bar and climbed on top of the picnic table, turning my back to Eddie Franklin and the blinking Dairy Queen sign that now seemed like it was there only to taunt me.

My fingers were so cold and stiff that I put the white paper bag between my teeth and grabbed the stick with one hand and pulled the ice cream out, revealing the most beautiful Dilly Bar I had ever seen. The curlicue was perfectly shaped and positioned right in the middle of the bar. The chocolate was smooth and seamless, and the ice cream was just hard enough so I didn't have to wait for it to soften before my first bite. I ate the chocolate shell first and then let the ice cream melt on my tongue until it was so soft and creamy that it slid right down my throat.

Eddie was right about one thing. That was for sure. I had spent an awful lot of time on this table plotting and scheming my way out of here. But he didn't understand. He didn't understand that the day my mama died, I just wanted to go with her, and every day after that. Now she was back, Daddy was gone, and a baby was on the way. And somehow I felt more alone today than I ever had before.

Taylor's Ridge was hidden behind a wall of falling snow and gray, heavy clouds. I looked down at what was left of my Dilly Bar and wondered if Eddie Franklin looked up at that lonely mountain. Did he ever find himself sitting up here on this picnic table, eating his very own Dilly Bar with the snow swirling about his head? I guess I already knew the answer.

I figured Eddie Franklin must have been a lot like my own great-granddaddy, who walked over that ridge to come and do the Lord's work. William Floyd never doubted where he was meant to be, and I don't think Eddie has, either. And yet that's all I've ever done, doubt where I'm meant to be. My body began shivering and shaking, but I wasn't cold anymore. I felt warm, wet tears streaming down my face, stinging my cheeks as they fell. With the very last bite of my Dilly Bar melting in my mouth, I became more convinced that my life was about to change in a way that I had not come close to imagining. And I had a strange, call it prophetic, feeling that I was heading into a storm of biblical proportions.

I stepped down from the picnic table and, throwing my ice cream wrapper in the trash, I looked back at Eddie Franklin. He was washing down the soft-serve ice cream machine, smiling as he stood behind the counter, moving his wet rag across the stainless steel.

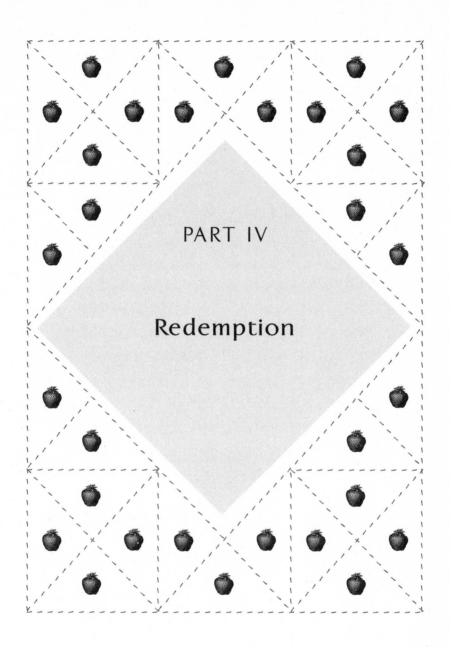

PART IV

Redemption

CHAPTER TWELVE

The Prodigal Daughter Claims
the Promised Land

Mama was sitting on the front porch by the time I got home. The house was lit up like a Christmas tree and I could hear Gloria Jean and Miss Mabie laughing inside the kitchen. They were probably sitting around the table, sipping the day's last cup of coffee, reminiscing about boys they had loved back in Birmingham. But Mama, wrapped snugly in a crocheted blanket, was sitting alone, swaying back and forth in one of the old aluminum gliders that Daddy had bought years ago at the Dollar General Store.

"How's that chair feel?" I asked her.

"Great," she said, obviously relieved I had spoken first.

"That was Daddy's favorite place to sit," I told her, knowing good and well that the wooden rocker was the only chair on this porch he ever sat in. I just wasn't sure how to talk to her about my daddy.

"Catherine Grace," Mama said with an urgent tone that told me she had been waiting a long time to say what was on her mind. "I have dreamed about this moment since the day I left Ringgold. I've practiced what I wanted to say to you for, well, at least a million times. But now that I'm here looking at you, I'm just not sure how to say it all."

I needed her to try. After all this time, I needed her to try. So I just stood there, waiting a little bit longer.

"You know, when I was your age, you were already one year old. I was so young, Catherine, maybe too young, too young to be a good mother. There were all these places I dreamed of going, places far away from Willachoochee and Ringgold. And there were all these things I dreamed of doing, and your daddy, God rest his soul, wouldn't hear of any of it. He said I took a vow before God to be a wife and mother and there was no going back on my word. I couldn't have it both ways, he said. But as soon as I made that vow, I started praying, begging the good Lord not to hold a six-teen-year-old girl to a promise like that.

"You know my own mama, your grandmamma, didn't understand me wanting to be a singer. She never had much money or much patience for my foolish way of thinking, and she figured your daddy was making me respectable or something.

"And your daddy did promise me something better than I knew, it just wasn't what I wanted . . . or it wasn't what I thought I wanted. A lot of mistakes were made along the way."

"Did Daddy hurt you? Was he unkind to you?" I asked, not certain I was ready to hear the answer.

"No. No. Get that thought out of your head. We just wanted different things, and he couldn't accept me not wanting his life completely. You have to know this, Catherine Grace, I never told your daddy I was leaving. It just happened. I was standing in the river, watching the leaves float away on the surface of the water, and something deep inside told me to run."

Somehow that revelation felt like a little blessing amid all the confusion. Just knowing Daddy hadn't helped mama with her drowning felt like a gift.

"Sometimes, Catherine Grace, you spend your life looking for the one thing you had all along," she said softly, a single tear rolling down her cheek. "I am just so sorry, more than you will ever know." Her body was shaking underneath her blanket, and I walked in front of her and got down on my knees. I took her hands into mine and I looked her in the face so I could see square into her eyes.

"Did you love me? I mean when you left, did you truly love me?"

She quit shaking and I leaned in even closer. Mama didn't flinch. She sat quiet and still as I moved my face directly in front of hers. I stared deep into her eyes, and for a minute, I knew I was looking right into her soul. Those beautiful brown eyes, every detail of which I had memorized in my sleep, were full of sadness. My mama's heart was broken too. It had been broken for a long time. I could see it for myself.

"I love you, too," I said, holding my mama's hands tightly in mine.

As I held my mama's hands, all I could think about was my daddy. He used to love to tell me the story of the lost sheep. He told me so many times I knew it by heart. Sitting here with my mama, I could hear him telling me again.

You see, there was a man who had a hundred sheep, but one of them wanders off. He loved all his sheep, and he left the other ninety-nine grazing on a hillside just to go looking for that one that couldn't find his way back home. When he finally finds it, he is happier about this one little lost sheep than he is about the other ninety-nine still grazing on the hillside.

Somehow I always figured Daddy was trying to tell me that I was that little lost sheep, trying to find my way back home. Maybe I am. But I think my mama was that little lost sheep, too. I knew she was back, I could see her plain as day. But I wasn't sure she had yet found her way home.

All the sadness I had been storing up wasn't all going to blow away tonight as easily as the wind blowing through my hair. But my heart wasn't hurting as much as it had the night before, and I had a feeling it wasn't going to hurt as much tomorrow night, either.

Mama and I sat on the porch for hours. She wanted to know everything about me, from my favorite color to my date for the senior prom. I told her about my shopping trip to Loveman's with Gloria Jean and about my pink dress. She smiled and cried at the same time, happy for my joy and sad that she had missed the journey. I told her about Hank and how we broke up and that he was dating Ruthie Morgan now. I told her that I missed him and had ever since that night back in June. We talked till my eyes and head began to hurt, neither one of us noticing that it was beginning to snow again and the ground in front of us was turning white.

But I couldn't leave. I wanted to know what Mama had been doing for the last twelve years. I wanted to drink it in slowly, savoring everything she said. She sang in a few bars in Nashville but never made it to the Opry. Mostly she waited tables at a restaurant near Music Row, serving Cobb salads and club sandwiches to fresh-faced music executives half her age. On the weekends, she sang at the Heritage Funeral Home. She said it was good money, and the grief-stricken weren't prone to complain about her performance.

Turns out the birthday cards I had gotten from my aunt in Willacoochee every year had come from her. At first she mailed them to an old friend who in turn would mail them to Martha Ann and me. Then about eight years ago, she moved back to Willacoochee to take care of her dying mama. She said they had never really gotten along, and, unfortunately, nothing changed much at the end. Anyway, she's lived there ever since, waiting tables, the only thing, she says, she knows how to do.

I wasn't sure if I was ever going to be able to accept or understand what my mama had done. But I guess I was coming to think like Martha Ann, I was just grateful to have a mama, good or bad.

Gloria Jean tapped on the front door and then opened it just enough to show her face. I waited for her to say something, but she was unexpectedly quiet. I think she was "drinking us in" as she'd say. I think she was drinking every last drop. Finally, she spoke.

"Ladies, I hate to call this evening to an end, but it's getting late and this cold air is not good for your complexions. And I know both of you want to look your best at the funeral tomorrow. The whole damn town's going to turn out for this one," Gloria Jean declared, as if we might actually be surprised by this announcement.

"Not every day the preacher's dead wife shows up at her husband's service, now is it?" laughed Gloria Jean, obviously looking forward to the day's events. I thought I might need to remind her that this was going to be a funeral not a wedding.

"Gloria Jean," my mama said, standing up and turning toward her friend, "I always knew you were the dearest person in this town, but Catherine Grace has been telling me, well, I need to thank you."

"Lord, for what?"

"For loving my girls."

"Oh Lord, Lena Mae, you are going to get me crying, and I sure don't want red, puffy eyes at that church tomorrow. Roberta Huckstep will be there and God only knows I have to look better than that old bat. Right, Catherine Grace?"

"That's right," I said, looking up at Gloria Jean. I could see her face in the light shining through the kitchen window. She wasn't wearing one lick of makeup. I don't think I had ever seen Gloria Jean without any makeup except that time she had her face covered with a bluish looking mud. But tonight, with her face bare, she looked absolutely beautiful.

The snow was falling harder and even the trees were turning white. Everything looked pure and peaceful. Suddenly I had that familiar, desperate urging to be with my sister. I got up and hugged Mama and Gloria Jean and then stepped into the warmth of the only home I had ever known. "Hey, would you do me a favor, Gloria Jean?" I asked, turning back to face her. "Tell Brother Bowden to get in touch with the minister in LaFayette first thing in the morning. He's welcome to come to the service, but I'll be delivering my daddy's eulogy." Then, with that said, I shut the door, leaving Mama and Gloria Jean staring blankly at each other, unsure of what to think.

Martha Ann was already asleep in my bed, having offered her own to Flora. I crawled in next to her and began stroking her hair. She turned her face toward me and asked what time it was.

"A little after midnight, I think."

"Lord, Catherine Grace, where have you been all day? I was getting kind of worried about you."

"It was a long way home, but I'm here." It had been six months since I left Ringgold, and yet the day I stepped on that Greyhound bus seemed like a lifetime ago. It surely had been a long way home, but it felt good being here, lying next to my little sister

"You know, Martha Ann, I'm not so sure a person can run away from home."

"What? Am I dreaming? You are Catherine Grace Cline, aren't you?" Martha Ann couldn't help but wonder.

"All I'm saying is that you can run away from a town or a house, but I'm not so sure you can run away from your home."

Martha Ann practically fell out of the bed. She sat straight up and turned on the light. She said she had to see my face to make sure I wasn't just joking with her. She wanted to know what had gotten me talking like that. I told her I wasn't really sure. Daddy would have said it was the Holy Spirit, but I think it might have been Eddie Franklin. Either way, all I knew was that I had spent my life begging the Lord to hear me out, to let me know He was out there somewhere, actually caring about what happened to Catherine Grace Cline. Turns out, I think He was talking to me all along, I just never bothered to listen to what He had to say.

"It's a funny thing, Martha Ann," I said, "how much time we spend planning our lives. We so convince ourselves of what we want to do, that sometimes we don't see what we're meant to do. Maybe Daddy was right, maybe I was meant to be here after all."

"What are you meant to do here, Catherine? Grow tomatoes?" she asked. "You'll never be happy doing that."

I wasn't exactly sure of everything, I told her. But it would come to me in time. I did feel certain of that.

As we snuggled in my bed, I could see the snow had stopped falling. The moon behind Taylor's Ridge was full and bright and the reflection of the moonlight off the snow made the sky so bright it was almost like day. For the first time, Taylor's Ridge was a comforting sight, like the earth's strong arm holding you close. I apologized to Martha Ann, thinking maybe I had forced my dream on her. Maybe I'd forced her to eat too many Dilly Bars.

CHAPTER THIRTEEN

The Sunday School Teacher's
Miraculous Reception

The next morning, everybody was buzzing around the house like a bunch of worker bees trying to please the queen. Miss Mabie and Flora and me had left Atlanta so quickly I hadn't really thought about what to wear to the funeral. Daddy would insist on me wearing black, I knew that much, and I'd spent the last half hour rummaging through my sister's closet looking for a black skirt to go with the black silk blouse I had bought for work. Martha Ann was frantically hunting for a pair of nylons that didn't have a run. I could hear her cursing and slamming drawers all at the same time. And Flora was already frying bacon, hollering for everybody to come and eat a hot bacon biscuit before putting on our funeral clothes.

In all the rush I hadn't really given much thought to

poor Miss Raines, at least not up until now. I found one of Martha Ann's baby dresses hanging in the back of her closet. And all of the sudden, looking at the delicate smocking and the little yellow ducks embroidered along the hem, I wondered who was going to help Miss Raines dress her baby. We were about to bury the one man she truly loved, and she was having his child. I knew she was sitting in her house all alone, with a pile of damp Kleenex growing by her side.

Gloria Jean said she had heard from Ida Belle who had heard from Ruthie Morgan's mother that Miss Raines would not be attending daddy's funeral, thinking her presence might be too uncomfortable for the Cedar Grove congregation. She was going to finish up some packing and then head on down to Summerville. Surely, the sweet Sunday-school teacher with the big, blue eyes didn't think she needed to keep pretending she had a fiancé named Donald.

I needed to talk to Martha Ann. She had given up her search for a new pair of nylons and had shifted her attention to putting on her makeup. She was standing in the bathroom in front of the mirror. Gloria Jean had picked up some new waterproof mascara for us at the Dollar General Store. She said crying for the dead was not a good reason to let your makeup run all down your face, and she made us promise we'd only use the Maybelline she left sitting on the bathroom counter.

Martha Ann was struggling to open the cap. I told her to run it under hot water and see if that would help. She kept fiddling with the tube of mascara as I started talking, telling her how worried I was about Miss Raines and her little baby. After all, that baby was our kin, too. Martha Ann dropped the mascara in the sink. "Damn it. It doesn't run because you can't get it out of the tube to put it on your eyelashes in the first place."

"Hey, Martha Ann, did you hear what I just said?" I asked, taking the mascara from her hand and loosening the cap before giving it back.

"Yes, yes, I did, I'm sorry. I'm just kind of nervous," she replied, turning toward me and giving me her full attention. "Look, I'm worried, too. I have been for a long time. You know that. I just wasn't sure if anybody, other than you, would understand."

"Well, we're all that's left of our daddy, and I think we need to make things right for him. And the only way to make things right is for Miss Raines to be here with us."

"Yeah sure, I don't care if she comes to the funeral. I think she should be there."

"No, that's not what I mean. I mean she needs to be here, in this house, with us," I said real carefully.

"You mean live with us," Martha Ann repeated, just to be certain.

"We're her family now, and we need to help her raise our little brother or sister." There, I'd said it. But before I had time to worry about her response, Martha Ann squealed with excitement. She loved the idea of having a baby in the house. Then she suddenly hesitated, wondering where we'd put everybody, especially with Mama back at home. She was not willing to share her room with a new-born baby no matter how cute he or she turned out to be. I told her I hadn't worked out all the details yet, but kind of like the feeding of the five thousand, we'd take care of everybody.

On the other side of the door, I could hear Flora holler-ing from the kitchen. "Ya gonna need to keep up ya stren'th. Ya hear me?" She was on the telephone talking to Miss Mabie, who had spent the night with Gloria Jean. Flora was already pacing the kitchen floor, worrying that Miss Mabie wasn't getting herself something to eat. She had no more hung up the phone when Gloria Jean called, for the third time this morning. She wanted to make sure us girls didn't forget to carry a lace handkerchief as well as an extra bottle of Aqua Net. Lord only knows what she planned on doing with all that hairspray at Daddy's serv-ice. She told Martha Ann to come over with her nylons, and, with a little Revlon clear nail polish, she'd have those stockings looking as good as new.

I knew if I was going to get Miss Raines to the church, I needed to leave now, while everybody was tending to their own pressing needs. Flora had finally left the kitchen, and I could hear her in Martha Ann's bedroom grunting as she tugged and pulled her girdle up and over her tummy. Flora would insist on driving Miss Mabie's car to the church, especially with all this snow on the ground. I stood outside Martha Ann's bedroom door and told Flora to tell everybody that I'd meet them at the church, and not to worry, I was going to take Daddy's car. Flora yelled back from inside the bedroom, wanting to know where I was headed right before my daddy's funeral was about to begin. It wasn't right, she said, to keep the dead waiting.

I told her that I just needed a minute or two to myself. "You understand, don't you, Flora?" I said, not waiting for an answer. I headed down the hall, grabbing my heavy wool coat from the closet and then running toward the front door. But as I threw my coat over my shoulder, something caught my eye. Mama was ironing one of my dresses. I wanted to ask her why she was doing that. I already had something to wear to the church. But all I could do was stand in the hallway and watch her hand gently glide the iron back and forth, smoothing every wrinkle out of the fabric. Ruthie Morgan's mama had never ironed anything as perfectly as this.

She set the iron down and looked up at me. I smiled, letting her know how thankful I was, and then I turned back toward the door and ran out onto the porch. The steps were covered with a thin layer of ice and as soon as my foot touched the first step, I fell flat on my bottom. Thankfully, my heavy coat cushioned the fall, but I couldn't help but laugh, wondering if Daddy and his new band of angel friends had seen that from above. I kept my curse words locked in my mouth just in case and picked myself up and walked very carefully to the Oldsmobile. The door was frozen shut and I had to pull hard on the chrome handle, leaning my entire body away from the door. When it opened, I fell on my bottom again.

This time Martha Ann yelled from the bathroom window. "Your butt's going to be frost bit by the time you get to Miss Raines." I could still hear her laughing as she closed the window behind her.

I pulled myself up into my daddy's car and settled in behind the steering wheel. For the first time since hearing that my daddy had passed, I truly felt his presence, his gentle, comforting presence. I put the key into the ignition and waited for the engine to warm. I didn't need any shivers down my spine to tell me that I wasn't traveling alone.

I backed the car out of the driveway and then headed toward the church. Cedar Grove's brick exterior stood out like a monument on the snowy, white ground. The black hearse was already there parked alongside the building, waiting to carry daddy's casket to the cemetery. I wondered if the men from the funeral home were going to be able to get my daddy in the ground, considering how freezing cold it was. I whispered I'd be back and then turned left and headed into town.

It felt like Christmas Day. Every building was closed and shut tight; even the lights at the Dairy Queen were turned off. Everybody in Ringgold was on his way to say good-bye to my daddy. Everybody but one, and I had to go get her.

When I pulled in front of Miss Raines's house, I could see boxes neatly stacked on her front porch. She was standing in the picture window, staring out at nothing. She jumped when she saw the car, obviously startled at the sight of my daddy's Oldsmobile. I climbed out of the front seat, this time leaning on the hood of the car to steady myself as I walked toward the curb. She was already standing on the porch waiting for me, holding out a hand to guide me up the two final steps to her house.

"Catherine Grace, what are you doing here? You should be at the church by now."

"Well, since it's my own daddy's funeral, I don't think they'll be starting without me. You're right, I do need to be heading that way, but I needed to say something to you first," I said, not giving her the opportunity to interrupt. "Martha Ann and I have been doing some talking, and we agree that there's not going to be a funeral if you're not there. So get your coat, and let's go."

"Catherine Grace, that is very kind of you girls, but I don't think the rest of Cedar Grove is going to feel too good about me showing up at Reverend Cline's funeral. They don't want to think your daddy had anything to do with this baby. Apparently they want to think I just miraculously conceived this child or, at the very least, went up to some bar in Chattanooga and let the first guy who asked me to dance knock me up. Oh Lord, I'm sorry, Catherine, I don't normally talk like this. I just haven't been myself lately."

"Miss Raines, of course you're not yourself. You're pregnant, and Flora says any woman who has a baby growing in her is sure to be acting like a crazy person. And as far as all those other people are concerned, well, I guess they'll just have to go find themselves another funeral to cry at if they don't want you there because I'm not leaving without you. Now get your coat. It's really cold out there." Miss Raines stood perfectly still, unable to speak or move, but I could see the tears starting to well up in those beautiful blue eyes of hers.

"Listen. I know that for a long time I was plain rotten to you, just downright mean. Truth be told, I always liked you. I was just so mad that my mama was gone, and I found it was easier to be ugly to you than to my own daddy. It wasn't right. But you're family now, and you need to be at that funeral today—for Daddy, for Martha Ann, for me—and most of all for that little baby inside your tummy. And after the service, I've got news for you, Miss Raines, you're coming on home with us. You don't need some imaginary husband in Summerville. You need a family, now more than ever.

"Now go get your coat because I'm really not leaving without you. And it really is cold out there. Besides, I sure would hate to have to call the sheriff out in all this snow to come and put you in that car, and you know good and well he'll do anything for Reverend Cline's little girl," I said with a big grin on my face.

"Well, in that case," she said, crying again so that I could hardly understand what she was saying, "I guess I better get my coat." As she walked past me, she reached out to hug my neck but suddenly lifted her head as if she had heard a frightening noise. "Oh Lord, Catherine, what about your mama? What's she going to think about me showing up at Marshall's service?"

"I'm sure she's feeling a bit out of place herself. Ida Belle and Brother Fulmer thought it was best we forewarn the congregation, for fear somebody might have a heart attack seeing her alive and all. So don't worry, she'll be fine with you being there. Who knows, seeing you two together may be enough of a shock to leave even Roberta Huckstep speechless, for once."

By the time Miss Raines and I pulled into the church parking lot, we could hear the piano playing inside the church. Thankfully, Mrs. Gilbert was in town and she had arranged a collection of Daddy's favorite hymns. I could hear the last notes of "I'd Rather Have Jesus" trail into the beginning of "When the Roll Is Called Up Yonder." Miss Raines and I helped each other climb up the cement steps to the door. Brother Fulmer had carefully scraped off the ice and sprinkled the steps with rock salt. We could hear the salt crunching underneath the weight of our bodies.

As I pushed on the door of the church, I saw Martha Ann standing guard in the entry. She grabbed the door from the inside and pulled it open, and there in the entry of my daddy's church stood Miss Raines and me and Martha Ann and Lena Mae, the four women Daddy loved the most. We walked toward the center aisle and I could see my daddy's casket covered with a blanket of red roses. I took a deep breath, needing a moment to remind myself that my daddy was the one we had come to bury. Then we stepped into the sanctuary, standing side by side.

The church fell completely silent. Mrs. Gilbert even missed a few notes on the piano but quickly picked up her place and continued to play. As we walked down the aisle, I could feel everyone staring at us. I could hear Roberta Huckstep's familiar gasp, but I just smiled. I reached for Martha Ann's hand, and she squeezed it tight, reassuring me of what I had come to do.

CHAPTER FOURTEEN

You Will Be Like a
Well-Watered Garden

Gloria Jean and Miss Mabie and Flora were already sitting in the first pew. Gloria Jean stood as we approached, hugging each one of us as we reached the front of the church. When she wrapped her arms around Lena Mae, you could hear everyone's surprise rush through the air. For Gloria Jean, that was nothing more than encouragement, and she opened her arms even wider toward Miss Raines.

I waited for the music to soften, then I walked up three final steps and, for the first time, took my place behind the pulpit. I stroked my hand across its top, feeling its uneven surface where years of Cline men pounding their fists had left an impression. When I was little, I would sit at the base of the pulpit waiting for Daddy to finish talking to anyone who needed his ear. But I had never stood here with something to say, and in that moment, I realized what an ominous responsibility it was being Ringgold's preacher. I looked at Mrs. Gilbert the way my daddy used to do, and she softly brought the hymn to a close.

"Good morning, everyone, thank you for coming today. I hope you feel like I do, that I'm here not to say good-bye to my daddy, but to celebrate his life. I'm sure some of you are struggling with my daddy's death—and his life— right now. Heck, you may be even questioning your own faith, a little uncertain of what or who to believe anymore.

"My daddy liked to preach the parables. Of course, you all know that as well as I do. He always told Martha Ann and me that Jesus understood that children, even the grown ones, learn best when listening to a story. One of Daddy's favorites was the Parable of the Weeds, and it was always one of my favorites because Daddy told it in a way that I could really understand. I want to share that story with you now if you don't mind.

"You all know that my granddaddy loved his garden. He loved to tend to each and every one of his plants almost as much as he loved and tended to all of you, but most of you probably know that, too. But did you know that his garden was his secret hiding spot, where he went to think and rest and praise the good Lord? I'm not sure if my daddy told me that or if I just figured it out for myself.

"Anyway, what you might not know is that one day a real Cherokee Indian came over from the Sequatchie Valley to give my granddaddy a purple tomato plant. That's right.

A real Cherokee gave him that plant as a gift for praying his little Indian boy, who was sick with a high fever, back to health. Granddaddy loved that vine because, as Daddy told it, it had come from the goodness that can be done in the world.

"But when he planted it, even though the tomatoes were sweet and plentiful, hundreds of weeds sprouted up around the vine, trying to strangle it to death. Every day Granddaddy pulled the weeds that had grown up during the night. Every day he pulled the weeds that were trying to choke the life right out of it. He never turned his back on that vine.

"I think we're kind of like that garden. Some of us here at Cedar Grove are trying to grow strong beautiful tomatoes, and some of us are like the weeds, trying to choke the life out of everybody else. My daddy was a good man. He was a good father. And he was a good preacher. Brother Hawkins, you know that firsthand. Daddy stood by you when your daughter went down to Texas to birth her little baby. And, Deacon Evans, wasn't it Daddy who went and smoothed things over with your wife when she locked you out of the house after you lost all your savings at the dog track down in Florida?"

I could see each and every person sitting before me starting to squirm for fear I was going to continue calling the roll of sinners, so to speak. But I didn't need to. They knew they were in no position to be casting any stones.

"But one thing's for sure, my daddy wasn't perfect.

Miss Raines's growing belly is testament to that. My daddy loved Miss Raines. He had loved her for a long time. It's just a shame he couldn't have loved her honestly. I think when my mama left, well, my daddy just wasn't able to admit to all of you that his sweet young wife wanted more than he could offer. I don't know, maybe he thought that if he couldn't make things right with his own wife, then none of you would ever trust anything he had to say about loving one another. So he let us all think she drowned.

"And now I wonder, with an innocent little baby on the way, if up and dying wasn't the only way my daddy could keep from disappointing all of you here at Cedar Grove. That's how much he loved each and every one of you. And I think if we turn our backs on our sisters, on Lena Mae and Miss Raines, then we are no better than the weeds choking the life out of those beautiful vines."

When I looked up, Mrs. Roberta Huckstep was holding her head in her monogrammed handkerchief. Everybody was tearing to one degree or another. So I just stood there for a moment, just like Flora would want me to do, giving everyone a chance to let the sadness pour out of their bodies.

I looked to Mrs. Gilbert, and she began to play "Just As I Am." At first the sound of the piano merely muffled the noise of a crying congregation. Then one by one, people began to sing, finding comfort in the words that surely now, more than ever, were a comfort to my daddy.

Just as I am, and waiting not
To rid my soul of one dark blot,
To Thee whose blood can cleanse each spot,
O Lamb of God, I come! I come!

Just as I am, thou wilt receive,
Wilt welcome, pardon, cleanse, relieve,
Because thy promise I believe,
O Lamb of God, I come! I come!

I could hear Brother Fulmer's deep baritone voice roll through the room, and even Mrs. Gulbenk's wavering soprano sounded pretty today. In fact, the entire congregation sounded different, sweeter, purer. And slowly one voice among all the others became stronger and clearer, one beautiful voice that belonged to my mama.

All these years, I couldn't remember what Mama's singing voice sounded like. Lord knows I tried to remember, but the voice I kept hearing in my head all these years was just one I had heard on the radio. Turns out, my mama sounded like an angel, a heavenly angel. Mrs. Gilbert started playing real softly so her voice could be heard above the others. And one by one, every voice at Cedar Grove grew silent, leaving my mama alone to serenade my daddy as he made his way through the Pearly Gates.

The sound filling the church that day surrounded me completely. I felt warm and comforted. I felt loved, the kind of love that comes only from your own flesh and blood—and those who love you as their own. I had spent a lifetime trying to get away from this place. Funny thing, you can run away from your family, and you can run away from dreams, but, like Daddy kept trying to tell me, there's just no running away from your destiny. I knew where I needed to be.

For a while after Daddy's funeral, everybody in Ringgold was real nice to one another. Ruthie Morgan's mama and some of the other ladies at church even hosted a baby shower for Miss Raines. Ida Belle spent two whole days making little cookies in the shape of baby bottles. Ruthie Morgan, who I started calling by her first name only, crocheted a white blanket for the baby, using a design Mrs. Gulbenk found in an old Simplicity pattern book. Brother Hawkins built a rocking cradle for the baby, and his wife painted Noah standing in his ark across the headboard. They laughed that it wasn't as good as a felt board, but they figured a Sunday-school teacher wouldn't want to waste any time in teaching her little one the Bible.

Mrs. Huckstep stopped by regularly for a month or so to bring a macaroni casserole or a vase of fresh flowers, just to brighten our day, she said. And oddly, it did. But it seems that people can only act right for a little while before their old ways get a hold of them. Probably for the best anyway. I imagine Mrs. Huckstep might have combusted herself if she hadn't finally opened her mouth and let all that gossip she had been bottling up since the day Daddy died drain out. She tried her very best to convince every churchgoing lady in town, which would be everyone but Gloria Jean and Mrs. Dempsey, that their dear departed preacher was seduced by the beautiful Sunday-school teacher nearly half his age. Women from Alabama are like that, she'd say.

Miss Raines said she had expected that kind of talk, and I think sometimes, late at night, she wondered if it was true. I kept telling her that Daddy loved her and she needed to hold her head high. Besides, I told her, no one pays Mrs. Huckstep half a mind anyway, especially now that she is consumed with planning Emma Sue's debutant party. Heck, when I was little, I figured everybody believed every word that came out of that woman's mouth. Now I know that there are very few people in this town who really pay much attention to anything Mrs. Huckstep has to say; even her precious little Emma Sue seems to ignore her most days.

Flora and Miss Mabie stayed for another three weeks or so. And even though they may not be living under the same roof with us on a daily basis, Flora and Miss Mabie are part of our lives for good now. They drive up from Atlanta every month for a visit. Miss Mabie always stays with Gloria Jean, and Flora sleeps with me, just in case there's a thunderstorm. As soon as Flora walks through the door, she heads straight to the kitchen to warm up the stove, then spends the day cooking biscuits and pineapple upside-down cake.

Miss Mabie and Gloria Jean have become real good friends. Truth be told, I think Miss Mabie is the first true friend Gloria Jean has had in a long time, since Lena Mae floated away. The two of them sit around the kitchen table and talk about old times for hours on end. I saw them drink an entire bottle of Boone's Farm wine one night when they got to talking again about old boyfriends down in Birmingham, a very favorite subject of theirs. Gloria Jean even invited Meeler up from Dalton just so he could meet her dear friend Miss Mabie.

Miss Raines settled into the Cline house rather nicely. She and the baby have Daddy's room, although it hardly looks the same with her pine furniture and pink chintz curtains hanging on the window. Flora loves tending to Miss Raines as if she were her own daughter. Heck, she doted on that woman every minute when she was expecting, rubbing her back and feeding her tummy. When that little baby finally came after one very long night in June, Flora was there to catch her. Miss Raines took one look at her baby's sweet round face and named her Flora Grace Cline. Flora took that little girl in her arms and cried like a baby. She said she never dreamed she'd know the day when a white mama would name her baby after a black woman like herself.

Even now when Flora comes to Ringgold, she makes Miss Raines eat and rest, and while Miss Raines does what she is told, Flora rocks the baby in her big, strong arms, comforting and soothing her just the way she did me the day my daddy died. Flora and Miss Raines are the two best mamas little Flora Grace could ever hope to have.

Martha Ann didn't go back to school till the first of February. She said she wanted to spend some time getting to know her mama, and who could argue with that? She and Mama took long walks and spent hours looking at the same old baby pictures of the two of us. Sometimes we'd play a game of Monopoly or stand in the kitchen and cook. But the rhythm of our bodies being together never beat quite right, and most of the time, Martha Ann kept to herself, reading her books. Mr. Boyce stopped by faithfully every week to give my sister a new book or two, mostly ones written by famous women like Jane Austen and Sylvia Plath. Mr. Boyce said their lives were filled with angst and he thought Martha Ann might find it helpful to read what they had to say.

When she started back at school, I got in the habit of walking her there myself, not that she needed an escort or anything. But it is the one time of the day when we are completely alone. We talk about Mrs. Gulbenk and football and Daddy and anything else that comes to mind, but mostly we talk about Martha Ann's dreams. She says she wants to live in a world of words. She just hopes it's not that far from home.

Mr. Boyce thinks Martha Ann needs to start thinking about college. He wants her to talk to a friend of his at Vanderbilt. He thinks she could get a scholarship.

Mama left, again. She didn't drown, not this time. She just got on a bus and headed back to Willacoochee. She tried to stay and make a life with us, but too much time had passed. The more Martha Ann and I talked about our memories, the more she realized what she had missed. Our childhoods were gone, and she could never have them back. I doubt Mama is ever going to forgive herself. That happens sometimes, Flora said. "The good Lord is full of grace but sometimes a person will just whip himself senseless before taking the forgiveness that He offers up for free."

Daddy always said he was working overtime to save God's children from a life of eternal damnation. But now I'm thinking Daddy may have been wasting his time because it sure seems like some of us spend most of our days walking through hell right here on earth.

I keep Lena Mae's special box in my room. It blends in with all the other treasures that have found their place back on the top of my dresser. Our mother still sends us a card on our birthdays, and sometimes she even calls us on the telephone. But our mama drifted away a long time ago.

After she left, I spent more time with my friend Lolly. I finally told her that she deserved more than a crystal vase, and then I gave her my three blue vinyl suitcases. I told her I didn't need them anymore, but I thought maybe she did. It took her five whole weeks to pack those bags. Slowly and deliberately she chose each and every piece of her life that she wanted to take with her. I've heard that her mama hasn't been doing well since Lolly left town, but

I don't know if she really misses her or just misses beating up on her.

As for Catherine Grace, well, I decided it was time I planted me a garden.

After Daddy's funeral, something drew me back to the land my granddaddy loved so much, right behind Cedar Grove church. I still say a little prayer before stepping into the dirt, just like I did that very first time so many years ago. I planted one tomato vine in Daddy's honor and one purple tomato in Granddaddy's honor. That's right, Catherine Grace Cline is growing her very own tomatoes.

I also planted some corn along the garden's western edge. I water and fertilize that corn so it's certain to grow thick and tall, the perfect spot where I can go and think about each and every passing day. It's not a hiding spot or a place to run away from fears and painful memories. I let those go the day we put my daddy in the ground.

I don't even need to sit on top of that picnic table anymore. Oh, I still stop by the Dairy Queen every now and then and eat a Dilly Bar, but mostly I just talk with Eddie Franklin. We have a patient ear for each other. We talk about profound things, like the meaning of life and how to form the perfect curlicue on a chocolate-dip cone. He let me try making my own one day, but the ice cream fell out of the cone and into the pot of melted chocolate. We had to empty the entire pot. Eddie hasn't let me try that again.

But most of my garden is planted with strawberries,

beautiful, red, juicy strawberries. Brother Fulmer let me borrow a little land from him where I've planted another couple hundred plants, maybe more. I harvest strawberries all summer long, freezing thousands of them by the time the first frost forces me to stop. By the end of the day my hands are blood red, permanently stained with the juice of my berries. Gloria Jean says my hands may remain a bright shade of pink till the day I die. That would be fine by me.

Come September, I spend most of my days in the church kitchen, where I've found the space I need to work making some sixty jars of Preacher's Strawberry Jam every single day. Gloria Jean taught me how to make jam, but my time at Davison's department store taught me how to make it special. And now my jam is shipped to gourmet food stores throughout the South, including the specialty food department at Davison's department store. Mr. Wallis said he was proud to carry my jam in his store. He said he knew I was going to make something of myself someday. He even invited me down to Atlanta to greet the customers and personally sign my jars of jam.

Ida Belle helps me out when she's not busy cooking church dinners. And Miss Raines and Gloria Jean keep track of the orders and the payments. Next year we're planning on buying another stove so I can increase my annual production by some fifteen hundred jars. Who would have thought that big-city folk would consider my jam to be a gourmet food product?

Hank comes by to see me every morning and every evening. He loves to watch me working in the garden. He says he can't get enough of looking at the big-city girl down on her knees with her hands buried in the red, rich Georgia dirt. Of course, Hank doesn't have far to walk. He's been preaching at Cedar Grove for the past ten months. The search committee was looking for a new preacher and asked Hank, since he had been Young Life leader and all, if he would consider preaching a couple of Sundays.

Brother Fulmer said the first time he heard Hank behind the pulpit, he thought he was listening to his dear friend, the great Reverend Cline. Before long, Hank knew he was meant to be a preacher, not a dairy farmer. The committee called off their search.

Everyone at Cedar Grove would love to see the two of us get married. Of course, only time will tell, but seeing Reverend Cline's daughter as the preacher's wife, well, they seem to think it'd be like carrying on the family name or something. Hank's mama keeps reminding me it was always her dream that the two of us would find our way back to each other. She says we're almost there.

Maybe. But dreams are a funny thing. Not so long ago, I was consumed with my dream, so consumed that I saw any other possibility as a disappointment. I was convinced that the Lord didn't *giveth* much of anything. I was convinced that He just spent all His time taking away, especially from Catherine Grace Cline.

Daddy said that Jesus talked in parables because people have a tendency to hear but not listen. They look but don't see. I guess I was no different than anybody else. I looked and looked for that dad-gum golden egg, and I finally saw it, just like Daddy said I would. Funny thing is, I didn't want it anymore.

Acknowledgments

Neither Catherine Grace nor I would have found our places in the world without the following people:

Shaye Areheart, my editor, whose wisdom and kindness and passion for things Southern has made her as much trusted advisor as friend.

Barbara Braun, my agent, who pulled me from the slush pile and gave me this opportunity to tell a story. I am forever grateful for her faith in me and her constant guidance and sage advice.

Bonnie MacDonald, reader, mentor, counselor, friend, who has read so many words I have written, generously providing countless hours of instruction from the grammatical to the spiritual.

Lee Smith, who not only taught me to diagram a sentence in the seventh grade but has continued to teach and inspire.

My big sisters: Mary Hall Gregg, Alice Gregg Haase, and Vicky Gregg; and all my Bradford-Street girlfriends: Suzanne Holder, Lisa Morse, Athena Wood, Tricia Partridge, Jane Herzog, Susan Regas, Cindy Norman, Michelle Doney, Sally Storch, Carey McAniff, and Michelle Whang whose early readings and enthusiastic encouragement were as reassuring and comforting as the discovery of the perfect tomato.

Fred Gregg, the big brother Catherine Grace never had.

Mark Wax and Mark Herzog, the movie men who thought it best I write a book.

Anne Berry, always patient with even the simplest of questions.

Claudia, who snapped her mother's picture.

My husband, Dan, and daughters Claudia, Josephine, and Alice, who took care of themselves and gave me hugs when the gang in Ringgold demanded all of my attention.

And, of course, my mother, Mary, and father, Fred, who made me go to church every Sunday.

And my grandfather, Pop, who took me to get a Dilly Bar.

About the Author

SUSAN GREGG GILMORE has written for the *Chattanooga Times Free Press,* the *Los Angeles Times,* and the *Christian Science Monitor.* She lives in Nashville, Tennessee, with her husband and three daughters. This is her first novel.

About the Type

The text of this book was set in Berthold Baskerville Book, Günter Gerhard Lange's twentieth-century revival of John Baskerville's original mid-eighteenth-century design. Lange revised Baskerville's typeface to allow for modern technologies while retaining the graceful characteristics of the original design. Due to greater contrast in its strokes, Lange's Baskerville Book is a bit lighter in weight than regular Baskerville, and its cursive capitals, particularly J, K, N, T, Y, and Z, reflect John Baskerville's background as a handwriting teacher.